Blue Christmas

DIANE MOODY

O Come, O Come Emmanuel,
(Veni, Veni, Emanuel), lyric author unknown,
translated from Latin to English by
John M. Neale in 1851. Public domain.

A Quiet Simple Kiss, original lyrics
© Diane Moody

Always and Forever, original lyrics
© Diane Moody

It Is Well With My Soul, lyrics by
Horatio Spafford, 1873. Public domain.

Love You Forever, original lyrics © Diane Moody

Cover design by Hannah Moody

Photo 62065102 © Guasor | Dreamstime.com
Photo © sylvanworks | istockphoto.com

DEDICATION

To Hannah

my beautiful daughter,
my pride and joy,
my inspiration.

Diane and Hannah 2003   Hannah today

AUTHOR'S NOTE

A little background on this story . . .

Once upon a time there lived a beautiful young teenager in our home, our daughter Hannah. Like so many others her age, she was smitten—make that, *obsessed*—by a band whose music topped the charts and won Grammys by the armful. The band was made up of five young men, some of them not much older than she was. Their pictures covered her bedroom walls so completely, you'd be hard pressed to know the color of the paint on those walls.

When she was still too young to drive, I chauffeured Hannah and her girlfriends to see her band in concert in our city. A couple years later she won a local radio contest by plastering the outside of our home with banners and posters and enormous pictures of her five beloved singers. The prize? Two front row tickets when their new tour came to town, and she took me as her special guest. What a precious memory that night was, sharing it with her. I don't think she stopped grinning the entire evening.

And I'm pretty sure the cute dark-haired one winked at me. Actually, he might have winked at me two or three times. Or maybe he just had something in his eye.

For Christmas that year, I wrote a story for her about a young woman named Hannah, a college senior who inadvertently meets her former teen heartthrob—one of the boys in the band—quite by accident. I didn't know it then, but it would one day be labeled *fan fiction*. Who knew such a genre existed? I printed off the short story, tied it with a red ribbon, and slipped it under her door. She *loved* it. Then she shared it with her friends who all pleaded, "Write more! Write more!" (No sweeter words to an author's ears.)

And so I did. In installments, I wrote the story you're about to read with the help of my daughter. We'd pile up on the sofa when she came home from school and brainstorm plot lines and story ideas. Good times.

The internet had just exploded on the landscape of our lives, and Hannah found an online website featuring these fan fictions stories about "her" boys in the band. She submitted my story and suddenly, girls all over the world were begging, "Write more! Write more!" We would eventually register more than 80,000 hits on that page over the course of the next year. I received more than *one thousand* fan letters via email along the way.

And to my surprise, some of them even asked questions about the thread of faith we wove into that love story. Those were my favorites.

Of course, the story on the following pages has changed a lot from that first version. The band and its members have all been fictionalized, and the character of Hannah is much different than *my* Hannah, who is now grown and married and completely amazing.

And last I looked, the walls in her loft apartment don't have a single picture of those boys in the band . . .

PART ONE

CHAPTER 1

Chapel Hill, North Carolina

"These cranberries are rancid. I want my money back." The old man straightened his back in defiance.

Standing behind the grocery counter, Hannah Brooks exhaled as she tried to carefully guard her words. "And I told *you* I'll be happy to give you your money back, but I need to see your receipt. It's store policy. Otherwise, how do we know you didn't buy those from another store? I mean no disrespect, sir, but there's no way you bought those here two days ago. Look at them—they're mush!" Fingers splayed, she pinched the edge of the bag and dropped it back in his hands. "And for the record, we don't even carry that brand." She stared him down and watched the crimson darken his face.

He wiped his brow with a wrinkled blue bandana then jammed it back in his coat pocket. "I demand to speak to your supervisor."

"Fine. I'm sure he'll be more than happy to talk with you when he gets back."

"And when will that be?"

"Next year. He's on vacation." She flashed him a smile then busied herself wiping down the glass-covered scanner beside her register.

"Then who's in charge here?"

"I am."

He turned to the well-dressed woman behind him, clearly hoping for some reinforcement. She looked unimpressed when he stepped closer, waving a gnarled finger back in Hannah's direction as he repeated his complaint. Hannah recognized the woman as one of her regular customers, the kind who occasionally stopped by late at night for a carton of milk or loaf of bread. They'd always exchanged pleasantries, sometimes a brief chat if the store wasn't busy. She was always friendly, though Hannah realized she didn't know her name. Just another regular face in the Alexander's Grocery family of customers.

When the grouch finished wheezing his frustrations, the woman raised her eyebrows and glared at him over her half-glasses. "For heaven's sake, pops, it's Christmas Eve. Is a three dollar bag of cranberries really worth all this fuss?"

He growled a couple of colorful profanities in her direction then barked at her. "And who asked *you*? Mind your own business, broad!"

The woman shot a quick glance at Hannah then got in his face, her manicured nail poking him in the chest. "This IS my business. You're taking my time and you're irritating me. So take your silly cranberries and hit the road, Scrooge."

He clamped his mouth shut, clutched the berries to his chest, turned on his heel, and stomped out the door.

The woman looked at Hannah with wild eyes, then just as fast burst into laughter. Hannah welcomed the sudden break in tension and joined her until they could laugh no more. She pulled her thick brown hair into a ponytail and tried to regain her composure. "Honestly, there must be a full moon out there tonight. Do you believe that guy? So much for Christmas spirit."

The lady, her long blonde hair woven in an elegant French braid, nodded her head in agreement. "Wasn't he a trip? But I thought you handled him like a real pro . . . Hannah," she said, noting the engraved nametag on Hannah's dark green bib apron. "You were completely polite until he became unreasonable. So don't you give him a second thought. People like him live their whole lives just trying to aggravate the rest of us."

"I guess. All the crazies are out tonight, y'know? It's been like this all day. Does *everyone* wait to do their holiday grocery shopping on Christmas Eve? It's been a zoo in here." She scanned the jumbo bag of peanut M&M's. "Then again, *you* strike me as someone who's had her shopping done for weeks, and I would bet this—" she held up the bag of candy—"is a stocking stuffer for someone very special. Am I right?"

The woman's face warmed as a smile graced her gentle features. Tiny laugh lines fanned her soft blue eyes. "You found me out. My son is coming home tonight and I completely forgot his favorite candy. I know it's silly—he's 27 years old. Not exactly a little boy any more. But it's one of those holiday traditions, and I couldn't help myself. I hardly get to see him anymore, so I've got to spoil him when I can, right?" Her smile faded when she looked back up at Hannah.

Hannah realized the tears pooling in her own eyes must have caught her attention. She felt a tear break free just as the woman reached for her hand and patted it maternally.

"Why, what's the matter? Did I say something wrong?"

Hannah wiped her eyes with the back of her other hand. "Oh no, really—it's me. I've been so depressed all day." She felt the catch in her voice. The sound of it destroyed what little resistance she had left. "I mean, it's Christmas Eve and I'm stuck here for the holidays. I'm the assistant manager—this is just a part-time job while I'm in school . . ." The words gained momentum as her misery spilled out, but she couldn't help herself. "But Jim, my boss, had a sudden death in his family. He had to go—it's not like he had a choice. And I'm next in line, so it fell on me to work through the holiday weekend."

Her nose ran like a faucet and she hiccupped, trying to catch her breath. *Oh brother. I must sound like such a whiner.* She paused to take another breath, sending a new wave of tears down her face. "My whole family is away in Colorado on a skiing trip. I was supposed to go, but I just couldn't do that to Jim. And my best friend Kylie went home to be with her family for the holidays, and here I am." She took a deeper breath this time and looked up at the woman. "Listen to me, carrying on like some blubbering idiot. I'm sorry, I really am."

"That's okay, sweetheart, you just blubber away."

"No, I didn't mean to drag you into my stupid little pity party like this. It's completely unprofessional. I'm so sorry."

"You didn't drag me into anything. There's nothing worse than being separated from family, especially during Christmas. But surely you don't have to work tomorrow, do you?"

"No, the store is closed for the day, thank goodness. I should be grateful for that and just get a grip."

The lady looked around this way then that. Finally, she looked back at Hannah. "Since it appears I'm the only customer left, I have a wonderful idea." Her eyes sparkled with excitement. "What time do you get off?"

Hannah wiped her eyes and nose with the hem of her apron then looked at the clock on the wall. "Actually, we're closed now. I didn't realize it was so late."

"Perfect!" She clapped her hands for emphasis. "How would you like to join my husband and me for a Christmas Eve service at our church? It starts in about an hour. Then we always have a quiet dinner at home after the service. I would *love* for you to join us."

Hannah shook her head. "Oh no. I mean, that's really nice and all, but I just couldn't. I wouldn't want to impose on your family like that. No offense, but I hardly know you."

"Nonsense. We're old friends! I see you in here all the time. We've talked about everything from the weather and football to Carolina politics! That's more than some married couples talk in a lifetime, by the way."

Hannah watched her, the gentleness of her eyes, her easy smile. She was certainly no one to worry about. The small diamond cross hanging from a delicate chain on her neck shined like a beacon of reassurance. Still, Hannah wasn't used to taking risks with a near stranger. Much less a near stranger's family.

"Besides, I told you my son is coming home. He'd be thrilled to have someone his own age around. Especially someone as pretty as you."

Hannah could feel the heat warm her cheeks. She averted her eyes, closing the register and turning off the light above her. "Look, I know you mean well, but I'm not really comfortable with matchmaking, if you know what I mean. But thank you any—"

"Matchmaking? Who said anything about matchmaking? Although, I must say you are a refreshing change from some of the bimbos he's brought home."

An unexpected scenario tiptoed through Hannah's mind . . .

"Mom? Dad? I'm home!" shouts the handsome son as he throws open the front door. "I want you to meet someone. Bambi, this is my mother and father. Mom, Dad, this is Bambi." His eyes turn to Hannah who sips eggnog,

seated on the sofa between his parents. "And who is this? Picking up strays again, Mom?"

An involuntary shudder raced down Hannah's back. She shook her head again, this time with resolve. "No, I just don't think it's a good idea. But thank you anyway."

"Hannah, I simply won't take no for an answer. I'll go wait in my car out front. You close up, do whatever you have to do, then come on out when you're ready. We have lots of time. We can even stop by your place if you'd like to change or freshen up." She rounded the end of the counter and gently looped her arm through Hannah's. Her eyes were warm and sincere. "Please say you'll come."

In such close proximity, Hannah caught a familiar scent. It was the same cologne her mother always wore. That was all it took. Suddenly the fatigue and stress overwhelmed her. The thought of going home to her lonely apartment for what was left of Christmas Eve depressed her even more. "I can't believe I'm saying this, but yes—yes I'd love to come."

"Wonderful! Now just take your time, and I'll go pull my car right up by the front door. Oh, this is going to be just perfect!"

"Are you sure we have time to run by my apartment?"

"Absolutely. I'll follow you, then wait in my car until you're ready. No problem."

Hannah couldn't help smiling. As she pulled out her keys to lock up, a thought crossed her mind. "Wait! I don't even know your name!

"Just call me Laura. We'll make all the introductions later. Now go!"

The church engulfed Hannah in a wave of sentiment that overpowered her. Soft candlelight danced across garlands of pine and ribbons of deepest crimson. An endless sea of poinsettias covered the bank of stairs leading up to the platform at the front of the sanctuary, a brilliant contrast to the ivory robes of the choir members now filling the loft. The crowded auditorium fell silent as the choir sang with hushed anticipation.

O come, O come, Emmanuel
And ransom captive Israel
That mourns in lonely exile here
Until the Son of God appear
Rejoice, rejoice, Emmanuel
Shall come to Thee, O Israel
Rejoice, rejoice, Emmanuel
Shall come to Thee, O Israel.

Hannah closed her eyes, breathing in the peacefulness. A slight nudge on her arm interrupted her thoughts. Sneaking a sideways peek at Laura, she looked into what must surely be the kindest face on earth . . . eyes sparkling, reflecting the warm glow of candlelight, her brows raised high in childlike pleasure. She patted Hannah's knee.

"I'm so glad you came," she whispered. "We're going to have such a good time."

"Shh!" Laura's husband pretended to scold them, making a valiant effort to act stern.

Frank had joined them at the church only moments before, arriving late from his own last-minute shopping. He put Hannah at ease immediately with a warm hug and genuine smile. She found his dashing good looks of no surprise—she would have easily paired him with Laura. His premature but striking white hair, cut short along with his neatly trimmed beard, offered a fatherly appearance that put her at ease the moment they met.

Now, after his feigned attempt at the reprimand, he winked then looked back toward the front of the church.

The rest of the service melted into Hannah's memory. It ended all too soon as candles were passed to everyone while the entire congregation and choir sang *Silent Night* a cappella.

"Where is that son of ours?" Frank asked, as he escorted Laura and Hannah back to their car. "I was hoping he'd show up in time for at least part of the service."

Laura chuckled. "He'll be here. He's probably already home and raiding our dinner as we speak." Laura chuckled.

Hannah felt her heart flutter, still apprehensive about spending the evening in the home of these strangers. No, they weren't strangers. They were far too friendly for that. Still, it was Christmas Eve, and she wasn't at *all* sure about meeting their son.

"Hannah, you'll just love Jason," Laura began. "But I have to warn you—he can be a heartbreaker."

Hannah felt the flutter twist into a strangling knot. "Heartbreaker?"

"Oh, you know what I mean. He's got his daddy's charm—"

"—and his mother's smile," Frank finished. "But I'll keep an eye on him for you, Hannah. Don't worry. One wrong move and I'll—"

"Oh, right, Frank," Laura chided. "You never laid a hand on him his entire life. He never got a whoopin' unless I gave it to him, thank you very much. But of course, that's why he worships the ground I walk on." A mischievous grin mimicked her playful eyes.

"That he does, I must admit." Frank stepped between them as they walked across the parking lot. He draped his arm across his wife's shoulders, then looped his other arm through Hannah's. "But stop boring our friend here with all this chatter. Hannah? You just come on home with us and relax, all right?"

She hoped her face didn't mirror the uncertainty she felt, despite the lopsided grin she managed to fake. The sound of her accompanying laugh was lame even in her own ears.

What in the world have I gotten myself into?

CHAPTER 2

She wasn't prepared for this. There was no way she could have prepared for this.

Laura's car slowed as her husband's shiny black Jaguar preceded them at an enormous security gate which opened regally before them. The long driveway stretched ahead under a canopy of barren winter branches covered with tiny white lights.

"Oh my . . ." *Who* are *these people?* Something flitted through her mind but she couldn't put her finger on it. Like a thought just out of reach, it teased her with uncertainty. She chose to ignore it and instead, drink in the warm hospitality of her new friends.

"Oh now, don't get too impressed," Laura responded. "After all, it's just wood and brick and mortar like any other house. And we're just ordinary people like everyone else. This house was a gift to us, if you can believe it. And, well frankly, how in the world would you turn down a gift like that?"

"A *gift*?" She couldn't help but laugh. "I feel like Little Orphan Annie going to Daddy Warbucks' house for the first time. It's like a dream or something. I'm beginning to think I must have scanned one too many turkeys on that register tonight."

Whoa. As the house came into full view, she felt her jaw drop as she stared at the most magnificent home she'd ever seen. Decked for the holidays with thousands more of the miniature white lights, it seemed to stretch on forever. "It's so *beautiful.*"

"Well thank you! I absolutely love Christmas, Hannah, and this house is so easy to dress up. I'll take you on a tour once we get inside. Since the minute I saw the architect's plans, I've felt like a kid in a candy store. Do you ever feel that way? Like you just want to pop, you're having such a good time?"

"You mean like now?"

Laura laughed, her head falling back against the headrest. While Frank pulled around to the four-car garage, Laura parked her Lexus in the circular front drive. Heading toward the elegant front porch entry, she wrapped her arm around Hannah's waist. "I'm so happy you decided to join us. I want you to just relax and make yourself at home. Okay?"

Hannah smiled in return. She couldn't even think how to respond. Laura pulled off her glove to punch numbers on a pad, disengaging the security system, then threw open the front door. Hannah's eyes opened wide to take it all in.

"First things first," Laura offered, taking Hannah's coat. "Why don't you go have a seat in the family room here, and I'll get us something to drink."

Entranced by the festive surroundings, Hannah descended three wide steps into the oversized living area. The dying embers of a fire glowed from a huge stone fireplace, the focal point of a room filled with comfortable sofas and overstuffed chairs. In the corner stood a massive Christmas tree, loaded with ornaments and tinsel, bows and lights, the star on its highest branch almost touching the two-story beamed ceiling above. She breathed in the fresh pine scent as Laura lit several candles around the room, chattering about her fondness for all things Christmas.

Frank strolled into the room, his purpose clearly evident as he added more logs onto the fire, then stoked it into a hearty blaze. "There, that's more like it." He turned his attention to the elaborate music system, pressing a couple of buttons. The room filled with an orchestral version of *I'll Be Home for Christmas.* He tossed a wink toward her as he turned for the kitchen. "Now, what can I get you, Hannah? Coke? Coffee? Perrier? Eggnog?"

Eggnog? No eggnog! "Um, Perrier would be perfect. Thank you."

"No problem. Sweetheart? How about you?" he asked, stealing a kiss on his wife's cheek as she clicked off the portable lighter.

Looking around the room to make sure she'd lit all her candles, she followed him into the kitchen. "I think I'll wait and have a cup of coffee. It's all ready to brew if you'll just flip the switch on the coffeemaker."

"One Perrier, one coffee, coming up."

Hannah looked around the room as she slowly lowered herself onto one of the sofas, finally giving in to the fatigue tugging at her. She missed her family. She missed Kylie. Her best friend would be so proud of her for being so . . . *spontaneous.* Kylie never met a stranger and never missed an opportunity for a new adventure. She'd always been the wilder one, often grabbing Hannah's hand and dragging her into crazy situations. Hannah made a mental note to try to call her when she got home and tell her about these people and their outrageously gorgeous home. Maybe someday, she could introduce Kylie to Laura and Frank.

Laura quietly slipped back into the room, a Christmas apron now wrapped around her. She set a plate of cheese and crackers on the coffee table, grabbing a bite as she turned to leave. "Now, don't by shy, Hannah. Help yourself. It'll be a few more minutes until I have everything on the table. You must be starving."

"Now that you mention it, I guess I am. Thank you." She reached for a cracker, then stopped. "Laura? I don't know what to say. Meeting you, then meeting Frank, then that wonderful church service . . . and now all this . . . well, it feels a little like heaven right now. I've been so buried with finals and working so many hours . . . and now all of a sudden that's all behind me and I'm here and—"

"And we're thrilled to have you," Laura answered, sitting on the arm of the sofa. "I'm awfully sentimental when it comes to holidays, and I meant it when I said no one should be alone for Christmas. We're used to having a houseful around here, so you're doing us a favor just by being here. Now, go on and kick off your shoes, if you'd like. Put your feet up, sweetie. We want you to feel perfectly at home while you're—"

"MOM!"

Laura halted, her face lighting up like the twenty-foot tree in the corner. "He's home!"

"Mom! Dad? I've got someone I want you to meet!"

The previous vision swept through Hannah's mind. The son. The bimbo. The snide remark about Mom picking up another stray . . . Panic sucked the breath out of her. She dropped her head into her hands, moaning out loud. *Oh no, God, please don't let this happen. Just let the floor open up and swallow me before—*

Suddenly, something furry and frantic and wiggling out of control accosted her. Hot breath panting anxiously against her nose then over to her ear sent a cruel shiver up her back just before a wet, slobbering tongue lathered the side of her face.

"What in the—"

"Baby! Come here! Down, girl!"

"Jason! What on earth is going on?" Laura's voice sliced through the pandemonium.

Hannah's arms shielded her face from the ongoing bath. Every time she tried to look out at the face behind the voice, she was met with a ridiculous black snout and pink tongue that seemed intent on licking her from one ear to the other.

"Baby! Now stop it! Bad girl!" But the commands got lost in the infectious laughter of Frank and Laura's son. "Mom, this is Baby. She was a gift from some girl I met in Montana, and I fell in love with her the minute I laid eyes on her. Well, I mean Baby—not the girl, of course." He dissolved in laughter at his own joke.

"But Jason, make her stop!" Laura scolded. "For heaven's sake, can't you make her mind?"

"BABY!"

The puppy seemed to snap to attention, going stiff on her lap. Suddenly, it was lifted away from her. Hannah attempted to untangle her hair from her face as she came up for air. Goose bumps raised on her skin as she rubbed her face, attempting to wipe away the doggy germs.

"Whoa—Mom!" The laughter beginning to subside. "Aren't you going to introduce me? Who is this?"

"Yes, but first give me a hug, you big lug. It's about time you got home!" Laura teased.

"Nice entrance, hotshot," Frank bellowed. "Give your old man a hug while you're at it."

Hannah could hear the three of them as they shared a welcome-home embrace. *Oh great, and now I'm intruding on a Norman Rockwell moment.* She avoided looking at them, postponing the inevitable introduction as long as possible. Shaking off the last remnant of a shiver, she focused on wiping the dog hair off her slacks and tried to make herself presentable.

Laura made the introduction. "Hannah, I want you to meet our son, Jason. Jason, honey, this is Hannah—well, good grief. I never did ask you for your last name!"

Hannah started to say her name when she finally looked up, her eyes locking onto his face—a face so familiar she froze. She knew that face—the bridge of his nose, the sandy brows, the shaggy blond hair, the famous green eyes, the tiny smile lines edging them. She felt the heat crawling up her neck as she tried to answer. "Juh . . ."

His eyebrows arched. Just like his mother's only moments ago. His eyes danced, just as Laura's had danced. *Those eyes I once adored such a long time ago . . .*

In a millisecond she was swept back in time.

She was sixteen in a huge arena filled with thousands of screaming fans. The stage exploded in pyrotechnic wonders, backlighting the five singers as they finished their final encore. *Out of the Blue,* the hottest singing group to crash the music culture, was on its latest world tour. Their ground-breaking stage performances had energized sold-out crowds around the world for over ten years. Whether seated on stools singing ballads in perfect five-part harmony or spread across the stage like wild men tearing through one hit after another, *Blue* always delivered. Thrilling young and old alike, they consistently offered a diverse range of musical styles, catapulting them to the top of the charts year after year.

On that night so long ago, Hannah saw her idols live in concert for the first time—a moment she would never forget as long as she lived. She had edged her way closer to the stage desperately hoping to get a closer look at Jason, Gevin, JT, Jackson, and Sergio before they disappeared from sight. Earlier she'd worried that her white down jacket made her look like the Stay Puff Marshmallow Man. Now, lost in a sea of hysterical fans, she was glad she'd worn it. Because even as she waved eagerly at lead singer Jason McKenzie praying to get his

---

attention, her jacket must have caught his eye. He pointed straight at her, his face breaking into that huge, to-die-for smile as he waved back at her. His hands slid back over his heart in a gallant gesture of genuine star-to-fan appreciation. She waved back, forever changed.

JASON MCKENZIE KNOWS I'M ALIVE!

Then, just as quickly, the memory vanished. Six years had passed since that night. And even though she'd lost track of her favorite singers as the demands of college and work dominated her life, now it all made sense. The pieces of the puzzle fell into place in a frenzied blur.

Laura and Frank. THE Laura and Frank McKenzie, parents of her childhood idol, Jason McKenzie. How could she have missed the connection? The palatial estate. Even the peanut M&M's—every devoted *Blue* fan knew it was Jason's favorite candy.

Now, here she was—in the home of Jason McKenzie and his parents as their personal guest on Christmas Eve.

With a face washed in dog slobber.

CHAPTER 3

Jason watched her struggle. Her mouth worked the letters but failed. He took in the sparkle of her eyes and didn't miss—what was it?—innocence? Something fresh and sincere in those soft hazel eyes. She tucked a strand of her silky brown hair behind her ear as a shy smile tugged at her mouth. Tiny dimples accented a face he found altogether enchanting. *Yes, that's what she is— enchanting.* He'd heard the term used in a movie he watched on the tour bus just last week. Now he knew exactly what it meant. He noticed the navy wool slacks and the cream turtleneck sweater that draped her slim figure perfectly. He didn't miss the highlights in her hair, like fine strands of gold reflecting the candlelight around them.

She tried again. "Ja . . ."

"Your last name is James? Jacobs? Gentry?" he asked, scratching his head.

She fell back onto the sofa. "Ja . . ."

This was too much fun. The long road trip had exhausted him, but the quest of this mystery girl in their home somehow reenergized him. He handed the squirming puppy to his mother. "Mom, this is Baby. Pretend she's your granddaughter and get acquainted."

"Oh Jason, why on earth you decided to bring home a puppy I will never know," she grumbled with just a hint of humor on the edge.

He sat down beside their guest, draping a brotherly arm around her shoulder in a gesture he hoped would relax her. "Look—Hannah, is it?" She nodded, her eyes glued to his. "This happens all the time. No big deal. It still embarrasses me but—"

"Embarrasses *you*?" she croaked.

"Progress! She speaks!"

"I can't . . . I mean . . . but you're . . ." Hannah gasped. "Oh, this is just *too* embarrassing. I . . . I'm *so* sorry. Of *course* I know who you are. You must think I'm like one of your groupies—" she stopped, realizing what she'd said. "No, no I didn't mean that. I'm sorry! I mean, your *fans*. Of course. *Fans*. Groupies are just so lame. Silly, really, don't you think?"

Her nervous laughter cracked him up, along with that face turning deeper shades of red. She closed her eyes, raising her hands in surrender and shaking her head in obvious, utter embarrassment. He pressed his lips together trying not to laugh.

"Um, I didn't mean that there's anything wrong with groupies, of course. I used to be one. Well, I mean, I wasn't *really* a—"

There it was again. That funny, nervous laugh. She dropped her head in her hands, hiding her face from him.

He got up, sliding onto the coffee table directly in front of her, popping a slice of Monterey Jack in his mouth as he pushed the plate aside. "Okay, let me help you." He pried her fingers away from her face and took both of her hands in his. He finished the cheese and looked at her, face to face. "Hannah, it's nice to meet you," he said softly. "Now the way I see it, you must be someone *very* special to have an invitation from my mom and dad on Christmas Eve. And if you're special to them, then I should make an effort to get to know you too. Now, tell me—how do you know my parents?"

She was looking him over. He watched her glazed eyes move from his hair to his chin to his mouth . . . He suppressed another smile. Ordinarily, this kind of reaction got old fast. Real fast. But tonight he was intrigued. *Who is she? Who is this unexpected guest on a night Mom always reserves for family only? And why is that face so fascinating?*

He patted her hand. "So are you from around here? Do you work at Dad's company?"

She tried to answer. Something resembling a croak erupted from her but nothing more. He looked at his parents for answers, but then it hit him. "WAIT! Are you from UNC? A college girl stuck in town for the holidays?"

A grin spread across her face. She nodded her affirmation.

"For real? No way! That's great! We have a Tar Heel in the house, people! Man, I love UNC. One of these days I'm gonna go back and get my degree. Isn't that right, Dad?"

"Jason, will you quit peppering our guest with all your questions?" his mother admonished, moving behind the sofa where Hannah sat. "I've met Hannah several times before, and this evening I invited her to join us for the service at church and dinner here at home. That's all you need to know right now. We'll have plenty of time for you to get acquainted. Now go do something with this dog and clean up. It's time for supper. Go on, now," she ordered, holding the squirming puppy out toward her son.

He looked back at Hannah and gently squeezed her hands. "Apparently duty calls. I'll be right back."

Laura took Hannah by the hand, helping her off the couch then leading her into the kitchen. "Now, just remember. He's a normal person like anybody else. He's really just a kid. *My* kid. And while he's home, we don't do the celebrity thing, okay?" She was quite serious. "I guess I should have warned you about Jason, but then I hate to be presumptuous and assume everybody knows who he is. I take it you're familiar with *Out of the Blue*?"

This time Hannah laughed out loud. "You could say that."

"Well, trust me. All that crazy lifestyle may look glamorous but it's a hard way to live. And we don't cater to *any* of it when he's home. So just relax. All right? You're a lovely young lady who is our special guest tonight, and we want you to feel right at home like part of the family."

Laura pointed Hannah to her seat at the kitchen table, set with Christmas dishes, colorful plaid napkins and a cluster of candles and holly at the center. Somehow the serenity of the setting helped calm Hannah's nerves. She started to take her seat then remembered the slime of puppy germs on her hands. Holding them up in silent explanation, she laughed at Laura's reaction then headed for the sink.

"By all means," Laura answered. "In fact, I think I'll join you." They scrubbed Baby's remnants off their hands, sharing the pump soap dispenser. Laura faked a shiver, still laughing.

"I know. I love dogs, but I'm a neat freak about clean hands," Hannah said. "Guess I must have listened to Mom more than I realized." She dried her hands on the fresh dish towel Laura offered her.

"Good girl. Your mother would be proud. Now have a seat and we'll eat before it all gets cold. Jason! Frank? C'mon, guys, we're hungry!"

Jason flew into the room, sliding across the hardwood floor in his socks. He rushed toward the table, then threw his leg over the back of the chair and flopped into his seat. He looked up grinning at Hannah, then turned to face his mother and father. They weren't smiling.

"Oh, sorry. I forgot." He got up, stepped away from the table and turned back around, his hands folded against his waist. "Mother? Father? Hannah? Good evening." Then, with the most elegant of manners, he lowered himself into the chair, snapping his cloth napkin into the air before gracefully placing it across his lap. "Shall we dine?"

Mr. and Mrs. McKenzie and their son reached out to hold hands for prayer. Jason held out his hand to Hannah, that mischievous smile taunting her. She slowly placed her hand in his, hoping and praying she wouldn't pass out at his touch. His fingers wrapped around her hand. Still smiling, he winked just before bowing his head.

And as her heart hammered against her chest, Hannah listened in wonder as her childhood idol—whose face once lined her bedroom walls and starred in a thousand of her dreams—began to pray.

"God, you're so amazing . . ."

Hannah recognized it immediately. That familiar sensation of being on the outside looking in. In a situation, but like some surreal, out of body interlude, merely observing the whole scene even though her body continued to interact. It felt so strange.

Such was her experience at dinner with the McKenzies. She listened, she spoke, she laughed, and she ate as if in a dream. Then, somewhere between the main course and dessert, she realized she was starting to rejoin the little party. Or maybe it was the reassuring touch from Laura when she served her that cup of coffee. The fog cleared and there she was—no longer shocked and nervous about whom she was with, but simply enjoying a quiet dinner with a remarkable family.

Well, *sort* of quiet.

As the four of them passed dishes of hot fruit salad, smoked ham, sweet potatoes, and angel biscuits, Jason talked non-stop. In between he wolfed down his mother's cooking like he hadn't eaten in months. Hannah hung on every word as he rambled about her teen idols, his closest friends. He bounced from one subject to the next, covering everything from JT's latest tattoo (don't ask) to the two teenage girls who broke into Jackson's hotel room while he was in the shower.

"So these two girls are standing there in the bathroom, screaming and laughing and begging to take some pictures, and Jackson is going nuts! 'How'd you get in here?'" Jason mimicked his best friend's voice. "'Y'all get out of here! This isn't funny!' He kept yelling and those girls just kept giggling and squealing." He hooted with laughter. "Oh my gosh, it was *hilarious.*"

"Oh, for heaven's sake, Jason," Laura interrupted, not amused. "Where was your security? I thought they locked down your floors at the hotels. How did this happen?"

"That's the funny part, Mom. That whole penthouse floor was ours. I mean, not just the five of us, but the whole entourage. The band, the back-up singers, our lead group, everybody. And we've got strict rules about who does and does not get on those floors when we travel. But Frito, one of our tech guys, had met these two girls after the show. You've gotta know Frito—he's from some other planet. He can fix any musical instrument as fast as any pit crew at Daytona. He's incredible, but when it comes to fans, he just doesn't get it. He's clueless.

"So these girls are flirting with him down at the Hard Rock after the show, and he's just putty in their hands. He's falling for all their bull, thinking he's just all that. And all the while, they're just scheming to get to *us*. Duh? Kids pull this stuff everywhere we go. He should have known better, but he's only been with us a few months. He never had a clue how devious these kids can be. So Frito soaks it all up, loving every minute of the attention these girls are dishing him. He swears he never told them he was part of our crew. But I guarantee they knew all about him *long* before that night. Knew just where to scope him out after the show, the whole nine yards.

"So they sweet talk the old Frito Bandito," Jason postured, imitating the girls, his voice in a ridiculous falsetto. "'We really love you, man. Pleeeease take us up to your room—we just wanna hang with you, man!' And Frito melts like butter on a hot biscuit, and off they go. He sneaks them up the elevator—mind you, you have to have a special key for that elevator. Then they hang out in his room for a few minutes until he goes into his bathroom to take a leak—"

"Jason—"

"Sorry, Mom." He winced at Hannah then continued, never missing a beat. "He goes to *relieve* himself then comes out and guess what? Miracle upon miracle, they're gone! Ya think?"

He stopped to shove a generous fork full of ham into his mouth. Frank took the opportunity to get a word in. "Your mother's right, Jason. What good is your security if you can't even trust your own crew? You may need to think about getting a new security team. And I hope you've disciplined this Frito guy."

"Oh, you could say that. Gevin went ballistic. He was furious."

Hannah visualized Gevin Michaels, oldest of *Out of the Blue* at 33, with a deep bass voice as smooth as velvet. The decisive father-figure of the group, Gevin usually called the shots when it came to organization and details, with the help of the management team that oversaw their every move. Tall, with spiky black hair, thick eyebrows, and a close-cropped beard, Gevin's maturity was no hindrance to even the youngest of fans. He had an equal number of "MARRY ME, GEVIN!" signs in every audience, just like the others. He was also Jason's cousin, nephew of Frank and Laura.

"Gevin? I would think Jackson would be the one who was upset," Laura countered.

"Jackson? Come on, Mom. Jax? You know how he is. He loves all that attention. He's still laughing about it."

Hannah had always adored Jackson Greer. The baby of the group, joining when he was only sixteen, Jackson had all the right stuff: messy white-blond hair, cobalt blue eyes, a raspy tenor voice with an endless range, and an outrageous sense of humor.

Jason continued. "Of course, I guess if Frito hadn't come when he did and snatched them out of there, Jackson might not be laughing. He would've been pretty ticked if they'd gotten pictures of him in his *nakeditity* and sold them to the *Enquirer*."

"Well, hey, inquiring minds want to know," Hannah quoted.

Jason paused then smiled at the unexpected joke. "Well, Hannah, is that a fact? Would you like to elaborate on that a little?"

"Uh, no . . . I don't think so," she laughed, embarrassed again. She faked a cough then plowed on, avoiding his teasing eyes. "But I'm curious. Is it always such a circus when you're on tour?"

Jason nodded. "Oh, the stories I could tell you, girl. Most of the time it's so surreal it's hard to even believe. People are *so* crazy. They will do *anything*. You cannot believe some of these kids. Mostly the younger ones. I'm talkin' girls like twelve, thirteen, fourteen. But you've gotta watch those middle-aged housewives too."

"You're serious?"

"I'm tellin' you—they're the most dangerous because they have the money to finance the chase. It's unbelievable the lengths some of them will go to. But y'know what? Most of the time we get a kick out of it all. I mean, it's just part of the package. We've learned to expect it. But there are times—sometimes when you're already exhausted and you've been away from home for too long—that's when it gets old. And those are the times you have to consciously fight your thoughts and those feelings of anger or frustration. And you have to realize that these fans, even the crazy little girls, are the ones who buy the music, buy the concert tickets, the whole enchilada. And then you just take a deep breath and go on."

"And those are the times when you head home for a little sanity, right?" Laura reached over to squeeze his hand.

He lifted his mother's hand to his lips and kissed it tenderly. "No place I'd rather be, Mom."

"How long will you be home, son?" Frank asked.

"I'm trying to stay for a week or so if we can make some schedule changes. We're supposed to do some studio time but none of us are in the mood. We're all too tired. We scattered in five different directions for Christmas so I doubt we'll make it to the studio. But as far as I know, everyone's still planning to be here for New Year's."

Laura stood up and began to clear the dinner dishes. Hannah started to join her when Jason placed his hand over hers. "That's okay, you're the guest. I'll help her."

She bit her lip, chiding herself for still melting at his touch.

Laura pinched his cheek. "Such a good boy," she bragged in a borrowed Yiddish accent. "He sings, he dances, he washes the dishes—what more could a mother ask for?"

"Grandchildren?" Frank quirked a hopeful smile.

Jason cleared his throat, ignoring the question. "So Mom! What's for dessert?" He picked up his plate and Hannah's.

Stacking the dishes in the sink, Laura looked over her shoulder at the towering son behind her. "Chocolate pecan pie. What else?"

"Sweet! You always come through for me, woman! Hannah, wait 'til you taste this. It's incredible. It's a good thing Sergio isn't here. We wouldn't get a bite."

"How is my favorite Spaniard?" Laura asked as she cut into the dark pie.

Sergio Cruz, the handsome European hailing from Barcelona. Everyone said he looked like a young Antonio Banderas, the movie actor. Hannah pictured his curly black hair usually worn in a pony tail, the dazzling smile, and the dark bedroom eyes that had stopped hearts all over the world for years. The mere sound of his accent used to make her knees go weak. She caught herself twisting her napkin.

"I'm not sure, Mom. You know Sergio. Totally unpredictable. He's supposed to be in Hawaii but then he could show up any minute. He's fine, I guess. Although I don't care much for his current steady squeeze."

Laura placed the dessert plate on the table before her husband. "Well, as I recall I didn't care much for *your* last 'steady squeeze' either." She shot a look at Hannah, rolling her eyes.

"Gee, Mom, and wouldn't I *love* to spoil this perfect evening with a rowdy discussion about my ex-fiancée." Jason served Hannah her pie then sat down to his own. "I don't *think* so."

That's when Laura gently placed her hand on Hannah's shoulder and looked kindly into her eyes. "Would you like some coffee, sweetie?"

Hannah couldn't explain it. The term of endearment, the touch of a mother's hand on her shoulder. The hospitality of this kind woman and her family, the palpable love between the three of them. The surprising ease she felt in Jason's presence. Hannah felt like she'd been wrapped in a warm blanket of love, at ease and completely comfortable here. The nervous butterflies seemed to have vanished.

She looked deeply into those compassionate eyes. "Laura?" she whispered. "Thank you."

Laura leaned over to hug her. Hannah blinked away the moisture in her eyes, avoiding the long familiar eyes she felt upon her. When she finally looked up, she smiled back at Jason. He ducked his head, absently picking at his pie with his fork. After what seemed like an eternity, he peeked back at her under his brow and flashed a quick smile before refocusing on his dessert.

What was that all about?

Beside her sat one of the most famous celebrities of the music world. The sandy blond hair—characteristically unruly, of course. The pronounced jaw line and exaggerated dimples, and the greenest eyes God ever made, set in a perpetual smile. Though she had adored him for more years than she cared to admit, she had never before met Jason McKenzie in person. For all she knew, he could have been conceited, arrogant, and none too happy to find a stranger at the family dinner table tonight. Yet, here he was, as normal and down to earth as anyone she'd ever met.

Stealing glances at me like a shy school boy?

"Honey, that was outstanding," Frank said, interrupting her thoughts. "And to think you did it all by yourself."

"Hey! I still know how to put a meal together," she teased. "Just because Jason insists I hire a little help around this big ol' house doesn't mean I've forgotten all my old recipes."

"Laura, thank you so much," Hannah added. "Thanks for inviting me to join you all tonight. Everything was *so* good. They're right—you're an amazing cook."

Jason snorted and leaned toward her. "You should see what she does with lima beans. To *die* for."

Laura sighed audibly. "Jason, would you leave the poor girl alone?"

"Actually," his eyes twinkled with mischief. "I was thinking I'd challenge her to a game of pool. You like to play, Hannah?"

"Me? Well, yeah, but I need to go. It's been really nice but it's getting pretty late."

Frank stood up, coffee mug in hand. "I was just thinking about that. It's almost one o'clock, Hannah. I think you ought to stay over instead of getting out on the road tonight. Jason could take you home if you're not comfortable with that. But I'm a bit uneasy for anyone to be out on the streets this late, especially during the holidays. Most folks don't know when to draw the line on their holiday cheer, if you know what I mean."

Laura jumped at the idea. "Frank's right. And besides, that way you can spend the day with us tomorrow if you don't have any plans."

Hannah's heart began to pound a little harder. *Christmas with Jason McKenzie and his family? No, no, no.* "No, no—that would really be too much," she said, begging off as best she could. "I just couldn't—"

"Nonsense. Sure you could," Jason said. "You're just afraid I'll beat you at pool, aren't you? A little chicken, are we? That's it, of course. You're chicken." His eyes taunted her. "Bawk bawk bawk . . ."

Throwing all her inner restraint out the window, she took the bait. "You're on."

"Whoa! Sounds to me like you've played a little pool before?"

"Well now, you'll just have to find that out for yourself, won't you? But weren't you doing the dishes for your mother tonight? I wouldn't want to keep you from your obligations."

"Hardly," Laura balked. "I wouldn't let him near these good dishes. Hannah, go on and get him out of here for me. You two have a good time. Frank and I are going to turn in for the night. Jason, show her to her room. Why don't you put her in JT's room?"

"Excuse me?" Hannah coughed. JT Malone—the bad boy of *Blue*. Numerous body piercings, tattoos, and hair color that changed almost weekly. His husky baritone voice was the perfect compliment to their legendary harmonies, and his renegade reputation earned him recognition as "the wild one."

Jason laughed at her again. "No, silly, you're not *rooming* with JT. Mom's got all the guest rooms designated for the guys. They all show up at one time or another and she insists on making them feel at home. You don't mind staying in JT's room, do you? I promise he's not here at the moment."

"Oh, I guess I can stand it," she teased. She tried to hide her embarrassment at the mistaken assumption.

"Come on." Jason grabbed her hand. "The pool table is downstairs. You'll love the game room. Wait 'til you see what Mom's done with it."

CHAPTER 4

Stepping down the last three stairs into the expansive game room felt like stepping into a museum. That's because it *was* a museum. Laura had covered the walls with professionally framed photographs documenting the entire history of *Out of the Blue*.

"This is amazing! Look how young you guys were!" Hannah laughed, pointing to an early cover on *Teen* magazine. "JT without tats or piercings? This must have been a nursery shoot."

Jason set up the billiard balls. "I know, doesn't he look like a big baby? Check that one out over there," he pointed with a cue stick. "Get a load of Jackson. I don't think his voice had even changed yet. *'Never gonna leave you, baby . . .'* he mimicked, croaking the *Blue* hit like an adolescent.

"Stop!" She laughed. "Besides, you don't exactly look like an old geezer either, Jason. Is that peach fuzz I see on your chin here?" She leaned closer to examine another group shot.

"Ouch? Pretty fast with the comebacks, are we?"

Hannah looked from picture to picture, enthralled with the captured history of the group she had once followed so faithfully all those years. Photos of the five at dozens of music award shows, appearances on television and concert stages, and many from photo shoots that adorned magazine covers for years. Among them, Laura had included enlarged personal snapshots the guys had taken—horsing around backstage, at recording sessions, on the tour buses as they traveled.

It was almost more than she could absorb. She took a deep breath, pinching herself to make sure this wasn't still a dream. She leaned forward for a closer look at a picture of Jason holding hands with a long-legged blonde beauty in a short, tight leather skirt.

"Ah, Jennifer, isn't it?" She started to glance over her shoulder but jumped when she discovered Jason standing right behind her. "Whoa, how long have you been standing here?"

"Long enough. I love looking at all these old pictures. Mom is so good about keeping up with all our stuff. And to answer your question, it just didn't work out."

"What didn't work out?"

"With Jennifer. You'd have liked her. She's terrific. We had a lot of good times together. I'm telling you, she's crazy. You wouldn't believe the pranks she used to pull on us."

Hannah noticed a far off look on his face and decided to leave it alone.

He inhaled deeply. "But, y'know what? Sometimes these things just aren't meant to be. She was ready to settle down and start a family and I wasn't. I mean, the way I see it, I've got to ride this train as long as I can. Or at least until I know it's time to get off. We're still friends and we occasionally keep in touch. She's engaged to an attorney in Nashville. Nice guy. I'm happy for her."

"No regrets?" Hannah turned back to the gallery.

"No regrets. A hard lesson to learn, but I knew in my heart it wasn't meant to be. Believe it or not—and you may have trouble understanding this coming from me— but I really try to keep tuned in to what God wants me to do with my life."

She turned to question his statement, lifting a brow.

He returned the suspicious expression then headed back to the pool table. "I know—kinda weird, huh? The thing is, I'm not a freak about my relationship with God or anything, but it's definitely important to me. More than anyone knows."

He picked up the eight ball, tossing it gently from one hand to the other. "There just came a time when I knew deep down it wasn't gonna work out with Jennifer. I fought it, but I knew it wasn't right. And I think that's why I have no hard feelings or regrets." His tone changed. "So I said to her, I said, "Jennifer? *'If you're really gonna leave me, just do it and go, 'cause I ain't gonna cry, I'll just get on with the show!'* ""

"You've got to be kidding. I had no idea that song was so personal!"

He was laughing again. "Yeah, well, it makes for easy lyrics. What can I say?" He made a silly face, as if he'd been found out. "But wanna know the truth? I still feel like a little kid living this dream life. I'm having way too much fun. One of these days, I'll know it's time to walk away from it and . . . I don't know, just grow up? But I'm in no hurry. Now c'mon, let's play some pool here. What's your wager?"

Hannah walked over to the opposite wall, selected a cue stick and chalked it. "I don't know. What did you have in mind?"

"If I win, you hang out with me for a few days."

WHAT! He might as well have karate-kicked her in the gut—the air sucked right out of her lungs. For a second, she thought she'd faint right there on the pool table. *He's known me a total of two hours and now he's ready to spend a few days with me? Jason McKenzie wants to hang out with* ME?! She tried to hide her shock, turning her back to avoid his probing eyes, continuing to chalk the cue stick.

Remnants of Laura's warning bounced around in her head like an echo chamber . . . *heartbreaker, heartbreaker, heartbreaker* . . . She kept her back to him to buy more time, taking a deep breath and a hard swallow to stop the tornado in her head. She kept moving, hoping he'd think she was just getting ready for their game of pool.

Think, Hannah, think! These guys can have any girl they want, anywhere, anytime. Women throw their panties at them on stage, for crying out loud! Which means Jason is just coming on to you because that's what he's used to. It isn't you. It's the whole adoring fan thing. He expects you to drool over the chance to hang out with him. Don't do it! Don't you dare! You're not some adolescent groupie! Just turn around, hold your head high, and show him what you're made of!

Hannah turned slowly, still chalking the cue in a grand attempt at nonchalance. "Let me get this straight. If you win, I spend some time with you over the next couple of days."

"I think a week would be more suitable."

"A week."

Not a couple days. A week. He wants a week.

He made his way toward her side of the table, touching her elbow gently to move past her. She inhaled the musky scent of his cologne. He was humming. He started to dance with his cue stick. Over-animated, suave moves that made her laugh out loud. And it felt *so* good to laugh. She felt muscles relax, easing the tension.

Then again . . .

The battle in her mind continued. *He is genuinely nice. He's polite. He comes from a good home. I mean, the guy loves his mother!* She felt her head nodding in rhythm to the debate ping-ponging in her head. *And let's face it. He is flirting with you. How long has it been since anyone other than Ed, the dinosaur janitor, flirted with you? Huh?*

"So is it a deal?" he sang, turning to lunge his cue-stick dance partner in a dramatic dip.

Be cool. Unimpressed. "I was expecting something like doing your laundry or giving you a foot massage."

"Ooooh, now that could be nice—"

"In your dreams, McKenzie." *That's it, that's it. Nice and cool . . .* "I'm pretty good at pool. I'll take the bet. But let's see—how about if *I* win, you sing me a song. An original song that you make up, right here, right now. All by yourself. No fancy equipment. Just you and your guitar. Let me see just how good a musician you really are."

"Piece of cake. With the addendum that if I lose, we play double or nothing for a second chance."

"You're on. Break 'em."

"Stand back, girl. You're about to witness poetry in motion." His tone changed. He became the announcer. "The master takes his stance. He carefully stretches across the edge of the table, positioning every muscle for optimum effort . . . he draws back . . . and in a single, fluid motion—"

"He misses the ball by a mile!" she shouted. "Way to go, Jason. Oh, this is gonna be way too much fun. Move over, Beethoven. Let me show you what 'poetry in motion' *really* looks like!"

34

"That was beautiful, Jason."

He set the acoustic guitar back into its case. "You're just saying that. You're mocking me 'cause you beat the snot out of me over there."

"No, I'm not. Of course, it's not a spontaneous original, so you still owe me. And probably big time, since you tried to cheat me with a Jason classic. But I've always loved that song. Why didn't you guys ever release it as a single?"

"How do you *know* that song?" He noticed the blush creeping across her face again and realized how much he enjoyed such innocence. Such a refreshing change.

"You played it on your first televised Fox Family concert."

"You're right—I'd forgotten all about that. We never released it because I was the only one who liked it. The guys gave me so much grief about it. But it was one of the first songs I wrote, and it still means a lot to me. So I'm glad you liked it. Even if it wasn't *spontaneous.*" He rolled his eyes. "Oh well, at least I know there's two of us on the planet who like it. Which tells me something else about you."

"And what would that be?"

"We have a history together. We both like the same music."

"That would be an understatement," Hannah laughed. "Confessions of a former groupie and all that." She tucked a strand of hair behind her ear and darted her eyes away from his.

He leaned back and smiled at her. In fact, he realized he couldn't stop looking at her.

What is it? Why is this girl getting under my skin? I don't even know her. She's kinda cute . . . and the gawking is long gone, thank God. But just look at her—

she's relaxed like she's been here a thousand times before. What's that about? And why did Mom invite her over here tonight anyway? That's so not Mom.

He watched her squirm under his gaze.

She looked away, stretching her arms over her head, yawning. "What time is it anyway? I can't keep my eyes open."

Jason peeked at the clock over the counter. It's only 2:30. The night's still young!" He stood up. "And don't you even think about pulling that sleepy stuff. You promised another game if I lost." He headed back to the pool table. "You owe me a game."

"No way. I'm beat. If you'll recall, I put in a full day at work before your Mom kidnapped me."

"Oh yeah, poor baby. And here's where I'm supposed to get all sympathetic and understanding, right? Forget it. Look, I'll get us something to drink and make some popcorn. Mom keeps the kitchen down here stocked. What do you want—a Coke? Dr. Pepper?"

He could tell she was exhausted but he couldn't help it. He didn't want the night to end. He watched her tortured yawn and felt a twinge of guilt for keeping her up, but it passed.

Hannah burrowed into the sofa, dropping her head back against the cushions. "How come none of those fan magazines ever told what a cruel person you are?"

"Because I'm not. I'm just stubborn. Now what'll it be?" He moved back toward the sofa, standing beside her. He noticed her long lashes fanning the top of her cheeks as her eyelids drooped then closed. She was just so . . . natural.

That's it. That's what makes her so different. She's natural. Not forced. Nothing striking or stunning. Just fresh and natural. And extremely appealing.

"Hannah, don't you fall asleep."

Nothing.

"Don't you even think about falling asleep."

Nothing.

"HANNAH!"

"What?!" She jumped with a start. "Don't do that! Jason, you scared me to death!"

He grabbed her hands, pulling her to her feet. "You've gotta wake up, woman! You see, I'm just a poor, poor boy who needs a little company here. Can you hep' me out, ma'am? Won't you hep dis po' boy?" He batted his eyelashes at her, plastering a silly grin across his face as he backed up, pulling her along to the bar. "Pweeze keep wittle Jason comp'ny, pweeze?"

"Now, that's pitiful. Just pitiful. Don't tell me that actually works on some of your fans?"

He deposited her on a bar stool then stepped behind the counter. "Sorry. State secrets. I could tell you but—"

"—you'd have to shoot me. Right. That's okay. I don't really want to know."

"So? What's your poison?"

"Coke straight up with a side of popcorn. And back off. I'm a witch when I'm tired. Just ask my little brother."

"You have a brother? Come to think of it, we've talked about me all night." He handed her a tall glass of iced Coke. "Typical. Because, of course, it's *all* about me." He dropped his head in mocked shame. "I'm so sorry. Tell me about your family, Hannah. What's your brother's name?"

"Greg. He's a linebacker for FSU."

"Get outta here! Your brother plays for FSU? He must be good."

"Yeah, he's great. He drove me nuts when we were kids. But then I gave him a lot of grief too."

"Any other brothers or sisters?"

"Nope, just Greg. And then there's my mom and dad. They still live in Dallas where I grew up. Dad has his own business, an internet company. Mom's in real estate. Loves it. Then there's Sassy, our Maltese. She's getting up there in doggy years, but she's still part of the family. I had her up here at my apartment for a while, but I'm gone so much with work, it wasn't fair to her. I took her back home to my parents at Thanksgiving."

"Yikes! I just remembered Baby! I'll be right back," he yelled flying up the stairs. In a few moments, he was back. "You won't believe this—she's all curled up, sleeping on top of the comforter, right between Mom and Dad. I can't believe it!"

"I take it your folks like dogs, huh?"

"Yeah, but I've never known Mom to let one sleep on her bed. Must be that Christmas spirit she always gets. Which would explain the extra place setting at the table tonight."

She blushed. He loved it.

"Okay, now where were we? Oh, you've told me about your family, but what about you? What are you majoring in?"

"Journalism. I like to write. Mostly freelance. I've had several pieces published already, but—"

"What kind of pieces? What do you write?"

"You name it. Mainly human interest stories. I've done some interviews for the paper. I did a piece on the history of McMurphy's that was—"

"You mean the coffee shop over by the campus?"

"Yeah, that's the one. It's been around for almost a hundred years and has a fascinating list of people who've worked there while they were in school. Quite a history—

two United States senators, a Supreme Court judge, and five NBA players. That was a blast to write—and what exactly are you grinning at?"

"You. Did you know your whole face lights up when you talk about your writing? It's like a hundred watt bulb just clicked on inside you. You really love it, don't you?"

"Yeah, I guess I do. It's a tough business to break into, but I love it. Sometimes there are so many different things floating around in my head I want to write about or research that it almost feels like I'm going to explode. My fingers can't fly fast enough across the keyboard. I'll get absolutely lost in what I'm writing and realize that hours have flown by and I didn't even know it."

"That's *exactly* how I feel when I'm writing music." Jason rounded the bar and pulled up a stool beside her. "Sometimes I forget to eat or sleep or anything until I finish a song—"

"—and when you do, it's like you've given birth to your own child, right?"

"Well, yeah, but then I've never experienced childbirth so it's a little hard to say."

"Jason!" she laughed. "I haven't either, thank you very much. But you know what I mean."

"Well, for what it's worth, I think that's totally cool that you have such a passion for what you do. Stay with it. Don't ever give up. Make a living doing the thing you love to do most? It's the only way."

She watched him take another shot.

"And that, my dear lady, is how you win at pool. Ha! You're mine. ALL WEEK!"

Hannah's jaw dropped. "That is so unfair! You cheated."

"What? I beg your pardon. I do not cheat. Not at pool. Not at anything."

"You did too! You distracted me with all these questions. That's not fair. I demand a rematch."

"Too late. Besides, I'm exhausted. It's now 3:35 in the morning. I can't believe how inconsiderate you are. You come into our home, you eat our food, then you have the audacity to keep me up all night after my long drive up here. On Christmas, no less."

He finished putting away the cue sticks, continuing his faux rant. Then, digging his hands dug deep into his pockets, he slowly walked over to stand beside her. They leaned against the back of the sofa. "By the way, Merry Christmas, Hannah." His eyebrows danced in mischief.

Hannah shrugged in resignation. She nodded, folding her arms across her chest and peeking sideways at Jason, noting the smirk still spread on his face. "Merry Christmas, Jason. I suppose you still believe in Santa?"

"Well, of course I do. How else could I explain you being here?"

Their eyes locked for only a second before she attempted a smile then looked away. Suddenly his arm was over her shoulder.

"See, I don't think for a second that Mom really conned you away from that grocery store."

Heartbreaker, heartbreaker, heartbreaker . . . The warning pounded against her ears again like a fog horn. *Careful, Hannah, careful.*

"I know for a fact that Santa dropped you off earlier this evening just before I came home. How do I know that, you ask? Because on my way home, I said a little prayer."

She made a face and started to interrupt—

"Don't laugh. It's true. I did. I asked God to make this a very special Christmas. Not just for me but for my whole family. And I walk in the door and there you are. Part of the family on Christmas Eve. How else would I explain it?"

Her cheeks warmed. "Jason, I think you need some sleep."

"I do. And so do you. But I have a favor to ask."

"No, your dog is not sleeping in my room."

He tossed his head back laughing. "Sorry, she's already spoken for. No, this one's selfish. A Christmas kiss. You. Me. Here. Now?" He paused, his eyes pleading. "I could grab some mistletoe if that would help."

Laura's subtle warning about her son's charm echoed over and over in her mind. But she couldn't suppress the smile creeping up her face. *Good grief. We only met a few hours ago and here I am, dying for him to kiss me. Gotta be a dream. I'll wake up tomorrow and be totally depressed from the world's longest, best dream.* She felt him move a little closer beside her.

"Look, you probably think I'm being kind of forward. But seriously, I'm not talking any deep down, tonsil-washing kiss or anything."

She chuckled, uneasy by the intensity in his eyes. Then, the sweetness of his gentle smile—a smile so familiar yet so sincere—sent a surge of heat from her head to her toes.

"Just a little merry-Christmas-nice-to-know-you kiss. That's all," he breathed.

"You mean 'a quiet simple kiss'?"

His smiled broadened at her reference to one of his famous lyrics. "That's right. Just a quiet simple kiss."

No more voices in her head. No more excuses. She surrendered with the slightest nod of her head. She followed his searching eyes as he looked back and forth from her eyes . . . to her lips . . . to her eyes . . . She felt dizzy.

Finally, he leaned down, his lips warm and moist against hers. She closed her eyes in the closest thing to heaven she'd ever known. He exhaled, a quiet sigh escaping from somewhere inside him. And then it was over.

She savored the moment, refusing to open her eyes. "Never been kissed like that before," she whispered.

"Uh oh. Did I do something wrong?" he whispered back.

"Oh no. You did everything perfect. That's what I mean. It was . . . perfect."

He slipped his arm around her waist pulling her closer against his side. It felt so natural. Like a brotherly gesture.

Only better. *Much* better.

"Merry Christmas, Hannah."

"Merry Christmas, Jason."

CHAPTER 5

Hannah showered and slipped into the pajamas Laura had left for her on the bed. She was pulling on the thick chenille robe when she heard a soft knock on the bathroom door. Scrambling to wrap the robe around her, she answered, "Yes?"

"Hannah, it's me Jason."

"Jason, what do you want?"

"I was just thinking. Are you really that tired?"

"Yes, I'm exhausted. Why?"

"Well, hurry up and come out here and I'll tell you."

She looked in the mirror, realizing she'd washed all her makeup off. *Great. Now what?* She ran a brush through her hair then sighed, knowing it was too late for any beauty tricks. She gathered her clothes and opened the door. Jason sat on the floor of her room—well, JT's room—leaning against the wall spinning a basketball on his finger.

"Jason, don't you ever sleep? Do you know how late it is?"

He jumped up still playing with the basketball. "I know, I know, but you've got to remember my day is my night." His scrunched his face. "That didn't make any sense, did it?"

"Not exactly." She headed over to her bed. *JT's bed . . .*

"Okay. See, when we're on the road we're up all night and sleep most of the day. And it's impossible to get my times switched around. So downstairs, I thought I was tired until I realized I wasn't.

"You're not making any sense."

"I know. So I was thinking—well, I was just wondering if you wanted to watch a movie or something. There's a loft up here, just down the hall. Fireplace, entertainment center, you name it. C'mon, I can't sleep and I'd love the company. What d'ya say?"

"I'll probably fall asleep."

"That's okay. Just don't drool on the furniture. Or me."

"I'll try to remember that. Are you sure your parents won't mind? We won't disturb them, will we?"

"No, their room is way down the hall. The loft is great—it's my favorite room in the house. When the guys are here, it's where we hang out. Come on, I'll show you."

A fire crackled in the fireplace, the lighting was soft, and easy jazz filled the room over the sound system. Overstuffed chairs and sofas formed an intimate circle around the hearth. He opened a cabinet to browse an extensive DVD library.

"Jason, can I ask you something?"

"Sure. Shoot."

"You and Jackson and Gevin, JT and Sergio. What's it like being who you are? I mean, do you *feel* like megastars and celebrities? Or is it just a way of life that you're totally accustomed to. I can't even begin to comprehend what your life is like."

He abandoned the search and sat down on the sofa beside her. "Actually, every morning I wake up, look in the mirror and admire myself—the famous, good looking one in the group, of course. Then I call my chef, order breakfast in bed, and tell Giles the butler what clothes I want from my twelve closets." He propped his feet up on the coffee table in front of them. "It's a tough life, but somebody's gotta do it."

"Okay, okay, laugh all you want, but I'm serious. I'd really like to know." She stretched her legs out on the table beside his, crossing them at the ankles.

"I know, I know. I was just kidding. Look, I'm just as normal as you or anybody else on the face of the earth. I get hiccups, I blow my nose, I put my pants on one leg at a time just like the next guy. I'm sloppy and irresponsible at times. I get moody sometimes. I get tired of the guys I work with sometimes. They get tired of me. We argue and fight. Then we'll get over it and laugh about it and go on. I don't really know how to answer your question. This is my life and it's all I've known since I was just a kid."

He arched his back in a slow stretch. "But I'll never get used to the hysteria of all the fans. All the attention and hype. When that stuff hits, I mean, it's like life kicks into this surreal realm that's flat-out bizarre. It's sooooo strange. I can't even begin to explain it. Hannah, I will never understand why the five of us are anything special."

"You're kidding—right?"

"No, I'm totally serious. Why us? Why not five other guys? Okay, so we can sing and we play a little music, but c'mon—some of these kids throw themselves at us like we're some kind of gods. That part scares me. And I always have to wonder why all this happened? Why us? Why me?"

"That's the part I can't imagine, Jason. Does it get old? Do you wish it was different?"

"No, I can honestly say I love it. Like I told you earlier—doing something you love and making a living doing it? Well it's incredible. Being up on stage and singing and doing our sets—I feel so *alive*. I wish I could put you in my shoes so you could understand."

"But how do you stay so sane? It seems like most celebrities are so full of themselves they can hardly function. But you're so—"

"Watch it—"

"—down to earth. Meeting you, getting to know you— you're so *real*. I've been with you all evening, and I still haven't seen a trace of ego. How is that possible for someone who has millions of women all over the world obsessed with you?"

Jason laughed. "Oh yeah, millions. But you have to remember most of them are adolescent. They're just kids, Hannah."

"Not all of them. I've seen those pictures of you guys with the gorgeous models and actresses. Don't give me this 'just kids' bull."

Jason's face crimsoned. "Maybe not *all* of them. There are a few ladies out there. Okay, a *lot* of ladies. *Hordes* of ladies—"

"I get the picture."

"And I'd be lying if I said I didn't go out with some of them. All the guys have. But I'm tellin' you now—what you see on TV ain't what you get."

"What do you mean?"

"Some of them are really nice. Decent. All that. But the majority of them are unbelievable. They talk trash worse than any sailor. They'll sleep with anything that moves. And all they want is to be seen with us to get themselves in front of a camera. You don't know agony 'til you've been stuck with one of those losers. I guess what I'm trying to say, it isn't always what it seems to be."

"So how do you come out of this when the time comes? How do you go from being rock star to regular guy again? Is it even possible? Will there ever come a time you can just walk into a restaurant without being mobbed?"

"Oh yeah. Think about it. Remember NSync? Other than Timberlake, would you recognize one of those guys if he walked in the door right now? Or the Spice Girls? If you ran into one of them at the store, would you know who she was? See, right now it's hard to imagine going back to a normal life, but it'll come."

Hannah snuggled deeper into the sofa, wrapping her arms around herself. Jason grabbed a quilt off the back of the sofa and threw it over both of them. "Thanks, Jason. But how will you handle it in here?" she asked, tapping her heart. "How will you look in that mirror and say, 'nobody knows who I am anymore'? How will you accept that and be okay about it? Think about what a *major* adjustment that will be. I wouldn't think most people would handle it very well."

"I understand what you're getting at. I think about it all the time. But I think I'm going to be *so* ready for the change when it comes. Ready to live a normal life again. I also give my parents some credit for instilling standards in my life that keep me on a reality check. Since the beginning of all this. They hold my feet to the fire and remind me who I am. And they pray for me all the time, too. That makes a huge difference."

He tucked the quilt around his legs. "Now it's my turn."

"Your turn for what?"

"To ask you a question."

"Fire away," she moaned through a yawn.

"Right now, tonight . . . when you think about this—I mean . . ."

"You're stammering. Spit it out, McKenzie."

"When we met tonight, you were pretty star struck."

She snorted. "That's an understatement. Your point?"

"So right here, right now. Who are you with? Me the celebrity, or me, the son of the lady who came through your lane at the store? I guess I'm wondering if you can get past the other stuff."

She stared into the fire. Tough question. Throughout the night she had not once forgotten that this was THE Jason McKenzie. The butterflies, the adrenaline. He was, after all, the idol of her teenage years. His picture had once plastered the walls of her room; his songs, engraved on her heart forever.

Could she ever think of him any other way? He wasn't just any ordinary guy. To think of him as a regular person, someone she could actually be "friends" with? Good question. Tonight had been so amazing. He already felt like a friend. He made it so easy. So incredibly easy.

"Jason, it would be impossible for me to forget who you are. I've had such a ridiculous crush on you for so many years, it isn't funny. *Long* after all my friends outgrew teen idol fantasies, if you must know." She felt her cheeks warm again. "But after getting to know you tonight—spending this time with you and your family— it's like I've gotten to know someone else entirely. I can't separate *what* you are from *who* you are. But I can tell you this much."

"What?"

"I like the person I've spent this evening with. He's very real."

"Fair enough."

They talked for hours. They talked about life and dreams and family and friends. They never watched a movie. Hannah smiled at the thought. With sleepy eyes, she watched the fire slowly die, leaving behind only glowing embers coated with ash.

Around 8:00 on Christmas morning, Laura padded down the hall with Frank close behind her. Finding Jason's bedroom door open and his room empty, they also noticed Hannah's door was open—her room also deserted. They stopped by the loft, smiling at the sight. Tiptoeing over to the sofa, they discovered Jason sitting with his head tilted back against the cushions, his long legs stretched out on the coffee table. Snuggled beneath a quilt, Hannah lay with her head on a pillow in his lap, Jason's fingers woven through the dark tendrils of her hair. His soft snores made them smile.

Frank rolled his eyes. "My son. Ever the heartbreaker."

Laura sighed happily, wrapping her arms around her husband's waist. "She's a nice girl, isn't she?"

His warm smile answered her question. "Yes, and apparently we're not the only ones who think so." He nodded toward his son's sleeping image.

She suppressed a laugh, not wanting to wake them. "Not a bad way to start Christmas, is it?" she whispered in his ear.

Jason suddenly snorted out loud. His head moved in perfect rhythm as he mumbled in his sleep with the slightest hint of a melody. His lips continued to move, but they heard nothing. He was sound asleep.

CHAPTER 6

"Turn left at the light up there. The apartment complex is on the left. See it?"

Jason maneuvered his black Escalade into the turn lane. The overnight storm had left the roads patchy with ice. The SUV slid around the corner. "Whoa, baby! That was fun." His sarcasm penetrated the chilled interior of the vehicle as he regained control. "Guess it's been a while since I drove on icy roads."

"No, really?" Hannah feigned innocence. She smiled at his appearance, his wandering hair tucked under a backward UNC baseball cap. The cold air pinked his cheeks, his eyes shining and alert as he concentrated on driving.

"Well, of course, because I don't get to—"

"I was teasing, Jason. It's obvious you aren't used to this kind of driving." She shook her head. "Anyone ever tell you you're gullible?"

"Me? No way. I knew you were teasing. I did." He shot her a serious look. "I did!"

"Sure you did. But that reminds me of something I wanted to ask you. What on earth would make a rock star drive a long trip like you made yesterday? You drove in from Atlanta, right? Is that where you live now?"

"No, I live in L.A. I was in Atlanta for some meetings with one of our producers."

"So why didn't you just fly?"

"Simple. I needed the space. Time alone. Just me, my wheels, my tunes, and the open road. Driving gives me a chance to air out my brain, y'know?"

"Makes sense. Oh, that's my apartment there—the last one on the right. Just pull in the last space there."

He navigated into the space with great care, sliding only slightly to a stop. "Sit tight." He opened his door. "I'll get your door."

Another smile curled Hannah's lips. *Who said chivalry is dead?* She looked up just as he slid past her window and dropped out of sight. She threw open her door, finding him sprawled flat on his back.

"Jason! Are you okay?"

His eyes tracked slowly to hers. A second passed before they both burst out laughing. "I've fallen and I can't get up!" he wailed like a little old lady. "Can you help me, dearie?"

Hannah fell back in the seat laughing.

"It isn't *that* funny. A little help, here? I could use a hand, Hannah. That is, if you're not too busy?"

She couldn't stop her giggles enough to sit up. Her legs hanging out of the vehicle above him, she felt him tugging on her shoe.

"Hannah!"

Finally gaining composure, she sat back up and looked at him. "I don't know. I kind of like having you helpless."

"Come on, woman! Give me a hand."

She realized they must have looked like a Shriners clown routine at the Ice Capades as they slipped and slid all the way to her door. Her stomach ached from laughing so hard. "What I would give to have that on tape. It would get a trillion hits on YouTube."

"Very funny." Jason wiped the wet snow off his rear. "Everybody wants a piece of me, and you want—"

"*I want you, got to have you—*" she sang, exaggerating the reprise of the old *Blue* hit. "*—gonna get you, and what'cha gonna do about it, ba-by!*"

He grabbed her, his gloved fingers attempting to tickle her through her heavy coat. Hannah shrieked in protest. "Stop! Jason—no!" she yelled between gasping giggles.

He pulled her into a bear hug, face to face. "Shhhh! Do you want to wake the dead around here? Have a little heart for your neighbors, Hannah. Sheesh."

She struggled out of his grasp, fumbling with her keys, anxious to avoid another attack. Too late. She fell through the opening door, pushing him away at arm's length.

"STOP IT! I hate to be tickled! I mean it! Do NOT tickle me anymore!"

He held his hands up in surrender. "Okay, okay—I get the message." He looked around her apartment. "This is really nice, Hannah. Feels really—"

"Cozy? I know it's kinda small. But I'm not here that much. It's really all I need right now."

"No, it's nice. We've all built these absurd houses and we're never home either. A house is a house." He gave himself a tour as Hannah snatched up stray socks and blue jeans.

"Sorry for the mess, but I wasn't expecting company, for the record."

He balked with a snort. "Tell me you're not apologizing to *me*. I'm a pig. You should see my hotel rooms on tour. If we didn't have a stylist, I'd never get dressed on time. Kinda sad to be twenty-seven years old and still need someone to dress you."

"Somehow I doubt she minds."

"Actually she does. She gets tired of how childish we act most of the time. But hey, she gets paid a truckload for putting up with us. So what time do you want me to come back and pick you up?"

Hannah stopped, then slowly put the pile of clothes in an easy chair. "Look, Jason—"

"Don't even think about it. You're coming and that's settled. Mom would have a fit if you didn't."

"But it's your family. They're all coming over to see *you*. I'll just be in the way. I'd love to see you again, but maybe today's not the best time."

"Nope. I'm not leaving you alone on Christmas so forget it. You'll love my family. And they'll love you too. Besides," he added, turning back toward the door, "I won you for a week, and don't you forget it." He opened the door, tossing an arrogant glance over his shoulder.

"I don't know. I'll think about it."

"Gevin's coming over, y'know," he taunted her. "And I think JT might drop by. His mom is on a shoot over in Australia, so he said he might bring Tracey over. If you won't come for me, surely you'll come to meet the guys? Hmmm?" His eyebrows danced again.

She shook her head, her smile weary. "You never give up, do you?"

He tiptoed back to her, furiously mussed her hair, then headed back toward the open door. "Nope, I don't. How about I pick you up around 5:00? And don't make me wait. I'd hate to have to take back your gift."

"My gift?"

"Gotcha. Now I know you'll come. See you at 5:00. And get some sleep. I don't mean to be rude, but girl, you look beat." His face morphed into an *I'm-in-trouble-now* sneer. He narrowly escaped the pillow she threw at him as he slipped out the door.

Hannah fell onto her sofa. She grabbed another throw pillow, pounding her head into it over and over. "Have I lost my mind?!"

Hannah climbed into a purple pullover sweater as her cell chirped. She looked at the clock. Four fifty-five. Not good timing for a phone call. She wanted to be totally ready when Jason came. She plopped on the edge or her bed and picked up her cell. Her boss's name appeared on the screen. "Hi Jim. I didn't expect to hear from you so soon." She grabbed her black trouser socks then leaned over to pull one on.

"Hi Hannah, how are you?"

She grimaced, wishing she didn't have to be reminded of her long work week ahead. "I'm fine. How did the funeral go?" Another grimace. "Oh, I'm sorry. That's a stupid question—"

"Hey, it's okay. I know what you meant to say. The funeral went about like you'd expect. Sandy is still pretty upset, but that's normal under the circumstances, I guess. But I wanted to let you know I'm back."

"What?" She stopped tugging up the other sock.

"I decided she needed more time with her immediate family, and I wouldn't really be missed. And you know me—I get kind of twitchy being away from the store too long. Anyway, just wanted to let you know you can take the rest of the week off if you want. I really appreciate you stepping in to help out like you did. In fact, you'll find a nice little bonus in your next paycheck. I'm really grateful."

She jumped up and danced a silent victory jig, pounding her fists in the air. She paused to steady her voice. "Oh, well, that's—I mean, I'm sorry you felt you had to come back so soon. But are you sure you don't need me?"

"Yes, I'm sure. Take some time off. Enjoy your break. I'll give you a call in a few days. And thanks again, Hannah. Merry Christmas."

"Merry Christmas, Jim. Bye." She threw the phone on the bed and jumped in the air. "Yessssssss! Yes, yes, yes, yes, YES!"

Her cell phone rang again.

The doorbell rang.

Kylie's name flashed on her cell. Kylie! She hadn't talked to her since all this began! She had so much to tell her!

The doorbell rang. Again. And again and again.

"Yikes! Just a minute, Jason!"

She tossed the phone back on the bed, unanswered. *I'm sorry Kylie, I'll call you later, can't talk now, you'll understand when you hear what's been going on!* She hoped somehow her mental message would get to Kylie. *Yeah right.*

Hannah flew around her room, grabbing the rest of her outfit. She hopped on one foot then the other as she pulled on her black slacks then ran a brush through her clean hair. She brushed her teeth in record time then hurried to the door. She stopped, took a deep breath.

Be calm. Look relaxed. She opened the door.

"Why didn't you tell me there was a blizzard out here, girl? I coulda killed myself coming over here!" Jason stomped his shoes on the welcome mat before stepping into the apartment.

"I didn't know." She peeked out then shoved the door shut against the frigid air. "I slept all afternoon. Is it that bad out there?" When she turned around, he was there. *Right* there.

"Whoa—Hannah. You look amazing," he said, folding his arms across his chest as if studying her. "I mean *really* amazing. You clean up good."

Her face warmed under the scrutiny of his attention. "Well that's good to know. I guess?" Seeing such affection in those warm green eyes reduced her knees to linguine. "Um, so you think it's too dangerous to drive?"

"It's looking pretty bad. The roads aren't impossible but don't plan on coming home tonight. You'll be snowed in for sure." He took both her hands in his. "Which, of course, would be *such* a shame now, wouldn't it?"

The butterflies flitted through her stomach. She plastered a nervous smile on her face. "Give me just a second, will you?"

Hannah hurried to her bathroom, grabbed her small makeup bag and tossed it in her purse. *With these people, you never know when you'll be home again.* The thought scattered the butterflies on another round. Still, she couldn't help feeling excited.

Twenty minutes later they walked hand in hand to the back entrance of the McKenzie's estate. Hannah slowed her steps, her hand tugging Jason back.

He turned. "You okay?"

"I'm really nervous, Jason. All these people . . . I don't think I can do this."

He cupped her face in his gloved hands. "Look. You liked Mom and Dad, right?"

"Of course I did."

"So see? We're all related. We're just a normal family, Hannah. You'll do great. And I promise not to leave you stuck with any of them. Deal?"

She sighed, only slightly reassured by his promise. "Deal."

The evening was one of the sweetest Christmas memories Hannah ever experienced. Just as Jason promised, his family turned out to be a conglomeration of McKenzie warmth and kindness. They made sure to include her in their conversations, asking questions about her studies, her interests, her family, her plans. Jason kept his promise, staying close to her side, sitting on the arm of her chair or sprawled on the floor in front of her, leaning back against her legs.

After their traditional Christmas dinner of turkey and all the trimmings, the family relaxed around the spacious home. They talked, they watched football—just like any other family. Jason was right. They were just ordinary people like everyone else.

Well, *almost.*

"Hey, whassup! Anybody home?"

Hannah knew the voice immediately. In mere seconds she would meet another member of *Blue.* Gevin Michaels. She noticed her hands trembling so she intertwined her fingers, hoping to still them.

She watched across the room as a whole new flock of cousins and nieces and nephews and aunts and uncles spilled into the family room. Jason jumped up to greet them all, hugging kids and kissing aunts and uncles on the cheek. She spotted Gevin, a head taller than the rest of his family.

"Don't even *think* about it!" Gevin warned as Jason pretended he was going to kiss his famous cousin. Gevin faked a punch to Jason's stomach. "It's bad enough I

Diane Moody

have to work with you day in and day out. You'd think I could have a little space on Christmas."

"How's it goin', Cuz?" The teasing aside, they shared a hug. Jason cocked his head to one side and narrowed his eyes. "And what's with the silly grin?"

Hannah watched Gevin's face beam. Everyone called him the serious member of the band, but you'd never know it today. "What're you talking about? What grin?"

Jason twisted his head the other direction, curiosity still etched on his face.

"There's someone here I think you know," Gevin said. He reached back through the pack of people behind him, grabbing a hand the color of coffee with cream. Suddenly, a striking African-American woman squeezed through the crowd.

"Marissa!" Jason pounced on her, scooping her up in his arms. "What are you doing here? This is great!" As he hugged her, the slender beauty's wild curls danced all over his face. "What a nice surprise!"

"Sheesh, McKenzie, you guys sure have a lot of family," she laughed, looking over the crowd. "Who *are* all these people?"

She stepped back beside Gevin, his arm wrapping around her slender waist. "I talked Rissa into spending Christmas with me, family obligations and all, so here we are."

Hannah watched Marissa Shaw snuggle into the comfort of Gevin's arm. Back in her groupie days, she'd read about the talented tour manager for the band. She was known for her no-nonsense approach to management, keeping the entire production team in line and on schedule. Her peers maintained a healthy respect for her, recognizing her immense talent and vision overseeing one of the hottest groups in the industry. Quite a remarkable feat for a woman so young. But Marissa was also known to adore her "boys." With them

58

from the start, she was part of their huge success story. But Hannah had never known how beautiful she was—tall and graceful with arresting caramel eyes, flawless skin, and a captivating smile with perfect white teeth.

Hannah turned to notice the strange look on Jason's face. Then, as if snapping out of a fog, he suddenly faced her with blinking eyes. "I'm so sorry! Hey, Gevin—Rissa. I've got someone you need to meet." He grabbed Hannah's hand, pulling her into the circle. "This is Hannah. Mom picked her up at the grocery store yesterday and well, we can't seem to get rid of her."

"Jason!" Hannah laughed out loud, elbowing him in the ribs.

He put his arm over her shoulder. "I'm teasing. Well, sort of. Anyway, Hannah this is Gevin, but you probably already knew that."

Gevin's smile broadened as his eyes grew wide. "Nice to meet you, Hannah." He embraced her in a hug and pretended to whisper in her ear. "But I probably need to talk to you later about your taste in men." His thick eyebrows raised to acknowledge some inside wisdom. "We'll talk," he whispered loudly.

She laughed. "It's nice to meet you, too, Gevin. But I'd be a little skeptical of advice from a family member. Gene pool and all that."

He threw his head back laughing. "Point well taken!" He turned to Jason. "Sharp girl. Though what she's doing with you baffles me."

Marissa reached out her hand toward Hannah. "Nice to meet you, Hannah. Looks like you and I are the only sane people in the crowd. I'm glad you're here. I was afraid I'd be suffocated by The Family." Gevin hummed the theme from *The Godfather* as Marissa crossed her eyes. "See what I'm talkin' 'bout, girl?"

Gevin grabbed her hand. "If you'll excuse us for a moment, we need to say hi to Aunt Laura and Uncle Frank. We'll be back in a minute."

Hannah sat back down. Jason slowly lowered himself on the armrest again, his arm landing across the back of her chair. He leaned over, whispering in her ear. "Something's up."

"What do you mean?" She felt his face against her hair, actually heard him inhaling the scent of it. An unexpected shiver trickled down her back.

"Gevin and Marissa have always been close. The two of them, I don't know—it's like they rule the roost. Y'know what I mean? They hang out and all that. But something's going on. I can tell by the way he's grinning. Like the cat that ate the canary."

"Aren't you and Gevin really close? Wouldn't he tell you if something was up?"

He hummed a few bars of something she didn't recognize, but the look in his eyes revealed a mind turning over every stone. "Maybe that's why they're here together. I guess we'll find out soon enough."

When the rest of the McKenzie/Michaels battalion said good-night and made their way into the driving snowstorm outside, Jason huddled next to Hannah, both shivering in the driveway as the last carload inched slowly out of the drive.

Gevin walked up behind them holding a plastic cup of Coke. "Geez, I thought they'd never leave."

Whomp! A snowball socked Gevin dead center in his chest. His cup flew into the air, Coke cascading through the flake-filled sky before drawing a brown dotted line across the snow-covered ground. In a fancy display of footwork, he fought to keep his balance, but lost. "Hey!" he protested, flat on his back.

Jason slipped into the shadows as Hannah leaned over to help Gevin to his feet.

"What's with you McKenzies falling flat on your butts all the time?"

Jason heard Hannah's taunt and the sound of their laughter, then watched as Marissa shuffled along the ice, joining them from the dark bushes on the other side of the sidewalk.

"Girl, you see what I got to work with?" She winked mischievously at Hannah. "These boys can't stand on their own two feet for nothin'!"

"Did *you* throw that? Rissa, you hit me! You knocked me down!"

Whomp! Jason ducked back behind the trees after lobbing a huge snowball that plastered the back of Hannah's shoulder. He watched her from his hideout.

"Ouch!" she yelled, turning to see where it came from. "Jason! I know you threw that! Come out here and fight like a man!"

He watched her lock eyes with Marissa. *Uh oh.* In a single fluid motion they charged for a bank of snow and the war began.

Their screams and laughter pierced the cold night air as the snow fell harder. Snowflakes stuck to their eyelashes and covered their hair. Marissa's tight curls looked like so many iced Tootsie-Rolls. Hannah's face glowed pink from the cold, her ears almost red. Gevin's beard looked like a frosted chocolate donut, his red nose easily rivaling Rudolph's famed snout.

The four of them poised in a face-off, each daring the other to throw one more snowball. Jason couldn't feel his fingers anymore, but he wasn't about to give in. He dug his hands back in the snow for one more missile, but they refused to cooperate. He rubbed them against his legs to get the blood circulating again.

Marissa stood up straight across the driveway, waving her hands in the air. "Truce! We're FREEZING! We gotta go back inside!"

Later, wrapped in quilts and sitting by the fireplace in the loft, they sipped hot cocoa and tried to stop shaking. They relived their battle, boasting and posturing about the promised rematch. Eventually, the conversation slowed.

Jason felt sleepy. The sound of the hissing fire lulled him into a relaxed trance. He looked up just as Gevin set his empty mug on the coffee table then moved to sit beside Marissa on the hearth. He watched his cousin cover her with his quilt and snuggle close to her. Gevin kissed her on the cheek and held her against him as they rocked to the music of Kenny G.

Jason watched them. An uneasy wave washed over him. Just like before.

He sat in the exact spot on the sofa where he and Hannah had fallen asleep the night before. She sat in the easy chair adjacent to him now. He caught her eye, patting the seat beside him on the sofa. She wrapped the quilt around her and joined him. He draped his arm around her shoulders, amazed how comfortable and relaxed he felt with her.

Was it only last night she walked into my life?

"Well, now, are we all comfy and cozy?" he teased.

Gevin and Marissa looked at each other then back at them. They nodded in unison.

He couldn't stand the suspense. "All right, you two. That's it. Out with it. What's going on?"

Marissa dropped her head, quietly laughing. "You tell him," she called up.

His heart pounded in his chest. "Tell me what?"

"Cuz, it looks like you need to get your tux to the cleaner's. Seems I'm in need of a best man."

Jason eyed his cousin then exploded in a wild outburst. "Get outta here! You guys are getting *married?*" His shout echoed against the beamed ceiling as he jumped to his feet.

Gevin wrapped both arms around Marissa. "We most definitely are." He planted a passionate kiss on her lips then stood into Jason's bear hug.

"I can't believe it!" Jason drew Marissa into the hug.

"I was *dying* to tell you earlier." Her eyes glistened with tears of joy, her voice husky with emotion.

Jason pulled back to look at her. "Rissa, this is fantastic! I've always thought you guys were perfect for each other!" He scooped her up in his arms, lifting her off the ground. "When did this happen? When did you—"

"It's been going on for a while," Gevin said with a shrug. "We just didn't want anyone to know until we were really sure ourselves. I proposed last night. You guys are the first to know." He paused for a split second, looking across the room. "And Hannah, I—"

"You don't even have to say it." She moved closer toward them. "This is confidential and I totally understand that. I won't say a word to anyone. I promise." Hannah could see the visible relief on their faces. She joined their communal hug. "Congratulations! To both of you!"

They settled back and talked incessantly. Jason pelted them with questions. When did they first know it was more than friendship? How did they hide it so well? Had they set a date? "So when are you gonna tell the rest of the guys?"

"Well, I was just getting to that." Gevin laughed. "We're hoping to tell them privately before the New Year's party."

"Good idea. That'll be a perfect time to make an announcement. Well, I mean, a private announcement. When do you plan to go public with this?"

The smile slowly waned from Marissa's face. This time it was Gevin who averted his eyes and looked down. "Well, that's just it, Jason. There's a little more to it than what we've told you so far."

Jason straightened his shoulders. "Okay. So what is it?"

Gevin glanced at his fiancée. She gave him a look of reassurance. "Go on," she whispered.

He looked across the room at his cousin. "The thing is—Jason, it's time."

The words hung in the air. Jason stared at Gevin. He felt a tremor grip him. *Surely he doesn't mean what I think he means?*

His gaze locked on Gevin's—the knowing look in his cousin's eyes he didn't want to see. Jason's mind refused to accept it. He shook his head, the slight movement screaming what he could not. *No! Not yet—not yet.*

He forced his thoughts on a desperate detour. A myriad of memories and concerts and appearances flashed through his mind all at once—those that had gone before and those that would never be.

This can't be happening.

He tried to tune them out, tearing his eyes away from Gevin and looking into the fire. He couldn't even breathe.

He felt someone take hold of his hand and gently squeeze it, an arm tucking beneath his. *Hannah.* He released a sigh, thankful for the air in his lungs. Thankful she was there for him. He lowered his eyes but couldn't bring himself to look at her. He patted his other hand over hers.

Seconds passed. The silence made him nauseated.

"Hannah, how about you and I go find some of that pecan pie Laura made?"

Marissa's hushed voice startled him. He felt Hannah squeeze his hand then pull away as she stood up. Out of the corner of his eye, he watched them slip out of the room and quietly down the stairs.

CHAPTER 7

Marissa touched her elbow. "I'm sorry, I just felt like they needed some privacy," she whispered.

Hannah didn't know what to say so nodded her reply.

At the bottom of the stairs, Marissa turned to face her. "And I hope you don't mind if I don't talk about it right now. This has been like an albatross around our necks, and I'd just rather not get into it. No offense, Hannah."

"None taken. But I'm just sorry it's been a problem when it should be the happiest time of your life."

"Yeah, that part pretty much sucks."

They entered the expansive kitchen. "Let me get us a couple pieces of that pie," Hannah said, grateful for the distraction.

"Sounds good. I noticed a cappuccino maker over there on the counter. I'm a pro with these things. You want some?"

"Sounds great." Hannah opened cabinets until she found the dessert plates then searched for a knife. She cut two small slices of the rich pecan pie then found a chilled bowl of whipped cream in the refrigerator. She dressed each slice with a dollop and set a fork on each plate.

Slowly, little by little, sitting on barstools at the granite kitchen counter, Marissa and Hannah got to know each other. Marissa's depth of character amazed Hannah. She found her laid back, easy to talk to, and extremely intelligent. Bright and lovely and deeply in love with Gevin Michaels. At the mere mention of his name, her eyes sparkled and conveyed more than her words ever could.

Anxious to change subjects, she pounded Hannah with questions. She seemed especially interested in Hannah's career plans and her writing. "I've got so many people I want to introduce you to. You like to do interviews? Write about people?"

"That's what I love more than anything, Marissa—"

"Please call me Rissa. All the guys do."

"Okay, 'Rissa.' She acknowledged the term of endearment with a smile.

"JT nicknames everyone he meets. First day I met him, he cut to the chase and I've been Rissa ever since." She wiped a streak of whipped cream from her lip. "But go ahead. What were you saying?"

Hannah sipped the cappuccino, wrapping her hands around the fat mug. "One of my greatest passions is probing people to find out all about them. What makes them tick, what their dreams are, that sort of thing, then put it on paper and communicate it in a way no one else has ever done. *Love* that."

Marissa took another bite of pie then jumped from her stool, dancing with head and arms in motion. "Hannah, fasten your seatbelt, girlfriend. Just say the word, and we'll introduce you to so many people, honey, your head will spin right off." They laughed, Marissa continuing to rock to some rhythm in her head. "But first I've got to ask you something."

"Ask me what?" Hannah asked, flaking the crust of her pie with her fork.

"You and Jason." She took her seat again, reaching for her cappuccino. "The thing is, the last time I saw him, there was no one special in his life. Hasn't been for quite a while now." Her eyes narrowed as she seemed to wait for answers. "He was dating a little, mostly publicity appearances, but nothing serious."

She set the mug down and faced Hannah with a curious bright smile. "Then, we come here and find this *sweet* angel of a girl who has quite clearly stolen the heart of our Jason . . . and *then* some. And the whole family already loves this angel. And I've just got to wonder, what did we miss? When did this happen!? Because I've gotta tell you, Hannah, these guys are my life. I love 'em all like they were my own brothers—well, okay, that's not *exactly* how I feel about Gevin now." She chuckled quietly and continued. "So, when all of a sudden, I see something going on with my man Jason, I wonder. Where did this come from? And who *is* this girl who's lighting up his eyes again?"

Marissa tented her fingers, resting her chin on them. "Hmm? C'mon, now Hannah. Spill the beans to Auntie Rissa."

Hannah traced the rim of her mug. "Oh, 'Auntie Rissa' is it?" She smiled back at the inquisitive face focused on her. "Geez, I don't even know what to tell you. This whole thing happened *so* fast. One minute I'm working at my store, the next thing I know, this kind, wonderful lady invites me to dinner—though I had no idea who she was, whose mother she was—then I'm sharing an intimate holiday evening with them when suddenly *my teen idol* appears, for crying out loud!" She covered her face with her hands, then raked her fingers through her hair. "I mean, how crazy is that? I still can't believe any of it. I keep waiting to wake up. Because it's got to be a dream. Has to be."

"Well, I'm here to tell you, this is no dream, girlfriend. No, ma'am, no way. And I might as well tell you, I've known Jason McKenzie a long time, and—" Marissa paused, cocking her head to one side. "I'm here to tell you, he's got it for you *bad!*"

Hannah blew out a troubled sigh, resting her hand on Marissa's arm. "No, no, Marissa—I mean Rissa—listen to me. It's not how it looks. Jason is wonderful. He's sweet, he's unbelievably *normal*, all things considered. But I'm not stupid. He's home on vacation, he's just being friendly since his parents invited me over and—"

"No way. Huh uh, I don't buy that for one minute."

"Be serious, Rissa! You've got this all wrong. His parents were so nice to me. I was having this stupid little pity party about spending Christmas alone, and then Laura showed up, and she took me to this beautiful candlelight service, and I met Frank, and . . . I'm not an idiot. It's just an exaggerated case of their holiday spirit, y'know? It's Christmas. People go out of their way to share their hearts and homes this time of year. And Jason? Well, maybe he's enjoying being out of the spotlight for a while and hanging out with someone who's . . . someone that's—"

Marissa waved her hand with attitude, letting Hannah know she wasn't having any of it. "Give it up, girl. Nice try. And if that's what you want to believe, then believe it. But I'm telling you this from someone who knows Jason. He's different with you. I've seen him with other women. I was there when he and Jennifer were tight. *This* is different." She drove home her point by tapping her manicured nails on the counter. "You gotta listen to me, honey. I won't tell you wrong."

Hannah took a deep breath, then slowly let it out, her heart pounding furiously. "Whoa . . . I don't know what to say." She felt a little dizzy. The butterflies stormed back in.

"Well, let me tell you one more thing about Jason."

"Go on."

Marissa laced her fingers together then stretched her locked hands high over her head. "Jason McKenzie is one of the most genuine people I've ever met in the business. Besides Gevin, of course," she smiled. "Jason has never been caught up in the garbage of our industry. He loves what he does—don't get me wrong. But what you see is what you get with him. No pretense, no façade, he's the real thing. I love him like a brother, and I have from the very beginning. And that's why I can tell you with complete honesty that he will not lead you on if there's nothing there. He might be gracious, he might be polite, but he would *never* take the time to get to know you like this if he wasn't interested."

Hannah scrunched her face. "But then why would Frank warn me that his son could be 'quite the heartbreaker'—I think that's how he put it."

Marissa smiled, her teeth gleaming against her lips. "Girl, that's what *everybody* says about Jason. It's because he's so nice, sure, but it's also because every girl this side of Moscow has decided he should marry her! Doesn't matter what age, they still think he's theirs. He's broken hearts all over the planet, and most of them are girls he's never met and never will. So chill. Just a generic, fatherly thing. Don't give it another thought."

Gradually, the smile faded from Marissa's face and her movements ceased. She looked up at Hannah. "I think they've talked long enough. C'mon. Let's go check it out."

Hannah pressed her eyes shut briefly, then followed her new friend up the stairs. They found Gevin and Jason sitting face to face, still in intense conversation. When the girls appeared on the stairs, they both leaned back, seeming to welcome the interruption. Marissa threw her a knowing wink. She knew these guys. There was no question in Hannah's mind she could read their hearts. Marissa walked over to the music system and loaded it with several selections.

A Motown melody filled the loft as Marissa turned, her body feeling the rhythm. Her long brown arms reached in the air as she moved to the familiar love song

"Anybody wanna dance?"

Gevin moved to her, pulling her into his arms then moving in rhythm with her. Hannah reached for Jason's shoulder, gently massaging it. "You okay?"

He brandished a tired smile. "I'm in shock, actually." He shook his head, tousling his hair and blowing out a long sigh. "But right now, we need a break. C'mere." He took her hand, leading her into a dance of their own. "I love this song." He sang the words as they moved together. In spite of the tension of the last hour, she melted at the sound of it. Especially when he got to the part about *my girl* . . .

First one song, then another and another. They laughed, they occasionally traded partners, they tried a few line dances from way back when, and they forgot their worries. For the moment, anyway.

Kenny G filled the room again and she was in Jason's arms. She rolled the cameras in her mind, wanting to seal this moment in her memory forever. This embrace. The made-up words he sang against her hair, words that touched her heart. They swayed gently to the sad melody of that amazing saxophone. Jason's voice caught and he sang no more. He held her, still moving to the music.

"Hannah," he whispered. "Stay close this week. Please?"

She wrapped her arms around his neck and pulled him closer, feeling the dampness of his eyes against her skin. "There's no place I'd rather be."

CHAPTER 8

The early morning sun sent a cheery glow through the kitchen's bay window, bouncing off the snow-covered landscape outdoors. Breakfast aromas filled the air as Hannah continued.

"So he's backing me up in this corner. Nobody's around, right? I'm scared to death but I wasn't about to let him know that. He's a defensive tackle. I stand no chance against this big ape. I figure he's got, oh maybe 150 pounds on me. My knees are Jell-O!"

She stood at the stove over a sizzling omelet sharing the story with Frank, Laura, and Marissa who all sat at the kitchen table over mugs of hot coffee. Dressed in gray sweats Jason had loaned her with her hair swept up on top of her head, she felt surprisingly relaxed and at home talking to these people.

"He's so close I can smell the bratwurst he had for lunch. He's saying, 'oh baby, oh baby, you know you gotta have me . . . I'll make all your dreams come true.' I thought I was going to hurl right there on his size 14 Nikes!"

She tossed some shredded cheese and bacon bits into the omelet then folded it, never missing a word. "And all of a sudden I remember the PE whistle in my pocket. He's moving in, got his hands up against the wall so I'm literally pinned like a prisoner, right? He leans his fat head down and starts whispering in my ear, 'c'mon baby, you 'n me, let's try a little play action pass of our own.'"

The groans of her small audience urged her on. Hannah grew more animated, waving her spatula in the air to punctuate every word. "I slowly reach down in my pocket, grab my whistle, and before he can say another word, I'm *blasting* that thing!"

Frank's roaring laughter bounced around the kitchen walls as Marissa doubled over with laughter.

"And it's *so* shrill and *so* loud, he's holding his ears and screaming at me—'Stop it! Stop it!' like some big 'ol sissy boy. But I just kept blowing and blowing, louder and louder 'til I thought for sure he was gonna cry for his mama." She scooped the omelet out of the frying pan and flipped it onto a plate, dropped the spatula, and turned to face them again. "And then?" She paused for effect.

"Then what?" Laura begged.

"I jerked my knee up in his nether lands."

"Oh no you did not!" Marissa yelled.

Hannah howled. "Oh, I most definitely did!"

Laura stopped laughing just long enough to add, "Oh, honey, that was very brave!"

Frank whimpered, cowering a little, the way men do when they hear tales of such strategic "targets," but his laughter never dissipated.

"He's lying there, all curled up in the fetal position, just moaning and groaning and carrying on like a big ol' baby. So I straightened my clothes, stood up all straight and said, 'Tommy Joe, you ever come near me again, I'll make sure you sing soprano for the rest of your sorry life. *You got that?'"*

"Oooo, Hannah! You are my hero!"

"Thank you, Rissa. I'll have you know, all he did was nod his pitiful head and drag himself out of there. But I can tell you one thing, that was the last time he ever said a *word* to me. He sees me coming in the hall and he bee-lines the other way. Does my heart good! Did my daddy teach this girl a thing or two or what?"

"I believe he did at that," Frank chuckled. "Good for you, setting him straight. Just remind me to walk on the other side of the room when you're coming *my* way!"

"Oh please, as if I'd ever have cause to set *you* straight?" Hannah passed a plate with the steaming omelet to Marissa. "Laura, what would you like on your omelet?"

"Just some of those bell peppers and cheese with a few sprinkles of bacon. Thank you, Hannah." She lifted her mug. "Marissa's looks yummy. I'm not sure I can wait." She quickly forked a small bite off Marissa's plate, barely escaping the playful swat in return.

Marissa moved her plate away from Laura. "Mama Mac, you keep your fork off my plate or I'll be showin' you a play action of my own. I'm just sayin' . . ." She flashed her a huge, mischievous grin.

Raising a brow, Laura feigned innocence as she continued to enjoy her stolen mouthful of cheesy omelet. When she followed it with a sip of coffee, she started to laugh, her coffee going down the wrong pipe. Her coughs echoed across the room.

Frank patted her on the back amidst the laughter. "You okay, sweetheart?"

"What's all the racket?"

Hannah turned to find Jason coming through the patio door. He pulled off his stocking cap and stomped the snow off his feet. She laughed out loud at the sight of him.

"What?" he asked, confused.

"Bad hair day, Jason?" Marissa teased. His hair stood straight up with static electricity making him look like a werewolf in an old black and white movie. Jason ducked for a peek in the mirror by the back door before attempting to pat it into place. He walked back into the kitchen. "Very funny. Glad you all had a nice guffaw at my expense."

Laura coughed once more, then asked, "Jason, what is all that noise coming out of your backpack?"

"Oh—Baby!" He turned around to reveal the tiny puppy's snout popping out of a pocket in his backpack. She yelped again in protest. "Okay, okay! I'll get you out."

He lifted the backpack off his shoulders and flipped it to pull the puppy out. "Baby and I took a long walk. Didn't we, Baby girl?" he cooed, rubbing noses with the miniature dog. "I thought she'd be more comfortable in here where it's all nice and warm. Have you looked outside? Do you believe all that snow?"

Frank stood beside his son. "It's incredible, isn't it? I can't remember the last time we had this much snow. Good thing you don't have to leave anytime soon."

Jason smiled at Hannah. "What am I smelling? Hannah? *You're* cooking? No way."

"Excuse me, but just because I appear to be a sponge around here doesn't mean I can't cook."

He walked up behind her. "Good morning, Hannah."

She turned to face him. "Good morning, Jason. You okay?" she asked quietly.

"You better watch your mouth, Jason," Marissa said. "This girl can *cook*. I'm here to tell you that's the best omelet I've ever had. Girl, where did you learn to cook like that?"

Hannah cracked another egg into the bowl. "When you're a starving college student, you learn to work with the cheapest possible ingredients. Eggs top the list. You should see what I can do with four-for-a-dollar mac and cheese."

"Uh-oh," Jason interrupted. "I do believe you're trying to come onto me now. Because I *love* mac and cheese."

Hannah wagged her head. "I know, I know—it was in all those teen magazines. My mom used to hassle me because all I ever ate was mac and cheese *until* she found out it was her beloved Jason McKenzie's favorite dish."

"Your *mom* is a fan?" He barked a laugh.

"Afraid so. She's hopeless. She took me to my first concert when you guys were on tour in Dallas and she's been hooked ever since. Even has all your music on her iPod. Listens to it all the time. But I drew the line when she put your poster in her and Dad's master bedroom."

His eyes popped. "Your mom has my poster in her *bedroom?*"

Hannah turned around to face him, tilting her head. "Jason?"

"Yeah?"

"Do you know what the word 'gullible' means?"

"Got that right," Marissa teased.

The grin on his face drooped. "Oh. No poster?"

Hannah picked up his hand and patted it. "No poster. Sorry, Jason. She really did have it bad for you. But then, what do you expect after writing a song like *A Mother's Love?* Every mother on the planet thought you were the perfect son."

"That's because none of them had to pick up after him," Laura quipped, taking the plate Hannah handed her. She reached for a piece of toast and took a bite as she stood. "I'm going to eat in the den while I read the paper, if you all will excuse me. After all, I'm on vacation now, too."

Jason snatched a chunk of cheddar then whined like a spoiled brat. "Where's *my* omelet?"

"I'm outta here too." Marissa put her empty plate in the sink. "Gevin's slept long enough. He's still sprawled out on the floor in the loft where I left him last night. I hope it's okay I snuck down the hall and found an empty bed to sleep in."

"Of course it is, Marissa." Frank said. "We're always happy to have you."

"Thanks, Frank. Well, we need to go back over to his mom and dad's house for a while. Though I have to admit, that houseful of cousins and munchkins makes this place a sanctuary. Don't be surprised if we show back up. But thanks for letting us crash here." Marissa gave Hannah a hug, Jason a longer one with a kiss on the cheek, then turned to leave the room.

"You and Gevin be careful out on those roads, Marissa."

"We will, Frank. See you guys later."

Frank stood, pushed his chair back, and began clearing the table. "Oh, and Jason, a word of advice, son. Keep the cook happy." He deposited the dirty dishes in the sink, then leaned over his son's shoulder whispering, "Two words: Tommy Joe."

As his father left the room, Jason lifted his brows, searching Hannah's face. "Tommy Joe? Something I should know?"

She laughed. "I guess not. Let's just say it's on a 'need-to-know' basis."

Alone with Jason for the first time that morning, Hannah started rinsing some of the dishes. "I told your mom you'd do the dishes for her. She was delighted."

Jason snapped her with a dish towel. "Ouch? Well, good morning to you too!"

"Don't be kissing up to my mama, Hannah," he chided.

She looked up at him, surprised at the tone of his voice. For a second her heart stopped. Then his face broke into his world-famous smile and she breathed again.

"You actually thought I was serious?" he teased, stacking the dirty plates beside the sink. "*Now* who's gullible?"

Silence.

"Hannah?"

She tried to smile. "Yeah?"

"It was a joke. You know it was."

She detected a sincere pleading in his eyes before turning her attention back to the dishes. "Jason, look— the last couple of days have been . . . unbelievable. I mean, I still don't totally know what's happening. How I got here, why I'm here with you and your family. But you've got to look at all this from *my* point of view. Two days ago I was just a college student trying to make ends meet working in a grocery store. Suddenly, I find myself in this make-believe world . . . but I'm still *me*. And when you said that just now about kissing up to your mom, I don't know, it just felt like an insult."

"But I didn't mean anything by it. Trust me on that."

"I know, but I also know how many girls and women out there probably *have* kissed up to you and your family and the other guys over all these years." She felt the agitation brewing inside. "The thing is, I don't *feel* like a groupie anymore, Jason. I'm not a little kid anymore. And this feels like . . . I mean, it seems like . . . only—"

"Only what?"

She paused, leaning over to put a wet glass in the dishwasher. "Only I don't know! How could I possibly know what all this means? Where all this is going? It's only been two days, Jason. *Two days.* And I feel like my life has forever changed. Like I'll never be the same."

He folded his arms across his chest, leaning against the counter beside her. He stared at his tennis shoes with absent eyes. "I know."

She waited. Nothing. "You know . . . ?"

He looked up at her. "I know what you mean."

His gaze penetrated her soul. If she didn't know better, thoughts were exchanged between them in spite of the silence.

She looked back at her soapy hands, blinking back tears she refused. "Why me, Jason? I'm a nobody. I'm just a girl who used to be sitting up in the nosebleed section at your concert a few years ago. Just one in a million. So why me? Why exactly am I here?" She was embarrassed to hear the words tumbling out of her mouth. She looked up and noticed a smile slowly warming his face.

His arms still folded, he reached over to pinch the sleeve of her sweats. "Truth?"

"Truth," she whispered as her pulse began to slow.

He pulled her toward him as she quickly wiped her hands on a hand towel. "First of all, don't ever—and I mean *ever*—refer to yourself as a nobody. Okay?"

She pressed her lips together for a moment. "Okay."

He wrapped his arm around her waist. "And second—the truth is, I have no idea what's going on. Nothing like this has ever happened to me before. *So many women, Hannah . . . I'd be lying if I said it was otherwise. Everywhere we go. But I never get involved with any of them. They just hang around. That's it. I promise you, it isn't *anything* like the tabloids portray. At least not in my case. I've gone out with a few—I told you that last night. The rest are just faces I don't even remember. I never took any of it seriously. Well, with the exception of Jennifer, of course.

"But this—with you dropping into my life like this . . . I don't have a clue. It was the last thing I expected to happen. But it has." He tipped her chin with his finger, their faces mere inches apart. "And I've gotta tell you, I like it. A lot. It feels right. And trust me—you are anything but 'a nobody.' If I wanted to get involved with a celebrity, I would. But I don't. Not ever again." His eyebrows spiked high on his forehead. A familiar expression she'd already learned to love.

"Just lose the 'kissing up' comments, okay?" she whispered.

"Okay," he mouthed silently.

"So what are we going to do today? Have you talked to Gevin yet?" She put the last dish in the dishwasher and closed it.

Jason drew in a deep breath. "No, I was going to, but I decided to blow it all off today. Until we talk to the rest of the guys, I want to pretend it never came up. Call me immature, call me in denial, but I just don't want to think about it."

"You didn't sleep last night, did you?"

"What gave it away? The bags under my eyes? Did I just snore through our conversation here? What?"

"Just a guess. But if you didn't sleep, maybe you should take me home and come back here for some rest."

"No way. That's the last thing I want to do. If I lie around all day, I'll go nuts. Let's go to a movie this afternoon. Maybe we can sneak in without too much hassle. I'll do the sunglasses and hat routine. And there's an Italian place here that I love. They're very discreet. I've got my own booth in the back. It's like heaven for me there. What d'ya say?"

"Works for me. Think I should wear a hat and sunglasses too? I wouldn't want anyone to recognize me."

His smile widened across his face. "You learn quick. Now let's get outta here."

"Well, it was worth a try!" Hannah screamed over the shrieks of the five adolescent girls surrounding Jason. He shrugged, resigning himself to the outburst around him. The young fans apparently spotted them as they left the theatre through a back exit.

Just then, a rotund redhead shot an elbow into Hannah's side, shoving her aside to get closer to her idol. "Jason! I love you! Sign my mitten! Please, please, please?!" The screaming continued with an unbelievable barrage of requests and adoration. Hannah stood aside, watching with amusement. Jason gave them his full attention, signing their purses and coats and bare hands. No wonder they loved him so much. Occasionally he came up for air and flashed her a smile.

Finally, he pulled himself free and reached for Hannah's hand, tugging her along as he took off running for his Escalade. Two freckle-faced twins hung onto the hem of his jacket, sliding across the icy pavement behind him.

"Don't leave, Jason!"

"Who's the girl?"

"Is that Jennifer?"

"Don't go! Please don't go!"

"Jason, come back!"

"WE LOVE YOU, JASON!"

They broke free, making a daring dash for the SUV they'd hidden behind a dry cleaner's next door. They jumped in and Jason roared the engine, the Escalade spinning a full 360 degree circle before stopping.

Hannah screamed. "Ahhhh! Jason! Be careful!"

"Whoa! That was GREAT!"

"What—the girls or the wheelie?"

"*Yeee-hawwww!* The wheelie, of course!"

"You know you're crazy, don't you?" She tried to catch her breath, laughing in the process.

"Is there any other way to be?"

"But I have to admit you were awesome with those kids. They adore you!"

"Yeah. Just call me kiddy bait. Me and Barney the dinosaur, we're right up there together at the top of the list."

"I'm just glad you're not fat and purple." She rubbed her mittens together, squinting to see out the window. "You sure you won't get mobbed at this restaurant?"

"Not a chance. Patty takes care of me. What are you hungry for? You like calzones?"

"Cheese only?"

"Is there any other way?"

An hour later, calzone crumbs dotted their plates, their glasses empty after two refills. Hannah had to agree, the food was outstanding. And his personally-proclaimed private booth in the back kept them secluded just as he'd said. They'd had no interruptions except for Patty's undivided attention. Jason wiped his mouth and sat back in the booth. "I'm stuffed," he moaned, rubbing his stomach. "I'll have to run ten miles to get this off my gut."

"Pssst! Max! Come back here!" A throaty whisper beckoned him from the kitchen.

"Max?" Hannah mouthed.

He grinned. "That's Patty's nickname for me. McKenzie. Max. Somehow she decided Max would be her cover for me and it just stuck. C'mon." He took her by the hand, leading her through the swinging doors into the hot kitchen. The strong scent of Italian spices filled the cramped room.

Patty hugged him again, patting him on the back like a child. "I just love this guy! He's like one of my own. I could just eat him up!" She laughed, pinching both his cheeks.

"I-wuv-woo-hoo, Paee."

Hannah laughed at his pitiful attempt to talk.

"Sing for me!" Patty wiped her hands on her apron as she stepped into her tiny office. "Pull up the soap, Max."

Jason grunted as he tugged a twenty-gallon drum of institutional detergent to the center of the room. Hannah found a pink vinyl chair in a corner and sat down. Patty emerged from her tiny office with a beat-up guitar case, handing it to Jason. "Max here gave me this years ago. It was his first guitar. I was hoping my Tony would learn to play, but all he plays is video games. Such a waste! So I keep it here for Max whenever he stops by. Go on, play me something sweet." She hopped up to sit on the counter, her legs swinging back and forth.

"Patty makes me work for my food when I come here. Won't take my money but always makes me sing. How about some U2? You up for a little Bono tune?" He started playing one of the group's classic tunes.

"No, no, no!" Patty groaned. "If I wanted Bono, I'd call Bono. I want Max."

Jason threw his head back laughing. "Oh, okay. U2, no Bono, huh? Then how about a little Rascal Flatts? I do a mean version of *Bless the Broken Road*. He sang the famous lyrics matching lead singer Gary Levox's exact tone and style.

"Stop! Honestly, Max—I'll never feed you again. I mean it! Now sing to me. *Your* songs. Don't make me hurt you." Patty forced a playful scowl.

His fingers strummed the guitar. He stopped to tune a couple of strings, then strummed again. The chords of the familiar song drifted around them making Hannah smile. One of her favorite *Blue* love songs . . .

> *There simply are no words*
> *To tell you how I feel,*
> *There simply isn't time*
> *To share what's in my heart . . .*

Patty moved to the music, at times closing her eyes and mouthing the words along with her Max.

> *A hundred songs of love,*
> *Or a thousand years together*
> *Could never be enough.*
> *So it all comes down to this,*
> *A quiet, simple kiss*
> *A quiet, simple kiss.*

She watched his fingers flying along the neck of the old guitar, a more classical version than the original recording. Hannah sang silently, drinking in the moment of this private concert, blushing at the memory of those words on Christmas Eve. He winked at her, a sly smile on his lips. He remembered too.

> *If only I could play for you*
> *The symphony inside my soul*
> *You'd hear the secret melody*
> *A lyric just for you from me . . .*

Patty and Hannah joined the sweet chorus, harmonizing the parts they knew so well.

> *But a hundred songs of love,*
> *Or a thousand years together*
> *Could never be enough.*
> *So it all comes down to this,*
> *A quiet, simple kiss*

A quiet, simple kiss.

"Whoa, you guys are *bad*." Jason shook his head, lowering the guitar into its case. "I mean, you really stink."

"Hey!" Patty hopped off the counter and thumped him on the back of his head. "You just get on outta here, Max. Nobody talks to me like that. Go on—get outta here. I mean it!"

She put her arm around Hannah as they walked out of the kitchen. "Listen, Hannah, you come back anytime. You and me, we'll put together a singing act all our own. We don't need him," she fussed, jabbing a thumb at Jason.

"Patty, don't you be filling her head with that stuff," he warned. He whisked Hannah away from Patty, then grabbed their coats as they passed their booth. "We'll be back! But Patty?"

"Yeah?"

"Stick to cooking. You sing like a *frog*!"

CHAPTER 9

The Chocolate Chip Cookie Dough now gone, two empty bowls coated with melted ice cream sat on the table between them. Hannah sat across from Jason at the tiny table in her kitchen.

"You said yourself when the ride was over, you'd know when to get off. Well, something like that. So maybe it's just time, Jason."

He tapped his spoon against the bowl with nervous agitation, his elbows resting on the table. Hannah could feel his anxiety. She leaned back in her chair, stretching her legs out under the table. Jason shifted his legs so they rested against hers. Unfortunately, one of his legs was bouncing in rhythm with the spoon.

His silence made her uncomfortable. *Extremely* uncomfortable.

Finally he dropped the spoon. He raked his hair with both hands letting out a frustrated growl. "No. No, it's *not* time. That's just it! Don't you think I would know it in my gut if it was? Wouldn't I have some inkling in my soul? *Something?* I mean, this hit me broadside. I had no clue it was coming! And I'm not gonna *let* it happen, Hannah," he snapped, shoving his chair back. "I'm not."

"Jason—"

"No, listen to me, Hannah. I told you—I stay tuned in to God. I really do. I'm not just saying it to sound like some righteous jerk. Ever since I was a little kid, I've known I could never make it without God. Ask my mom. She'll tell you. The guys will too—it's just part of my life. I know it doesn't fit with the industry we're in, but it's just who I am.

"And ever since this *Blue* thing happened, I've had my head on my shoulders, facing it straight out." He was roaming the small room, idly picking up utensils, an oven mitt, anything he came across. "I swear it, Hannah. From the beginning, I laid this whole thing at God's feet and said, 'it's all Yours.' So don't you think I would have known *something* was coming? Don't you think I should have had some kind of inner alert or . . . or *feeling* that something was about to happen? Like shouldn't God have given me some kind of clue?"

The total bewilderment on his face alarmed her. "I don't know, Jason. God's God. He doesn't *have* to do anything." She cringed at the tone of her sheepish response.

He started wiping the counter with a dishrag in wide, angry circles. "But still, think about it. I haven't exactly turned my back on Him, y'know? Or, I don't know, maybe I have. Maybe I just thought I was staying tuned in to Him. Maybe I screwed up and didn't even realize it."

"Jason, why are you doing this? First you're trying to blame God and now yourself? There's no way you could have known this was going to happen now. Gevin and Rissa want to get married. What's so difficult to understand about that? He's older, Jason. Why *shouldn't* he want to get married and settle down? I think it's great that he found someone like Rissa and knows this is the real thing. That's probably pretty tough to discern in your business."

He rolled his neck. Her comments clearly only agitated him more. She folded her arms across her chest and took a deep breath. *Just let him talk.*

He threw the cloth in the sink and turned around to lean against the counter, bracing his hands on the edge behind him. "I'm just not ready. Not now."

Her heart ached for the disappointment in his face, his every move. "Have you talked to any of the other guys yet?"

"No. I thought about it. Then I decided, why ruin their break too?"

His cell phone rang from the living room. "Geez, I don't even want to answer that." He looked up at her, his eyes asking *should I?* Hannah shrugged leaving the decision up to him. It rang, then rang again.

He left the room, his steps heavy. Hannah dropped her head onto her folded arms on the table. *Oh God. Please help him.*

"Hey! When did you get in? . . . Yeah? . . . Did Tracey come with you? Good, it'll be good to see her." Jason walked into the kitchen, holding the tiny phone to his ear. "JT," he whispered.

Hannah sat up. Jason crossed his eyes. The slightest hint of a smile crept up his face. He winked at her and her heart skipped a beat.

"Okay, we'll see you in a few minutes. Tell Mom to fix you guys a turkey sandwich or something . . . Okay, see ya, man." He disconnected and put the cell in the pocket of his jeans. "Well, Hannah, how would you like to meet JT Malone?"

"Hannah, Jason—come on in. Y'all want a sandwich?"

Laura was in her element. Dressed in a navy designer tracksuit with her blonde hair twisted in her signature French braid, she set plates heaped with sandwiches in front of her guests.

Hannah tried to swallow. *I can't believe it. I'm nervous again. After everything else, I'm reduced to a basket case of nerves. Trembling, no less!* She avoided eye contact with JT as long as she could, afraid she would blush twelve shades of purple.

Jason grabbed his buddy in a bear hug, slapping him on the back. "Hey JT . . . Tracey— get up and give me a hug, woman!" As Jason moved to embrace JT's girlfriend, Hannah took a chance to steal a peek at *Blue's* famous bad boy. With a huge smile planted on his face, he approached her. He was shorter than she'd expected, but well built. A thin dark beard lined his jaw, accented by multiple earrings on each ear. His close-cropped hair was a dark shade of burgundy. Suddenly she was gazing into those puppy dog eyes that made girls all over the world melt like butter.

Me included.

"And you must be Hannah." His raspy voice snapped her out of her fog. "Laura's been telling us all about you. I'm JT, Hannah, nice to meet you," he said taking her into a warm hug.

"Hi JT," she croaked. *Oh God, please don't let him feel my heart beating against his chest!*

"Hey, you're shaking! Come on in and warm up," he said, leading her by the hand toward the kitchen table.

Yeah, that's it. Shaking from the cold. Right.

"Mama Mac, how about some hot tea or something? This one's shaking like a leaf." He pulled the chair out for her and she sat down. She looked up to see Jason snickering silently behind JT's back. *Great. He knows I'm star struck.* She shot him a warning glare.

"Hi Hannah, I'm Tracey—and thanks guys for remembering to introduce me." JT's girlfriend was attractive in an eclectic sort of way, just as Hannah would have expected. Jet black hair in a short blunt cut. She had her own share of piercings, though most were tiny studs confined to folds of her ears. Her ready smile helped put Hannah at ease.

JT ducked behind Tracey's chair and wrapped his arms around her neck. "I didn't forget you, babe, you just beat me to it." He planted a kiss on top of her head.

"Tracey, you look really familiar," Hannah said, finding her voice again.

Tracey tugged at JT's tattooed arms around her neck. "I was a background dancer in the *Who's It Gonna Be* video. We hit it off from the moment we met, didn't we, honey?"

"That's it!" Hannah interrupted. "Tracey, you're the one he stepped on, aren't you?"

"You remember that? See, JT—she saw it too!" Tracey teased. "I told you guys we should've done one more take. Nobody listens to me!"

"I didn't *step* on you, Trace. You accidentally put your foot under mine," he corrected. He turned to look at Hannah. "Can I help it if she's a klutz?"

Hannah felt Jason's hands on her shoulders. "Tracey, the whole *world* saw him step on your foot, so don't let him give you grief about it." It was good to hear him laughing. She lifted her hands to rest on his.

"Hannah, the thing is," JT continued, "I'm surrounded by these wannabe dancers day and night.

They never listen to me, they never listen to Rissa or Gevin—"

Hannah looked up at Jason. A trace of pain dashed across his face. Just as fast, he covered with nonchalance.

JT stopped. "What?"

"So what made you guys decide to come up early?"

Nice cover, Jason, Hannah thought.

"Since you didn't show for Christmas I wasn't expecting you 'til the party."

Tracey reached for her glass. "I talked JT into spending Christmas with my family. We were there for a couple of days until he started climbing the walls."

He reached over to take her hand. "Yeah, one too many aunties and uncles for me. Hey, speaking of relatives—is the big guy in town?"

Jason took a deep breath and patted Hannah's hand then moved to his chair. "Yeah, Gevin stopped by with his family last night."

Silence.

Hannah watched as JT waited for more, his eyes squinting as he studied Jason. JT glanced across the table at her. She returned an innocent smile then looked away.

"Okay, JMac. What's going on here? Spit it out."

"I don't know what you're talking about."

"Oh yeah, right, and I don't like jewelry. What's the deal? Is something wrong with Gevin?"

"Not at all, JT. He's fine. Couldn't be better."

More silence.

JT shoved his plate aside. He folded his arms on the table. "Are we gonna sit here and play games all day or are you gonna tell me?" All pretense of humor had left his face.

"We'll talk later, man. Okay?" Jason answered quietly.

"No! I wanna know *now*. What's the matter?"

Tracey rolled her eyes. "JT, just chill—"

"Babe, if you'll please stay out of this?" his response, quiet and measured.

"I said later, JT," Jason interrupted, his tone stern.

"Geez, Jason, it's not a hard question. Knock off the suspense, okay?"

"I promised Gevin I'd let him tell you."

"Tell me what?"

Jason exhaled. He rubbed his face with both hands. He looked up at Hannah for support, then made the announcement. "Gevin's getting married."

"What?! *Gevin?*" JT bellowed. "Who's he marrying? I didn't even know he was—wait!" He snapped his fingers. "Just a minute. Rissa. It's Marissa, isn't it?"

Jason nodded his head, that sheepish grin on his face. "JT, you're too smart for your own good."

"Rissa! I knew it! I had a feeling about them . . . but man, has he been discreet or what? So when's the big day? When is he announcing it to the press? That snake! Why didn't he tell us?"

Jason was laughing. "Yo, JT! Chill! You're gonna hyperventilate if you keep this up."

"This is wonderful!" Tracey joined in. "What a perfect couple. I'm so happy for them! But what a surprise, huh?"

JT threw his head back. "Oh man, I'm in total shock here! Is Rissa in town? Are they coming over?"

"I'll call them and get them over here. He's gonna be chapped that I told you but, oh well." Jason pulled out his cell phone and auto-dialed Gevin's number.

JT was still shaking his head. "Oh my, oh my, oh my. This is unbelievable. Hannah, were you here when they told Jason?"

"Yeah, it was pretty incredible." She silently warned herself not to say too much. "I really enjoyed getting to know Rissa. She's so sweet. And they seem really happy together."

"They're on their way over." Jason closed his phone. "Sooooo .... looks like another long night, right Hannah?" His eyes widened again with mischief. She stood to slip beside him. He pulled her to his side. "Here we go again. Guess you better fasten your seatbelt, babe."

Babe? A tingle slid down her back. He'd never called her that before. *Maybe it's just the power of suggestion with JT saying that all the time.* Or was it something more?

Didn't matter. She liked the sound of it.

She liked it a lot.

They were settling into the loft when the doorbell rang. Just returning from the restroom, Hannah was closest to the front stairway. "Jason, do you want me to get it?"

"That'd be great. It's probably Gevin and Rissa."

As she skipped lightly down the steps, her cell phone vibrated in her jeans' pocket just as someone hammered the doorbell making it ring incessantly. She dug the phone out of her pocket, noticed it was a text message from Kylie. She started to read the message when she heard someone yelling, "Open up! We're freezing out here!"

"Come on in, I'm comeeeeeen—" Hannah flew off a step, her phone catapulting out of her hand as she bounced off every step on her rear end. It didn't hurt, but she felt like an idiot. When she finally came to a stop at the base of the stairs, she was too stunned to move. The front door opened.

Suddenly, imagining what she must look like, she burst into laughter. Hannah looked up through her tears expecting to find Gevin and Marissa.

"HAPPY NEW Y—whoa! Who the heck are you and *what* are you doing?"

Jackson Greer stopped dead in his tracks at the sight of her. Hannah's eyes flew wide open as she tried to catch her breath to stop laughing. Seeing his face for the first time—here like this—mortified her, making her laugh even harder.

"Hannah! Are you okay?" Jason's voice floated down from the top of the stairs. She looked sheepishly back at Jackson. One of his eyebrows was raised. He looked like he'd seen a two-headed freak at the circus.

But he's so much more handsome than any of those pictures I had plastered on my walls back home! I had no idea he was so tall. Course, anyone's tall from down here.

She tried to regain her composure. "Nice to meet you, Jackson. I'm—" She lost it again, the sheer embarrassment making the laughter wheeze out of her. The harder she tried to stop, the harder she laughed. Her stomach began to ache.

She felt Jason's hands under her arms attempting to lift her. He must have forgotten how ticklish she was until she lurched at him, still unable to catch her breath. Her sudden movement caused him to lose his balance so that he fell, landing right on top of her. He rolled back beside her, losing control as well. Finally, he caught his breath and looked up at Jackson. "Hey Jax, how's it goin'?"

A giggling face appeared peeking out from behind Jackson, her long brunette hair swinging as her head tipped sideways to see what was going on.

"Alli!" Jason shouted, "Come on in! I want you to meet Hannah!"

Another round of laughter made it impossible for him or Hannah to get up. She couldn't even see Jackson much less Alli for the tears blurring her eyes.

Alli tucked her arm under Jackson's, her smile broad. "Nice to meet you, Hannah. Wow, you make a great first impression."

"Yeah—unforgettable, isn't she?" Jason cried, finally catching his breath.

Hannah completely forgot about her cell phone and the message she never read from Kylie.

CHAPTER 10

Gevin and Marissa arrived moments later, joining the fiasco in the entryway. After massive hugs and high-fives, they all drifted back upstairs to the loft. Hannah couldn't believe the noise level coming from so few people. Then again, these guys were used to screaming fans and music at decibels beyond the endurance of the average Joe. Or Jane.

The pizza delivery guy unloaded an armload of pepperoni, supreme, and veggie pizzas which quickly disappeared.

"Tracey, what I don't understand is how these guys stay in shape," Hannah mused, wiping her mouth. "They're stuffing their faces every time I turn around. Jason's been eating since the minute we met—his mom's home cooking, her turkey dinner on Christmas day, Patty's calzones, ice cream—"

"Hey!" Jason jabbed her in the ribs. He stood up to strut like a WWF wrestler. "Do you see one ounce of fat on this body? Huh? I ask you—is this not a lean, mean fighting machine?" He continued posturing, striking all the signature body-builder poses.

"Jason, sit down. I'm still eatin' here. Do you mind?" Rissa shouted over the music.

And so it began. Jason stripped off his shirt and grunted like a linebacker, hopping onto the wide hearth. JT and Jackson followed suit, ripping off their shirts and throwing them like prizes to the girls who shouted fake groans in response, hiding their eyes from the onslaught of bare-chested men.

In one united effort, Alli, Hannah, and Tracey threw the shirts back at them with a barrage of cat calls.

"Put 'em back on!"

"I'm still digesting here! Do you mind?"

"Give us a break!"

Behind the pretense of complaints, Hannah couldn't help peeking at the idols of her adolescent years, admiring their muscles and biceps. *Don't know how they do it, but these guys obviously work out. A lot.* Realizing she was holding her breath, Hannah forced her eyes away from Jason's six-pack, then quickly looked back, trying hard not to stare.

And for the first time, she noticed the tiny line down the center of Jason's chest. A slender, pale scar, the remnant from surgery years ago to repair a hole in his heart. How well she remembered that scary event. Every *Blue* fan around the world held a collective breath as they waited for news from his team of surgeons. Had he made it through the surgery? Would he be all right again? Could he still keep up with the stress and rigors of the crazy lifestyle he led? She brushed off the memory, interrupted by Alli's laughter.

"How's a girl supposed to eat with all this going on?"

Alli's sarcastic remark brought Jackson off the hearth. He plopped himself on her lap, the image of wounded feelings.

"You're mocking me, Alli? Making fun of *me*? Your one and only? I—I think I might just—yes, yes. Here come the tears. Here they come. I'm crying here! You made me *cry*!" His sniffs and snorts didn't fool any of them.

Jason stepped down slowly, acting indifferent. "That's okay. I'm man enough. I can take it."

"Poor baby," Hannah cooed. "Did we hurt your little feelers? Come on, sit down and I'll make it all better." She patted the seat beside her. Jason wriggled his eyebrows at the others and squeezed in next to her in the Lazy Boy. "Yo, Jason—a little snug for both of us here. Do you mind?"

He grabbed her, plopping her on his lap despite her protests. "There. Now we're all better."

Gevin and Marissa shook their heads at all the antics around them. The two were stretched out on the floor, propped up on their elbows still eating. "What am I gonna do with these guys?" Gevin asked her as if overwrought. "I try and I try to teach these boys. Tell them it's time to grow up. And do you see what I get? It's nothing but work, work, work for me. Never a moment's rest."

Marissa wrapped her arm across his shoulders. "I know, honey, I know. And a fine job you do, baby. But look what you've got to work with? There's only so much you can do."

JT pulled his shirt back on. "Jax, I don't know about you but I'm still in shock about these two." He tossed a nod toward Gevin and Marissa.

Jackson, still sitting shirtless on Alli's lap, shook his head. "I know, man. All those months on the road, acting like such 'professional acquaintances.' Geez, guys—why all the secrecy? What's up with all the subterfuge?"

Gevin picked a piece of pepperoni and popped it in his mouth. "Jackson, where does it say we have to tell anybody anything, man? We just kinda liked the privacy, y'know? Right, Rissa?"

"Right, baby," she said kissing his greasy lips. "Guys, here's the deal. We didn't want all the hassle and hype and publicity until we knew we were really sure about it. You know how it is out there. We just decided to sit on it until we were ready to take the plunge. And when Gevin proposed—"

"—and she said yes—"

"Well, we decided it was time to move on to the next step. And here we are." She beamed, tapping her head against his.

JT sat on the floor leaning back against Tracey's legs. "Well, I can only speak for myself, but I couldn't be happier. Rissa? Gevin? All the best. I love you guys."

"Me too," Jackson said. "Hey wait—does Sergio know? Where is he, anyway? Still in Hawaii?"

Jason rolled his neck. "Yeah, last I heard from him, he was planning on staying most of this week. But he'll be here for the party on New Year's."

"I bet he's having a *wonderful* time."

Hannah didn't miss the sarcasm in Alli's comment.

"Don't you know it," Tracey groaned. "I'm just glad he's there and we're here."

"Wait, I don't get it," Hannah said. "What am I missing here? Who *wouldn't* want to be in Hawaii?"

They all looked back and forth at each other. Finally, Jason tightened his arms around her waist. "It's not Hawaii. It's Liza. And you've not yet had the pleasure of meeting the *lovely* Liza."

"Be nice, JMac," Jackson warned.

"Well, first of all, Hannah," JT began, "Liza is a party girl, okay? Let's just say the girl never met a bottle she didn't love."

"Whoa, baby, you're being way too kind," Tracey admonished. "Hannah, to put it bluntly, she's a lush."

"A drunk?" Hannah asked. "So does Sergio drink a lot too?"

"No, that's just it," JT piped in. "Serg rarely takes a drink. So we can't figure out why he puts up with her. We've all tried to talk to him about her, but he just blows us off. Which is not like Serg at all."

"So is she drop-dead gorgeous? Is that it?"

Alli laughed. "I guess that depends on your taste. The deal is, we're really not being mean. We all love Sergio. But we're concerned about him because she's obviously got some kind of major voodoo spell on him or something."

"Yeah, unfortunately she tries to cast that voodoo on the rest of us," Gevin said.

"What do you mean?

"It means she puts the moves on all the guys behind Sergio's back," Alli answered. "You wouldn't believe it."

"And Sergio refuses to see it," Jason continued. "He all but goes postal if you approach him about it. Won't talk about it. I'm sure it sounds like we're exaggerating, but we're not. She's unbelievable, Hannah. You've never seen anything like her. She's so—"

"Slick. That girl is downright slick." Marissa shook her head. "I've never seen anyone so blatant about it, and believe me—I've seen it all in this business."

Hannah took a sip of her Coke. "So what does Sergio see in her?"

"Beats me," JT answered. "I guess she's attractive enough, but that's not it. We're hardly naive, but let me tell you, she is one hot little number."

"You mean she's a hoochy-mama?" Hannah asked.

"A 'hoochy-mama'?" Jason laughed. "A *hoochy mama*? Where do you get this stuff?"

"Hey, it's not exactly Greek, Jason," Alli added. "And it certainly describes Liza."

Hannah felt something akin to dread drifting through her. "So how do you handle her when she's around?"

"It's not much fun," Jackson said. "We don't want to be rude for Sergio's sake.

But man, you sure have to watch out for her. You can't give her the time of day or she'll give you a little . . . *hooch*, is it?" he said, looking at Hannah.

"She gives *you* any hooch and I'll wrap your tonsils around your ears, Jackson Greer" Alli wrapped her slender fingers around his throat.

"Hey! What did I do? Can I help it if she thinks I'm sexy?"

Tracey and Marissa pelted him with throw pillows. Alli whacked him over the head with one of them, then narrowed her eyes. "One word, babe: Tonsils."

Jason leaned into Hannah who still sat on his lap. "Jackson and Alli have been together since they had side-by-side incubators in the hospital nursery."

"You're kidding."

"No, and he never ever looks at another woman because she's got this tight leash on him. The kind of leash you'd see on a rottweiler, y'know?" He continued, his words animated. "So it doesn't matter where we are— anywhere in the world—he never even *thinks* of window shopping, if you know what I mean. He's hopelessly smitten." Jason paused, then faux-whispered, "Not to mention *scared*."

"Very funny, Jason," Alli chided. "Thing is, Hannah, I don't *need* a leash on this guy. He loves me. Don'tcha, Jax?"

Jackson pretended to tremble. "Yes, ma'am. I mean, yes, dear. I mean—"

She whacked him again.

"See what I mean?" Jason whispered.

"Ah, Hannah, don't listen to Jason," JT said. "We all love Alli. She's like one of the family. When we got Jax, we got Alli. Package deal. They go way back and what they've got is the kind of love that lasts a lifetime. And it goes both ways, so don't you let Jason mess you up on that. Jackson's crazy about her."

Alli smiled. "Well, thanks, JT."

Jackson stood up and pumped his chest out. "Yeah, there's broken hearts all over the world because of this woman."

"Yeah, and they're all twelve years old," Gevin quipped.

The jabs kept flying. Finally, Jackson asked an innocent question. "So Gevin, when did you say the wedding is?"

Gevin and Marissa shifted their eyes to Jason, who in turn looked at Hannah.

"There they go again!" JT yelled. "What's up with you all?"

"What do you mean?" Jackson asked, pulling his Bucs sweatshirt over his head. He wiggled his back side, motioning for Alli to make room for him in the big recliner. In one motion, he plopped down and kicked the foot rest, throwing the chair—and them—back.

"It means, I asked the same question before you got here and all I got was a bunch of goofy looks and no answers."

"Gevin, maybe this isn't the best time to get into this," Jason said quietly.

Marissa squeezed Gevin's shoulder, then sat up. Gevin followed her motions and hung his arm across her shoulders.

"No, Jason, I think we owe it to JT and Jackson to get this out in the open."

A moment of silence passed.

"The thing is," Gevin began, "we haven't exactly set a date yet, but we have made a decision that's probably more important."

Jackson took the bait. "Such as?"

Marissa leaned into Gevin's shoulder. "Such as calling it quits," he said. "I want to move on with my life, guys. I *need* to move on. It's time."

Seconds passed. No one said a word. Hannah looked at JT. His jaw dropped at the announcement. She glanced over at Jackson and Alli. They were staring dumbfounded at Gevin.

Jackson finally broke the silence. "Excuse me?"

"I said, it's time for *Out of the Blue* to retire, guys. It's been an unbelievable ride, but it's time for all of us to move on. At least, I know it's time for me."

"Rissa? Is this your doing?" Anger coated JT's accusation as he lifted himself off the ground.

"Now, stop right there, JT," Gevin insisted. "That's not fair." His tone cut the air like a knife. Hannah felt Jason's hand tighten around her own.

"Well, what else am I supposed to think?" JT clenched his fists as he started to move around the room spinning a palpable angst. "Everything is great—we have plans and concerts dates and recording contracts . . . and now you tell us you're marrying Rissa and we're supposed to all give it up? I don't *think* so!" His chest rose and fell rapidly. "No, no, no. This is NOT happening."

"Okay, okay, wait a minute," Jackson said. "This is a joke, right Gevin? You're just putting us on, aren't you? Rissa?"

"He's totally serious, guys," Jason answered, his voice husky.

JT bolted toward Gevin who quickly stood up, towering over him. "NO WAY! You can forget it, man! We didn't come this far just to let it all go so you can run off and get married! Are you crazy? Rissa travels with us all the time anyway! So you get married! Why does anything have to change? What's the big deal?"

Gevin shook his head back and forth. "JT, you don't understand—"

"Well that's one thing you've got right! I *don't* understand! It doesn't make any sense!" A string of expletives flew from his mouth, one on top of the other.

Jason flew out of the chair, almost knocking Hannah on the floor. "Shut up, JT! You're not going to talk like that in this house. You got that?"

Jason's anger frightened Hannah. She wished she was anywhere but this room. She and Alli shared disquieting looks while Tracey dropped her head and covered her eyes.

"Guys! Settle down!" Marissa pleaded. "Just calm down. We've got to be able to talk this out."

"No! I have no intention of calming down!" JT blasted. "JMac—why aren't you backing me up? What's the matter with you? Are you gonna just stand by and watch everything we've accomplished get flushed down the toilet by these two selfish—"

"No, JT, I'm—"

"And what about you, Jax?" He stepped toward the recliner. "You just gonna sit there like this doesn't affect you?"

Jackson stood up, his face flushed. "JT, I'm as shocked as you are! I just—"

Gevin moved toward JT. JT raised his hands, warning Gevin not to come closer. "No—don't even try to candy coat this with a bunch of sappy big-brother crap. C'mon, Trace, we're outta here."

"C'mon, JT, we have to talk through this," Jason pressed. "Don't leave. That won't solve anything!"

"Fine! So we don't solve anything. I'm not gonna listen to another word. We are *not* quitting. And if that doesn't suit you, Gevin, then you can just stick it—"

"Knock it off, JT!" Jackson warned.

JT grabbed Tracey by the arm, pulling her to her feet. "NOW. Let's go, Trace."

Jason shook his head in frustration. He looked at Hannah, his eyes wild. "You can't talk to him when he gets this way. He's so freakin' stubborn!" he grunted, clenching his fists.

"Yeah, I'm stubborn and you're a wuss, JMac. You're lettin' him roll you over with this just like every other—"

"Shut up! Just SHUT UP!" Alli screamed. "You guys are acting like a bunch of jerks!" Tears tracked down her cheeks.

JT and Tracey thundered down the stairs. The front door slammed behind them.

"Oh my God, what's happening?" Jason cried. Hannah slowly got to her feet, cautiously reaching out to touch his arm. He turned to her, his eyes searching and moist.

Marissa folded her arms across her chest. "Well, that was . . . fun."

"He'll calm down," Gevin said. "He acted just like we knew he would. He just needs time to chill out."

105

Jackson pulled back, wrapping his arm around Alli's waist. "So . . . seriously, how are we going to handle this?"

Gevin took a deep breath. "We give it time. We talk it through. But we have to wait for JT to get a grip. And—we need to get Sergio back here as soon as possible."

Jason blew out an exasperated breath. "I'll try to track him down."

"And," Gevin continued, turning to look at Jason, then directly at Hannah. "We make sure this stays in this room." His serious tone alarmed her.

Jason pulled Hannah toward his side and looked Gevin in the eye. "You have my word. I think Hannah's already more than proven herself."

Gevin's expression softened. He leaned forward to kiss Hannah's forehead. "Thanks," he whispered, patting Jason's shoulder in reassurance. "Hannah, I'm sorry you had to witness this."

She nodded in silent response.

"Let's call it a night. I think we all need some sleep." Jason rubbed his eyes. "Hannah, you can have JT's room again. Obviously, he isn't using it tonight."

"I'll take Sergio's room, if that's okay," Alli said as she and Jackson picked up their shoes. They headed down the hall toward their rooms.

Hannah started toward the hall when Jason caught her hand and pulled her back. "Second thought," he began, taking both her hands in his, "I think I need to unwind a little first. Are you tired?"

She remembered Christmas night. They ended up here in this same room on the sofa right behind her. How deeply she had grown to care for this man in such a short amount of time—an *incredibly* short amount of time, she reminded herself.

106

She gazed at him, her heart aching for the pain etched on his face. "How about I make us some tea?" He nodded, a tired smile trying to form on his face. "Besides," she added, "the sun will be up in just a couple of hours. Who needs sleep anyway?"

CHAPTER 11

The next three days blurred together as they all waited for JT to thaw and Sergio to arrive. From time to time, they talked through every possible solution to the problems between them. But until all five members of *Blue* could sit down and talk, little could be done.

In the meantime, a unique bond of friendship surfaced as Hannah spent time with Marissa and Alli under the peculiar circumstances. They shared their hearts together as they watched the struggle continue among the guys. New to this odd little cluster of people, Hannah no longer felt like an outsider just along for the ride; she felt part of them now. The realization astounded her.

In the short time they'd known each other, Hannah and Alli became close friends. While Marissa never left Gevin's side, Alli and Hannah occasionally slipped out for a stop at Hannah's apartment or a cappuccino at a nearby café. They talked non-stop as if they'd known each other forever. Hannah loved hearing Alli's stories about the guys, about her life as the "unknown girlfriend"—her preference—and her feelings about what was happening. Alli, on the other hand, assured Hannah constantly of how "refreshing" her presence was, as she put it. And after knowing Jason for so many years, she made sure Hannah knew this was not a relationship that would just run its course and die out after the holidays.

"You're just what he needed, Hannah. Besides, I love watching the two of you together. If I'd handpicked someone for Jason, she'd be you. Totally."

On the morning of New Year's Eve, Laura finished putting away the breakfast dishes and served a fresh pot of coffee to all of them. Jason said he could never bring home too many of his friends. The party that night had been her idea and he'd gladly taken her up on it.

Laura set down her cup of coffee, finalizing the arrangements. "The caterers should arrive around 4:00 and have everything set up before anyone arrives, honey. I padded your number a bit so if a few more show up, we'll have plenty for everyone."

"Mom, honestly—we kept it small on purpose. Only a few of the guys in the band, some of the roadies . . . and a couple of the management folks who were gonna be in the area. Shouldn't be more than fifty at the most."

"Fifty?" Alli mouthed to Hannah. She rolled her eyes then slapped a fake smile back on her face. Hannah laughed silently.

"What?" Jason asked, noticing the exchange. "Alli, someone else you're wanting to invite?" he teased.

"Yeah," Jackson interrupted. "She invited some of the Bucs cheerleaders, but I said, 'Alli? No—*no* cheerleaders allowed. This is Jason's party!' She pouted, she whined, but—I stood my ground, JMac. No problem."

"Yeah right, big guy," Alli begrudged. "Like I would invite cheerleaders. In your dreams."

"Well, Jackson, if you want to invite the cheerleaders or the entire team for that matter, you just tell 'em to come on," Laura said. "I'd be happy to meet your friends.

And don't you let Jason give you a hard time," she finished with a wink.

Laura started to turn, then stopped, reaching into her pocket and pulling out a cell phone. "Oh, Hannah, is this yours?"

"I've looked everywhere for it!" Laura handed it to her. "Where'd you find it?"

"It was under the sofa. I found it when Frank moved the furniture out of the way for the party."

Hannah hit her forehead with the heel of her hand. "Oh, now I remember. When Jackson and Alli arrived the other day, I—oh, never mind. I'm just glad you found it." She pressed the side button and found six missed calls, twelve text messages, and five voice mails. *Kylie. She's gonna kill me.* She brushed off the thought and looked up. "Thanks, Laura."

"No problem, sweetheart. I'm just glad—"

"Thought you might like to see who I found at the front door," Frank interrupted, as he entered the kitchen, a funny expression on his face.

A head full of bouncing black curls atop a short, 5'2" frame came bustling through the door. "Hi everybody! We're here! We're here!" she squealed, her dark Italian eyes wide with excitement. "Did you miss us?" An exaggerated high-pitched laugh trilled across the room.

Liza. Has to be. Exactly as I'd pictured her.

Sergio appeared behind her, his huge grin expectant as he faced the roomful. "Hey guys, how's it goin'?"

Jackson and Jason jumped up to greet them. Hannah watched closely as they lightly embraced Sergio's girlfriend. She didn't miss the heated hug they received in response as Liza pressed her body against each of them.

She stole a look at Alli, that same fake smile plastered on her friend's face. "Liza. Nice to see you," she said, her tone flat. "Sergio, welcome home."

Sergio gave Laura a hug, which she returned warmly. "Sergio, we thought you'd never get here. What's Hawaii got that North Carolina doesn't, huh?"

Liza stepped between Jason's mother and her boyfriend. "Why, me, of course! Isn't that right, Sergi?"

Baby talk. I hate baby talk. Hannah's eyes locked with Alli's, communicating her disdain.

Alli's expression spoke volumes. *See what we mean?*

Laura made a valiant effort at remaining cordial as she stepped away. "Well, there you go," she remarked.

Hannah glanced up to notice Sergio looking straight at her. "And who is this?" he asked, the broad smile warming his face as he moved toward her with his outstretched hand. He was far more handsome than she'd imagined, his dark eyes the kind you could get lost in. Forever. He'd clearly spent a lot of time working out in a gym just like the rest of the guys. A *lot* of time.

Jason rested his hands on her shoulders. "Sergio Cruz, meet Hannah Brooks. Hannah, this is Sergio."

She took hold of his hand, surprised how firmly he gripped her hand. He leaned down to kiss her cheek. "Hannah, nice to meet you. This is great! It's about time someone took pity en este pobre perdedor!"

"Now, Sergio, Jason's not a loser," she laughed.

"Very funny, Sergio," Jason anguished in a sing-song response.

"¡Ah! Ella habla español. ¡Qué inteligente chica!" Sergio continued, praising Hannah's Spanish. "Inteligente y hermosa," he added, his eyes dancing.

"What did he say?" Jason asked her.

"He says I'm smart—"

"Smart and beautiful," Sergio completed. He wrapped his arm over Jason's shoulder. "Looks like Santa was *very* good to you, JMac."

"That, he was, Sergio. More than you—"

"Well, he was good to Sergi too, wasn't he, baby?" Liza interrupted, again stepping between Sergio and his friend. "We had a *wonderful* time in Hawaii with my family, didn't we?"

Sergio's smile struggled.

"Nice tan there, Serg," Jackson said.

"Nice tan, Serg," Alli added.

Sergio barked a nervous cough. "So when does the big 'par-tay' begin? And what was with all the phone calls, Jason? You knew I'd make it."

"*We'd* make it," Liza corrected, moving in front of Sergio.

Jason busied himself pouring Sergio and Liza mugs of coffee. "Have a seat, okay?" he motioned toward the big kitchen table. "Oh, nothing special's been going on around here . . . except that Gevin and Rissa announced their engagement."

"*What?*" Sergio cried. "I mean, that's great, but—what a shock! When did this happen? Are they here in town? This is amazing!"

"You *must* be kidding." Liza planted her fist on her hip. "Gevin and Marissa? You're not serious. Why on earth would he want to marry *her?*"

"Geez, Liza!" Sergio's snapped. "What's *that* supposed to mean? Marissa is terrific, and Gevin's a lucky man to have her. I can't believe you even said that." He looked around the table. "Hey, I'm sorry. Sometimes she speaks before she thinks."

She playfully slapped Sergio on the shoulder and looked around the table as well, though clearly not getting it. "That's not true. I know exactly what I'm saying, Sergi! It's a terrible match and Gevin must be out of his mind to even consider it. Oh, I know she's nice and all, but she's . . . well, for starters, she's *black*. Duh? As if no one noticed?" Liza smirked.

"Your point?" Alli shot back.

"My point being, it's the biggest mistake he could ever make. A white *Blue* member marrying a black girl? What was he thinking? I don't care if it is a new millennium, the *Blue* fans will never stand for it. Take my word, if he goes through with this, then *Blue* is toast. You might as well—"

"Liza, shut up. Just SHUT UP!" Sergio grabbed her arm and started to pull her up from her chair.

She kicked her chair back. "Don't you *ever* talk to me that way, Sergio Cruz!" She wrenched her arm free then jabbed him in the chest with her finger. "How dare you?! You ever lay a hand on me like that, and you'll regret it the rest of your life. You got that?" She stuck her face in his, then blew out a huff. "Oh, I don't have to put up with this. Where's my room?"

Frank cleared his throat. "I'll show you." He moved toward the door to the living area.

"The rooms in the guest house are ready, Frank," Laura said quietly. "Any room will do."

Once they were gone, Sergio immediately stood up, clearing his throat. He walked to the counter to pour himself more coffee. "Look, guys, I'm really sorry. I don't know what gets into her sometimes." His hands trembled as he carried the mug back to the table. He exhaled deeply. "Really, I'm so sorry. I'll talk to her when she calms down."

If he was hoping someone would fill in the gap, no one did. Eventually, Jackson changed the subject. "The thing is, Sergio, we've got a bigger problem than Gevin's engagement."

"What do you mean?"

Jason hoisted himself onto the kitchen counter. "Meaning, Gevin wants to call it quits. He's done."

Sergio looked around the room for signs of a joke. "You're kidding, right?

"Unfortunately, we're not," Jackson answered. "JT and Tracey were here just after Christmas. When JT found out, he blew up—"

"Can't say I blame him!"

"We haven't heard from him since, but we're hoping he and Trace show up for the party tonight," Alli added. "Geez, won't *this* be a party to remember."

"You can't be serious! Isn't this kinda sudden? I mean, did you know about this? You didn't agree to it, did you?" He continued looking at them, face by face. "Right? Guys, tell me you didn't go along with this!"

"No, Serg, we didn't," Jackson answered. "Nothing definite has been decided. But whatever we do, we can't give up. I think we just need to give it some time. We keep talking to Gevin about it, but we refuse to give up."

"Jackson's right," Jason added. "We can't give up. I'm thinking once it all settles down, Gevin might rethink this. I think he's just tired and all caught up in the happiness of his engagement and—"

"And you cut him some slack," Laura said. Standing at the sink, she turned off the faucet with extra force, then turned to face them. She looked from Jason to Jackson to Sergio and back again, wiping her hands on a towel. "I've heard all the ranting and raving for days now, and it seems to me you all need to back off and give him some space. Fighting about it day in and day out isn't going to solve a thing. Am I right?"

Jason let out a loud moan. "Of course, you're right, Mom, but—"

"No buts. Stop fighting and start talking. You're grown men now. Start acting like it. And that's all I have to say about it." She draped the dish towel on its rack then left the room.

"Yep," Alli started, "this will be one unforgettable New Year's party."

"Excuse me?"

Alli stopped dead in her tracks. Opening the door to her room, she found Liza unpacking her suitcase. Alli's things were in a pile on the floor. "What do you think you're doing?"

Liza continued her task. "I'm unpacking. Why should I stay in the guest house when everyone else is up here? The housekeeper told me this was actually Sergio's room, so this is where I'm staying."

Alli pressed her lips together, unwilling to engage the little tramp. Instead, she stared her down then turned, slamming the door on her way out.

Jackson turned the corner at the top of the stairs. "Alli, what's wrong?"

"She made herself at home in my room! Even though Frank gave her a room in the guest house, she decided to stay in 'Sergio's' room, so she just threw all my stuff on the floor like it was trash! Jackson, I cannot *stand* that girl. Make her leave! I don't care what Sergio says, she has got to go!"

Jackson grabbed her by the hands and dragged her down the hall to his room. "Shhhh! Alli, listen to me. I can't stand her either, you know that. But right now—with all this other stuff going on, can we just blow her off? I'll get your stuff out of there as soon as she leaves the room. How about I put you in with Hannah? It's just not worth a big fight right now. Everybody's already upset as it is."

"Yeah, but—"

"Just do me this favor, okay? Let it go, babe. Please? You and I both know Liza is a short-timer. You can see it in Sergio's face. I doubt seriously he'll keep her around much longer. So just be cool and let this go. For me, Alli. Please?"

"But you're just letting her win!"

"No, I'm not. I'm just trying to keep us all from killing each other right now. If we're going to survive—if the band is going to survive this—we have to let go of the little stuff and focus on what's important. Do you understand what I'm saying?" He pulled her into his arms. "Will you do this for me?"

As usual, he diffused her and she melted in his arms. Resting her head on his shoulder, she nodded in agreement. "Okay, but only because you asked me to. But that doesn't mean I have to like it."

"I know, babe. I know."

CHAPTER 12

Despite the underlying tension coursing throughout the McKenzie home, Hannah and Alli tried to make the best of the situation. They focused instead on helping Laura with last-minute preparations, then took their time getting dressed for the big New Year's party. The day before, they'd slipped out for a few hours to shop for the perfect party dresses. Alli said these parties were always dressy affairs, so they both tried on several long formal gowns until they found what they liked.

With her hair swept up on her head, Alli was stunning in a floor-length black sequined dress with spaghetti straps and a slit to just above her knee. The dress looked as if it had been made for her.

Hannah wore a slim-fitting satin dress in a deep sapphire blue, its bodice scattered with a splash of tiny rhinestones. Even her hair looked surprisingly good for a change, she thought, catching her reflection in the full mirror. She ran her hand through her long, thick curls cascading over her shoulders and smiled at her image. Butterflies flitted once again through her stomach, but she dismissed their presence, hoping the evening would be magical despite all the drama.

Diane Moody

Any traces of gloom lingering in the air at the McKenzie's completely dissipated once the party started. Dressed to the nines and feeling on top of the world, Hannah and Alli descended the staircase. They were pleased to find both Jason and Jackson waiting for them at the foot of the stairs. They turned simultaneously to look up just as the girls started down the stairs.

It was worth every penny Hannah had spent. Jason's lips parted, a smile slowly spreading as he drank in every inch of her. She peeked to see Jackson's eyes grow wide with the sight of Alli adorned like a goddess.

"Whoa," Jason and Jackson uttered in unison.

Hannah's heart skipped a beat as Alli squeezed her hand. "I'd say they like what they see, wouldn't you?" Alli laughed before rushing down the remaining stairs and into Jackson's arms.

"You can say that again," Jason whispered. He took Hannah by both hands, lifting them to wrap around his neck. "You look *amazing*," he said, suspending a kiss on her cheek.

"I could say the same for you," she whispered, not trusting her voice. "A man in a tux is a dangerous thing to behold, Jason McKenzie." His starched white shirt against the black tux accented his smile and sent a wave of goose bumps across her flesh. He was positively beaming—and his eyes were glued to her.

I can't believe I'm here.

With him.

Like this.

She closed her eyes, praying the moment would never end. When she opened them, she was surprised to find his eyes glistening with emotion. He hugged her again.

This time, he breathed the words against her ear. "I love you, Hannah."

She held her breath, afraid she must still be dreaming—this, the final scene before she would awaken to reality. But no, there was no mistake. She'd heard his words and felt them in her heart. *It's too soon . . . much too soon . . .* The warning raced through her veins faster than her pulse.

Then, she realized something. Not once in the week she'd spent with Jason had he ever been anything but truthful. And not just to her, but to everyone. It wasn't in him to lie. She knew it without question.

And she knew something else. Deep in her heart, against every ounce of practicality and logic and reason, she knew what she felt was real. Jason pulled back, looking into her eyes, searching for a response. Her chin trembled as she answered, "I love you too, Jason." She laughed even as a single tear escaped her lashes.

"Yessss!" He twirled her around in a circle. "Hannah, let's dance! You wanna dance? I feel like dancing!" He led her through clusters of people she'd never met until they were dancing on the impromptu dance floor in the McKenzie's great room. The music pounded as they moved to the rhythms surrounding them, lost in a love just discovered.

Jackson and Alli hadn't made it to the dance floor, however. Still standing at the base of the stairs, Jackson continued staring at Alli. He hadn't said a word but the love she found in his blue eyes said all she wanted to hear. Alli, normally not the least bit shy, felt light-headed. The depth of her feelings for this tall, handsome man she had loved as far back as she could remember was overpowering.

"I'm speechless, Jackson. You look so . . . *perfect.* I don't know whether to faint or ask for a table in the non-smoking section."

"I know. I feel like a penguin. But not too bad for a rental, eh?" he said, turning around to give her the full effect of his black tuxedo, tails and all. The black and navy paisley bow tie made her laugh.

Typical Jackson. Always the quirky, special touch.

He took hold of her hands again. "But you—whoa, Alli. Talk about speechless. I mean, one minute you're this skinny little teenager and the next thing I know, you're this gorgeous *woman.*"

"I guess we just grew up, didn't we?" She smiled, her heart filled with affection as she lost herself in the eyes she knew so well.

"Always mine?" he asked, the question their own private ritual.

"Always and forever, Jackson."

A gust of cold air blasted them as the front door flew open. "So is there a party here or what?" JT shouted, closing the door behind him following Tracey inside.

"JT! You came!" Jackson exploded, almost knocking JT over. "You actually came. Miracles never cease!"

"Easy, Jax! You know I never miss a party."

Alli was pleased to see him relaxed and obviously recovered from the bitter encounter days before. They welcomed JT and Tracey into the house as they blended into the mass of friends and family. Hannah and Alli giggled as JT took off his coat. Who but JT Malone would wear a purple tank-style t-shirt under his white tux jacket?. In minutes they were all dancing, the burden they shared momentarily dismissed.

Blue Christmas

Sometime later, Sergio and Liza finally made their entrance down the stairs. Hannah smiled, watching Sergio descend the stairs, his charcoal gray tux accented with an embroidered brocade vest beneath it. His warm Spanish eyes sparkled, but his smile seemed hesitant at best.

Then she realized she might be the *only* person even noticing Sergio Cruz.

On his arm, a spectacle descended the stairs with him. Dressed in a lipstick red sequined dress, Liza's neckline plunged to her waist revealing her quite-noticeable and no doubt surgically-enhanced cleavage.

Hannah felt sorry for Sergio the moment her eyes met his. Liza tugged him along like a forgotten stuffed animal. When they approached Jason and Hannah, Liza elbowed Hannah in the ribs, pushing her out of the way so she could hug Jason. He stiffened at her touch, quickly detaching himself from her.

"Oooh Jason, you look good enough to eat tonight. So handsome, baby!"

Hannah caught a whiff of something wafting around Liza and it wasn't perfume. *Whoa. The girl smells like a walking distillery.*

By the sickened look on his face, Jason noticed it as well. Hannah looked closer at Liza's face. Tiny pinpoint pupils. The whites of her eyes, streaked red like a road map. *This can't be good,* Hannah thought.

She wasn't the only one who spotted it. Jason stared intently into Liza's eyes. "Liza, are you all right? You look a little—

"All right? Just all right? Jason, are you blind? Look at me!" she took a twirl to show off her gown. "I'm fabulous!" Liza giggled at herself, taking Jason into her arms to dance.

"Whoa, Liza, hold on there." He pulled himself out of her clutches again.

"No! Stop being such a prude and dance with me!" She pressed herself against him launching into her own version of dirty dancing.

"Liza, no—not right now, okay?" he begged off. He reached for Hannah's hand and quickly distanced them from the dancing Italian queen.

"Oh SCREW YOU, Jason!" Liza flipped him off. "You're such a Boy Scout anyway. Why don't you and your little girlfriend just go off and . . . *hold hands* or whatever." She turned around, searching the crowd. "Sergi? Where are you?"

As Hannah and Jason moved across the room, they ran into Sergio. He was tugging at the collar of his shirt. Reaching out to hug him, Hannah smiled warmly at him. "Ah, Sergio, te ves incredible esta noche."

"No, Hannah—*you're* the one who looks amazing," he answered, holding her hand at arm's length, then kissing her hand in true European style. "Jason, you better keep an eye on her. She's *way* out of your league tonight, mi amigo."

"And don't I know it." Jason laughed. He leaned into Sergio, draping his arm over his shoulder. "Listen, man, I'm concerned about Liza. I'm sorry to have to ask but is she on something? She looks really stoned."

"Look, JMac, I'm really sorry about Liza. I don't know what—"

"Sergi! Come here!" Liza shouted. In a flash, she was in the middle of them, her eyes boring a hole through Jason and Hannah. "I want to dance. NOW." She pulled him toward the dance area. He looked back at them over his shoulder rolling his eyes.

Jason and Hannah watched as Liza thrust her arms high in the air, her dance moves so lewd they were almost comical. As she strutted herself in and out of couples, Sergio stopped to talk to one of the road managers. Eventually, his date disappeared in the crowd.

He didn't seem to mind.

"Well say there, JT. Where've you been all night?" Liza slid beside JT on the sofa, wrapping her arms around his elbow, pressing herself against him.

"Liza, do you mind?" JT moved over a couple of inches away from her.

She lifted the drink out of his hand and drained it, then spit it back into the glass. "What *is* this?"

"It's Pellegrino, Liza. What did you expect?"

"What's the matter with you people? This is *New Year's Eve*! Where's the booze? I feel like I'm at a church picnic here."

He set the glass on the end table, moving again to distance himself from her on the sofa. "It's a matter of respect. The McKenzies prefer not to have alcohol in their home and we respect their wishes, pure and simple. Everybody here knows that."

"But it's New Year's! We need to party, JT! C'mon, let's you and me blow this place and go find us a real party!" She placed her hand high on his thigh and tossed him a wink.

He picked up her hand and removed it from his leg. "Liza, there are plenty of after-parties planned tonight. Why don't you go find Serg and leave?"

She pouted, running her finger along the back of his hand. "I've got a better idea. Why don't you and I leave instead? I know you like to party as much as I do." She leaned in to whisper in his ear. "C'mon, let's go see what kind of trouble we can get into."

JT shook his head in amusement, Liza's face still nuzzled against his neck. "Girl, seriously, you need to chill, y'know what I mean?"

"What's going on here? JT?" Tracey stood before them.

Liza tossed her a glance, then dug in closer to JT. "Tracey, why don't you go find something else to do. JT and I are chatting."

JT suddenly stood up, reaching out for Tracey's hand. "No, I think we're quite through with our little discussion, Liza. See ya!" He tugged Tracey behind him to the middle of the dance floor.

She stopped. "JT, what was that all about?"

"Trace? Forget it. She's pathetic and not worth getting upset over. Dance with me, baby, and forget about her." He pulled her close into his arms. "Sergio needs to dump that girl. The sooner, the better. She's nothing but trouble. Big trouble . . ."

The crowd partied long into the evening. The endless trays filled with cheese and deli meats, fruits, chicken wings and marinated meatballs disappeared, along with all the fussy desserts. Laura and Frank hosted the younger crowd until around 11:30 when they called it a night.

As some of the guests left, the music gradually turned more mellow. Lights dimmed and shoes were kicked off as spirited conversations gave way to quiet chats.

Hannah and Jason shuffled upstairs to the loft, knowing most of the guys would have drifted there already. As they topped the stairs, they heard the heated voices of Gevin and JT.

"But you can't do this! It isn't fair!" JT grunted.

"That's where you're wrong," Gevin answered, his words measured. "Nobody ever said this was a prison we could never escape. JT, I'm *tired* of it. It's been ten long years and I'm tired. I want to marry Marissa and have a normal life."

"Then you're a traitor!"

"Stop acting like a child, JT," Sergio barked.

"Oh, so you're siding with him now, huh Serg?" JT turned on him. "You roll into town at the last minute and think you know everything that's happened here?"

"I know enough. I know that calling Gevin a traitor isn't gonna solve anything."

"Knock it off, you guys," Jason hissed. "I told you not to get into this tonight. This is not the time or place—"

"Jason, thank God," Marissa cried. "I've been trying to make them stop, but—"

"—but I still say it's *your* fault to begin with, Rissa!" JT yelled. "I mean, fact of the matter is, who the hell do you think you are anyway?"

"SHUT UP, JT!" Gevin got in JT's face. "I will not allow you to talk to her that way. Do you understand me?"

"Gevin, I'm gonna say it one more time," Marissa spoke with barely controlled anger. "Either work this out with him once and for all or we leave town. And I mean *now.*" Marissa stormed down the stairs.

Hannah took a seat on the sofa, cradling her arms around herself. Jason yanked off his tie and jacket as he approached the fireplace. "Geez, guys, can't you see what you're doing? I know we've got to talk this all out. But not tonight and not here! Is that understood?" He looked back and forth at his friends, the anger still burning behind their eyes.

He looked around the room. Alli was curled up in the easy chair, her lower lip trembling. "Alli, where's Jackson?"

"He went to his room little while ago. I'll go get him." She wiped her eyes as she left the room.

Approaching Jackson's room, Alli heard laughter coming from behind the door. Candlelight danced along the carpet under the half-closed door. Certain she had happened on to some renegade partiers, she started past the door.

Her breath caught. A black and navy paisley bow tie lay on the floor just outside the cracked door. Alli leaned over to pick it up. Soft murmuring drifted from the room.

" . . . but you know you want me, Jackson. You always have. I've seen it in your eyes a thousand times."

Alli stopped breathing. The speech was slurred, but she'd know that voice anywhere. She started to reach for the door handle but found herself paralyzed.

"I've seen you looking at me tonight, baby." Liza's voice faltered

She's crying? Why is she crying?

"Don't do this, Liza." Jackson's voice cracked. "I beg you, don't do this."

Oh my God. Alli watched her hand reach for the door knob as if it didn't belong to her. Liza's voice drifted through the slight opening.

"You like this dress on me, don't you? Did you know I wore it for you? Did you? I picked it out just for you, Jax."

"Liza, please."

"Sergi was always just for fun. But you knew that, didn't you?" Her voice grew more emotional.

Alli froze, hearing the desperation in Liza's sobs.

"You knew it was always you I wanted, didn't you? Because I've always known you wanted me. From the very beginning. Say it, Jackson. Tell me you want me."

Silence.

"SAY IT! I'm losing patience with you, Jackson. All my letters and emails, I've told you a thousand times how I felt about you. You *know* I love you."

"What are you talking about? You never wrote me."

"Of course I did, silly. I signed all my love letters—'Til death us do part.'"

"Leslie?" he gasped. "*You're* Leslie? The one who's been stalking me? Threatening me with all those deranged letters?"

"*Love* letters, Jax. Not deranged. I poured out all my love to you in those letters." She sobbed openly, hiccupping her words. "Leslie. Liza. Leslie. Liza. I thought for sure you knew. You *had* to know. Because you love me. I know you do. Now I'm only going to ask you one more time. Tell me you love me. Tell me now."

Silence.

"TELL ME!"

Alli couldn't control the shaking. A thousand thoughts pelted her mind. Slowly, she pushed the door open without a sound. She blinked back the tears blurring her vision. Wild images danced along the walls from a sea of candles lit all around the room. On the far wall in the corner, she could barely make out the image of two people. She bit her lip to keep her staggered breath silent. Slowly the images came into focus.

Jackson was pinned against the far corner, Liza's body pressed firmly against him. But it made no sense. Jackson was a full 6'4". Liza was so little. Why didn't he do something? Why would he allow her to—

"Jackson?" His name fell from her lips.

His eyes shot toward her. "Alli!" he gasped. "No! No! Get out of here!"

She shook her head. "Jackson? Wha—"

"Just turn around and leave. Now, Alli. LEAVE."

Alli tilted her head. *I'm dreaming. Surely this is a dream?*

Liza hadn't moved. She looked over her shoulder, casting a drunken glance at her. "You heard him. Get out of here." She paused a moment then yelled, "GET! OUT!"

Alli slowly shook her head, back and forth, trying to make sense of it. She searched Jackson's face, desperate for an answer. His eyes were tightly closed. "Alli, please leave," he pleaded, his voice catching again.

She backed out the door, one step after another. Suddenly she bumped into someone.

"Alli? What's wrong?" Sergio turned her to face him. "What's the matter? What is it? You're shaking like a leaf."

The words wouldn't form. She looked back at the room she'd just left.

He stepped around her, still holding her arm. "Alli, answer me! What's wrong?"

"Jackson . . . "

His puzzled eyes questioned her but she couldn't speak another word. He stepped toward the door into Jackson's room. Alli reached for his sleeve, tugging to warn him. He turned to face her just as the slurred speech continued inside the room.

" . . . because I've waited all this time. And now it's *my* turn."

At the recognition of Liza's voice, Sergio shoved the door open. "What's going on here?"

Liza jerked her head to face him, but remained pressed against Jackson's body. "Get out of here, Sergio. GET OUT!"

He moved closer, Alli right behind him. "Liza, what are you doing? Get away from him!"

"He loves me, Sergio. He always has. And I've been in love with Jackson. From the very beginning." She laughed, a wet rebuke. "You're such a fool. You never knew, did you? I *used* you to get to Jackson." She spewed out expletives alongside a sarcastic laugh. "You're *soooo* naive, Sergio. They all tried to tell you about me. But you wouldn't listen. You actually thought I loved you, didn't you? What are you, blind or just stupid?" Her crazed, inebriated laughter filled the air.

Sergio turned around to face Alli. She watched his jaw clench as he steeled his eyes.

"No, Sergio, don't—"

He turned like lightning, charging across the room toward his deranged girlfriend. "Liza, you—"

She stepped back, revealing the gun she held firmly against Jackson's stomach. Sergio stopped in his tracks.

"Stop, Serg," Jackson warned. "She's had it planted against my gut for the last ten minutes. She's drunk and stoned, and I have no doubt in my mind, she'll fire it." A bead of sweat trickled down the side of Jackson's face.

"STOP TALKING ABOUT ME LIKE I'M NOT HERE!"

"Jackson!" Alli screamed.

Jackson leaned his head back against the wall. "Alli, please, honey. Just back up and—"

"No!" Liza shrieked. "She stays right where she is. Nobody leaves 'til I say so now."

Alli watched Jackson swallow with difficulty, his eyes pleading with her silently across the candlelit room. Sergio pushed her back, forcing her to stay behind him.

"Liza, just put down the gun and let's talk about this," Sergio asked quietly. "There's no reason we can't work this out. You don't want anybody to get hurt, now, do you?"

"Oh, I don't know, maybe I do. Maybe I need to make sure Little Miss Muffet over there is never a problem for me again."

"No, Liza, leave her out of this!" Jackson begged. "Please just let her go."

Slowly blinking her besotted eyes, Liza turned once again to face Jackson. "Oh, I don't think I can do that, Jax," she said, pressing the gun harder against his stomach. "How can I ever be sure you're totally mine if she's still alive?"

Alli could hear Jackson panting. He lifted his eyes just as Sergio dived toward them. Liza grabbed Jackson's jaw, jerking it down toward her, then covered his lips with her own.

Sergio pounced against her back, screaming, "LIZA!"

But it was too late.

The shot echoed through the room. Jackson heard Alli's scream but she sounded far away. His breath knocked out of him, he blinked, trying to understand what had happened. It was only as he slid down the wall that he felt the searing pain in his stomach. He pressed his fingers against the pain. When he drew them back, his hand was dark and sticky. He gasped for breath but couldn't find it.

His eyes moved mechanically across the faces floating around him. Sergio's horrified eyes as he held Liza's arms behind her. Liza's twisted, satisfied smile. And Alli's contorted face, so close now though her cries sounded so far away . . .

Then it all went black.

CHAPTER 13

"Alli, move back. You have to move back." Jason spoke with quiet firmness as he gently pulled her away from Jackson.

"You need to get her out of here NOW," the paramedic instructed Jason. He and three others moved swiftly to assess Jackson's vital signs.

"I can't leave him, Jason! No! Please don't make me go!" she begged, screaming through her tears. "Jackson! Jackson! Oh God—please! No!" She shook violently in Jason's arms as he tried to move her out of the way.

"Shhhh, take it easy, Alli. The paramedics need lots of room if they're gonna help Jackson, okay? Shhhh . . . just try to take a deep breath for me, okay? C'mon, Alli. Jackson needs you to pull yourself together." He held her tightly in his arms, hoping to stop her trembling . . . and his.

When the shot first rang out, Jason and the rest of those in the loft flew down the long hall toward the sound of it. Laura and Frank bolted from the other end of the hall to find the heartbreaking scene along with the rest of them. Frank immediately called 911 as Jason, JT, and

Gevin raced to Jackson's side. Sergio quickly explained what had happened as he held Liza's arms in a vise grip behind her back, the gun kicked away from them across the carpeted floor. His anger and panic erupted as he shouted the accusations at the woman who remained silent.

Jason had worked swiftly alongside Gevin and JT to lower Jackson to the floor. They ripped open his shirt, the buttons scattering silently across the carpet like discarded pearls.

"Oh my God," Gevin groaned. Bright crimson seeped from the nasty black hole in Jackson's stomach.

JT patted Jackson's face. "Jackson! Jax, wake up, buddy! You gotta wake up!"

Jason looked across at Gevin and JT and saw his own terror mirrored in their faces.

JT continued. "C'mon, Jax! Don't you do this! Don't you even *think* about leaving us, man! JACKSON!" His voice cracked with despair.

Jason helped pull the blood-soaked shirt away from Jackson's wound. They unbuckled his belt, loosening his slacks to relieve any possible pressure. "Gevin, he's losing too much blood!"

"I know, I know. Where are those paramedics?!"

The commotion behind them answered the question as the medical team arrived. Frank and Laura tried to clear out the guests, instructing them to move quickly downstairs and out of the way. Red lights swirled through the windows as dozens of police cars swarmed the grounds responding to the 911 alert. Jason heard a police sergeant assuring his father they had called in extra back-up knowing the identity of the homeowners and guests. They would secure the property against curiosity-seekers or media who would arrive as soon as the news spread.

They handcuffed Liza who moved like a zombie as the officers pushed her out of the room. Her face registered no emotion whatsoever.

Jason spotted Hannah, Marissa, and Tracey huddled close together in the corner of Jackson's room, their hands locked tightly as they trembled together in tears. They watched in horror as the paramedics strapped an oxygen mask on Jackson's face and attached other monitors. Their medical terms meant little to the hushed people gathered in that room, but they didn't need to know the scientific language. What they saw was enough.

One of the paramedics hustled to get the stretcher from the hall, popping it to lock the wheels in place once back inside the room. As they secured Jackson's arms across his chest, they lifted him efficiently in one motion, placing him on the gurney. Strapping belts across him, they continued to work on him.

"Let's go—move out of the way, please," the female medic yelled. "Clear out, people! Move it!"

Suddenly everyone was in motion, all talking at once, making sure everyone had a ride to the hospital. Gevin wrapped his jacket around Alli, trying to keep her on her feet as they left the room. Jason joined Hannah and Marissa, quickly ushering them out of the room and down the stairs. In a matter of seconds they were all outside, blinded by the countless flashing red lights of all the emergency vehicles.

Jason shuddered as the scene unfolded.

Oh God, please tell me this is just a bad dream.

"C'mon, JT! Tracey! Hurry!" Jason pulled Hannah along with the others as they climbed into a limousine one of their guests had hired for the evening. Gevin and Marissa held Alli between them, gently pushing her into the car. JT and Tracey climbed in after them.

"C'mon, c'mon! Get this thing moving!" JT shouted at the driver.

"Wait!" Alli cried. "Where's Sergio? Where is he?"

Realizing he wasn't with him, they looked outside. "There he is on the porch!" Jason threw open the limo door. "Serg! Get in here! Hurry up!"

Sergio stood among the crowd of party guests, his hands dug deep in his trouser pockets and shivering in the cold night. He shook his head back and forth defiantly. "No," he mouthed.

Jason flew out of the car, racing toward the porch. He lunged at Sergio who bolted back, resisting Jason's efforts. "No, Jason, I can't go. This is all my fault! I can't—¡no puedo! ¡No puedo! ¡Oh Dios mio!"

Jason gripped Sergio's arms. "Just shut up and get in the car, Sergio. I'm not gonna listen to that kind of talk!"

Sergio fought back, his strength overpowering his friend. "No!" Angry tears coursed down his face. He stepped back, colliding into the strong arms of Frank McKenzie. Sergio struggled to get free, but Frank held him tight.

"Jason's right," Frank said urgently, just an inch away from Sergio's ear. "You have to go with them. This is not your fault, son. But this isn't the time for discussing who is or isn't at fault. You have to think of Jackson right now and nothing else. That's *all* that matters."

Jason could see Sergio's body relaxing. He looked at his father appreciatively. He wrapped his arm over Sergio's shoulder. They moved quickly toward the limo. As Sergio ducked into the long black car, Jason turned back toward his father. "Dad! Call Jackson's family. Get them here as fast as you can."

"Your mother is already trying to track them down. Go on. We'll join you shortly."

The door slammed behind Jason as the tires of the limo squealed in hasty retreat. Sirens pierced the air as a long police escort surrounded them. Hannah cried softly, her head on Jason's shoulder. He rested his head against hers, looking at Alli, sandwiched between Gevin and Marissa. Her lips moved silently as tears poured down her face. JT stared out the window, his body rocking in quick, jerking movements as Tracey held his hands tightly in hers.

Sergio sat in a side seat of the limo, his elbows resting on his knees, his head buried in his hands.

Jason wiped his eyes with the back of his hand. He let out a long breath then forced his eyes toward the side window as he prayed silently. In every direction, huge displays of fireworks erupted in the sky as the new year arrived. Jason's heart ached in his chest. Not since his own surgery years ago had he known such pain. But this was so much worse. Looking around he saw the fear on the faces of those he loved. He couldn't bear it. A lump the size of a baseball filled his throat, but he knew what he had to do.

"Oh Jesus," he cried. "Sweet Jesus, *please* . . . please save our Jackson." He stopped, unable to say more. Hannah squeezed his hand.

One by one, then simultaneously their prayers came together, reverberating through the car. They continued to pray as the sirens wailed in an eerie, strange accompaniment. They begged God for their brother. They cried out to God for a miracle.

Because tonight, it would take nothing short of a miracle to save Jackson Greer.

"As the world ushered in the new year, we here in Chapel Hill were shocked to learn of a tragic shooting this evening at the home of Frank and Laura McKenzie, parents of *Out of the Blue's* Jason McKenzie." The newscaster's face appeared somber as she spoke into the lens of the camera outside the hospital. "Details are sketchy but we have learned that a guest attending the New Year's party at the McKenzie's shot and wounded band member Jackson Greer. Greer was brought here to North Carolina Memorial Hospital where we were told just moments ago that he remains unconscious in critical condition."

The camera angle widened as it panned the hospital area. "Security is tight at the hospital as word has spread of the shooting. We are told that the four other members of the group arrived by limousine just minutes behind the ambulance carrying Greer. The police chief has asked that well-wishers and others respect the privacy of these celebrities and their families at this time of crisis by not coming anywhere near this medical facility."

Dozens of similar camera crews reported the story across air waves that reached around the world in a matter of minutes. Security tightened at the hospital as police officers sealed off the area.

Inside, doctors and nurses worked at a frantic pace to stabilize the young celebrity in their emergency room. Jackson was moved to a special intensive care unit. With immediate access to a private wing, those who waited for news of his condition were able to be together away from the public. The gracious hospital staff tried to make them comfortable, providing plenty of space and amenities for them.

The minutes ticked by agonizingly slow for those who waited.

Gevin grabbed the remote and clicked off the television. "Enough."

Hannah sat in a corner of the waiting room watching every movement and listening to every word. People spoke in urgent whispers, but mostly they were silent.

Occasionally, she would shake her head, as if doing so could wake her from this nightmare.

She felt uncomfortable and out of place. Yes, she had learned to feel a part of these people over the past few days. But now, in this highly charged atmosphere of crisis, she felt like an intruder. She thought briefly of slipping out and going home, but a nagging inner voice kept telling her to stay.

Jason needs you.

She wanted to believe it. She watched him across the room, clustered with the other guys as they took turns sitting with Alli. Hannah wanted desperately to comfort her new friend. But mostly she wanted to cling to Jason. Still, she couldn't seem to find the courage to invade their space. So she waited.

Kylie had called again. And again, Hannah had chosen not to take the call. How could she now? How could she explain all that had happened leading up to this? She knew Kylie would be angry with her, but now wasn't the time to worry about that. She would understand once they had a chance to talk.

Not knowing what else to do, Hannah closed her eyes and added to the silent rush of prayers. After a while, she felt someone sit down beside her. Before she opened her eyes, she breathed in the familiar scent of Jason's cologne. His hand reached for hers, intertwining her fingers with his. He dropped his head on her shoulder. She could almost feel the weight of his heartache in that gesture.

"You okay?" he asked quietly.

"Yes. I think. How are you holding up?"

"I just can't believe this," he began. "What if—"

"Shhh." She pressed her fingers against his lips. "Don't, Jason."

He exhaled deeply pulling her hand toward him, settling against her. "I just wish I could get in to see him. Just for a moment. I just need to see him breathing."

She tightened her grip on his hand. "Any word from his family?"

"No, I don't—"

The door opened as Frank and Laura arrived. Their eyes raced across the sea of faces looking for their son who suddenly appeared before them. He collapsed in their embrace. Hannah couldn't bear to watch as the three of them cried together. Gevin joined their circle, burying his head against his uncle's shoulder and weeping out loud.

The family shared quiet words and Hannah knew that Frank and Laura would be the strength they all needed right now. She was right. As the minutes slowly bled into long, unbearable hours, the McKenzies moved among the people assembled here for Jackson and encouraged them to have hope.

From time to time, the doctors would come in to report on Jackson's condition. Each time they opened the door, you could hear the collective intake of breath as they all feared the worst. And they collectively sighed in relief when they heard that he was hanging on. He was still unconscious, but he was alive.

Around 5:00 in the morning, Hannah made her way over to the coffee pot and got two white mugs, filling them with the fresh, steaming brew. She silently thanked God for the simple luxury of real coffee mugs, not the usual Styrofoam cups found in hospital waiting rooms. She walked slowly toward Alli. "Buy you a cup of coffee?"

Alli looked up, her eyes bloodshot and puffy. She nodded, reaching out for the mug.

"Alli, I couldn't begin to know what to say right now," Hannah said as Alli sipped the hot brew. "But I've been praying for you since we left the house. And I promise you, I won't stop."

Alli looked at her, the slightest nod communicating her appreciation. "Hannah, don't think I'm being ungrateful. I'm just trying really hard to stop all these tears, and—" She took a deep breath, shaking her head. "And I just—"

"It's okay," Hannah whispered. "I understand. You don't have to say anything. I just wanted to check on you. Is there anything you need?"

She closed her eyes briefly. "Actually, there is. Do you think we could get out of here for a few minutes? These walls are suffocating me."

"Sure. Let's take a walk down the hall." They moved toward the door. "Jason?" Hannah touched him on the arm as he sat talking to Gevin and Marissa. "Alli needs some fresh air. We're going to step out in the hall for a minute, okay?"

"Do you want me to come?"

Alli squeezed the back of his neck with her hand. "No, we're fine. We'll be right back."

They walked up and down the dark hall for half an hour. It felt good to be up and moving. Hannah let Alli talk. Sometimes they walked in complete silence. They were just heading back to the waiting room when anxious voices filled the hall ahead of them.

"Oh thank God, Hannah. It's the Greers!"

Alli flew into the arms of Jackson's mom and dad, immediately surrounded by his brothers and sisters. Hannah slipped back into the room to give them some privacy. It would only be a moment, because as soon as Hannah opened the door, Jason saw them too. He squeezed her hand before rushing into the hall. He was followed by Gevin and JT. Sergio remained on the floor of the waiting room. Frank and Laura sat on either side of him, no doubt trying to counsel him through the long hours of relentless, self-imposed questions.

Hannah walked back to the corner where she had originally been seated. Marissa plopped down beside her, folding her arms across her chest. "Oh girl, how in the world did all this happen? One minute we're dancing and laughing and having the best time . . . and then, the guys are fighting . . . and then that shot was fired . . . and it's like time just froze. And none of us have breathed since that moment." She shook her head back and forth. "I can't believe it. I just can't believe it."

"I know. It's surreal, isn't it? I think we're all still in shock."

"That we are."

Hannah thought for a moment then turned to face Marissa. "Rissa, can I be honest with you?"

"Sure, Hannah. Anything."

"I feel *really* out of place here. I'm trying to convince myself I should stay because of Jason. But I can't help feeling I've intruded on a great big family that's dealing with this horrible thing, and I just shouldn't be here."

Marissa's face clouded. "What in the world are you talking about? You *are* here because of Jason. And he needs you here. He needs you now more than ever. Just because you're new to this little soiree doesn't mean you aren't important to all of us. Okay? So just chill. None of us wanna be here, but we're here. And we all need each other. Okay?"

Hannah felt the burden lift off her shoulders. "Thanks. I guess I just needed to hear that."

"That's okay. Thing is, I've had my own doubts about being here. Ever since Gevin and I announced our plans, this whole thing has been one big mess. I knew it would be hard on the guys, but I never dreamed it would come to something like this."

"You can't blame yourself for any of this! Liza would have pulled that trigger regardless of what else was going on. She obviously had planned this—bringing a gun with her, cornering Jackson alone in his room like that. You and Gevin had nothing to do with it, Rissa."

"I know that, Hannah. But maybe we shouldn't have said anything. Just kept it to ourselves for now. I don't know. It's just all so crazy."

"I know. But the one I'm really worried about is Sergio. I see all that sadness in his eyes and it breaks my heart."

"Sergio's gonna need a lot of help to get through this. He's such a neat kid, y'know? He's got a heart the size of Texas and he's one of those people who's always happy just to be alive." Marissa smiled at memories obviously playing in her mind. "I just love him. Always have. Like a kid brother you just adore. He's so excited to be a part of this group. Loves every aspect of it. When the rest of the guys need a break from it and go off on vacation, he'll still make the award shows and do all the interviews. All by himself. It's like he can't get enough of it."

They looked over at Sergio, deep in conversation with the McKenzies. Laura held him close, her arm wrapped around his shoulders.

"He'll be okay, if he'll listen to Frank and Laura," Marissa continued. "They are so solid, those two. Now *that's* a model family if ever there was one. In fact, I'd have to credit the McKenzies with one of *Blue's* dirty little secrets."

"And what would that be?"

"Well, we don't make a big deal of it, but the fact is, most of us are pretty strong in our faith. A lot of people in the business are. It's not that we're ashamed or anything like that. Not at all. We just don't want to be put under undue scrutiny—dubbed 'Christians' and somehow categorized as freaks and never heard from again. And that happens a lot. Sad to say but Christians get verbally crucified every day in the industry. It's brutal out there. And, to be honest, we can help a lot more people flying under the radar, if you know what I mean. They let us into their world where they never would if we waved our Christian flags in their faces. Jason calls it *Christian espionage.* We just love 'em and try to be Jesus for them.

"But our faith is an integral part of what we are. Bet you didn't know that."

"No, I didn't. I mean, Jason has always been pretty outspoken about it personally, but I never knew about the other guys."

"Yeah, Jason's totally upfront about how much he loves God. He and Gevin were both raised that way, but Gevin's more private about it. It's there. Trust me.

"As for me?" A sassy lilt crept into her tone. "Little Miss Marissa here was singing in the Mt. Pisgah Missionary Baptist Church choir when she was only five years old." Her smile gently warmed her face. "And she knows the real deal when she sees it. The others—Jason made sure they're all 'glory bound,' as he calls it. You should see him do his crazy evangelist routine, Hannah. Girl, he cracks me up.

"But what I'm saying is, we all believe, we're just on different pages of the book, you know what I'm saying? None of us are saints—you can trust me on that one too. JT? Now, there's your bull in the china shop. JT wears his life on his sleeve. You always know exactly where he stands. He's got a lot of baggage—a lot of rough edges, and he's still got a lot to learn. He still struggles with some issues, but deep down, he's there. And Sergio and Jackson—they're both on board too, just low-key."

Marissa leaned back in the chair, relaxing her legs out in front of her. She closed her eyes, her head swaying ever so slightly as she hummed a quiet melody. It was a hymn but Hannah couldn't place it. The sound of Marissa's rich alto was soothing, calming Hannah's nerves. She felt her own eyes get heavy, giving in to the fatigue.

A few moments later she heard Marissa whispering. "Oh, Jackson, c'mon. Hang in there. We need you, baby."

CHAPTER 14

The sun rose on the first day of the new year.

And then it set again.

Jackson Greer held on, but he was somewhere far away in a world that wouldn't connect.

As his close friends and family settled in for the long vigil, they grew more quiet with each passing hour. The city of Chapel Hill reached out to them in gracious but unobtrusive ways. The hospital opened a hall of empty patient rooms for them, allowing them to sleep or shower in shifts. Flowers arrived by the truckloads. Huge bouquets and stuffed animals filled the waiting room and lined the long walls of the wing the employees now called Jackson's Floor.

The intensive care unit strictly limited visitation for all its patients, no matter who they might be. Throughout that first night and day, Jackson's immediate family, along with Alli, took turns visiting at the specified times. Later, the guys would be allowed a brief visit.

Around 10:00 in the evening, Jason stepped into the waiting room and called for Hannah. As they went out into the hall, he yawned deeply and wrapped his hand around hers. "I want you to come in with me to see Jackson."

She stopped. "No, Jason, it wouldn't be right. I couldn't."

"We've all had a chance to visit him, and it's my turn again. I want you with me." His eyes pleaded with her. "Change that—I *need* you with me, Hannah."

She studied his face. The pain and fatigue overshadowed the normal exuberance she found there. The deep creases of his brow seemed to be knotted permanently in place. She couldn't refuse him. She pulled him toward her, wishing to somehow give him the strength he needed. He searched her face as though looking for the hope he lacked, gently pushing her hair back away from her face. Finally, they turned and moved quietly down the hall.

As Jason slowly opened the door to Jackson's room, Hannah took a deep breath and silently asked God to give her strength. Alli sat beside Jackson's bed, her back to them, her hands wrapped around his lifeless hand. Jason motioned for Hannah to stand back with him, not wishing to intrude on Alli's privacy. He wrapped his arm around her tightly as they observed their two friends.

Apparently unaware of their presence, Alli laid her head against Jackson's leg covered by a blue blanket. Her body rocked slowly back and forth. They could hear her unsteady breathing. After endless moments of silence, she raised her head, gently caressing Jackson's leg. "Wake up, Jackson. Please wake up," she whispered.

Then they heard the faintest sound of her singing.

I could never love another
The way that I love you,
I could never face another day
Without you by my side.

Hannah recognized the haunting melody of the ballad though barely discernible—the first song Jackson had ever written, recorded by *Blue* on their sophomore album. His love song for Alli.

Now, as Alli struggled to murmur his lyrics, Jason stepped quietly behind her, Hannah close beside him. He gently squeezed her shoulder. She looked up at them with eyes so filled with pain, Hannah could barely stand to watch, her own tears racing down her face. She leaned over, hugging Alli as Jason covered them with his arms. No words were spoken. Instead, they simply shared the unspeakable sorrow as the medical machines beeped steadily around them.

After several moments, her friends still embracing her, Alli reached back out to hold Jackson's lifeless hand. She was rocking again, Jackson's song filling her. Her voice was raspy from too many hours of too much crying, yet she softly sang the words.

I will love you always,
Always and forever,
With every breath I take
I will love you—
Always and forever . . .

Jason pulled away from them, abruptly leaving the room. Hannah hugged Alli once more then quietly left the room. She found Jason standing in a dark corner, his head in his hands.

"Why, God? Why Jackson? *Please* don't let him die."

Hannah stood just behind him, wrapping her arms around his waist. He poured his heart out to God—begging and pleading. Hannah simply held him. She leaned her head against his strong back, feeling each ragged breath he took. When she finally opened her eyes, something near the window caught her attention. She squinted, trying to make out the movement of the images reflected in the glass. Gently pulling away from Jason, she moved toward the window.

What she saw took her breath away. "Jason, come here." She heard him sniffling. He didn't move. "Jason, please. You've got to see this."

Rubbing his eyes, he shuffled slowly toward her. "What is it?"

She reached for his hand, pulling him closer toward the window. "Don't get too close, but look outside." She watched his face as the dancing lights flickered against it.

When he finally realized what he was seeing, he let out a breathless gasp. "I can't believe it."

Below them, on a tightly secured hospital lawn, thousands of people covered the hospital grounds. In their hands, they held candles. Like tiny lights sparkling on a moonlit sea, they burned with one message: *We love you, Jackson.* Young girls clutched teddy bears, others held up signs of encouragement. *God, Please love Jackson tonight . . . Hang in there, Blue . . . We are Blue for You . . . Jackson, we want you back!*

Out of his tears came the sound of Jason's laughter. "Will you look at that? There must be thousands of them."

Hannah laughed too, feeling the healing balm of hope descending over them. She heard footsteps approaching them from behind.

"What is it?" Gevin asked, his arm around Marissa's shoulders. When they got close enough to see, the same shock registered on their faces.

"Oh my gosh," Marissa whispered. "Gevin, look at all of them!"

In moments, the others joined them at the window— JT, Tracey, Sergio, Laura and Frank, Jackson's parents and siblings. They all had the same reaction—at first shock, then overwhelming gratitude.

"Wait—I've gotta get Alli. She's got to see this." Jason peeled off down the hall. Moments later he returned, his hands pulling hers, dragging her against her will.

"Jason, stop it! I don't want to leave him. Please stop!"

"It's just for a minute, Alli. You need to see this. I promise you won't regret it." He escorted her to the front nearest the window.

Her expression melted immediately. "Oh . . ." It fell from her lips, nothing more than a breath. "I can't *believe* it. If only Jackson could see this." She smiled through her tears as Jackson's parents embraced her.

The friends and family members crowded close together in one collective hug as they watched the lights reflect on the faces of the faithful fans below. They wept through their smiles at the extraordinary gesture of love.

"Hey, look at that." JT pointed toward the right side of the crowd. "Over there on the side of that van."

A huge banner flapped in the brisk winter breeze. On a brilliant blue background, the bold white letters grabbed their attention:

DON'T GIVE UP!

WE LOVE YOU!

BLUE FOREVER!

"Do we have the most amazing fans, or what?" Jason sighed. He hesitated, then turned toward Gevin. Their eyes locked momentarily.

Gevin raised his eyebrows. "Yeah, Jason, we do. We have the most amazing fans." With that, he moved closer to the window, unlatched it and threw it wide open. At first, the mass of faces below didn't see them. Then slowly, like a giant wave, they began pointing up to the window where the cluster of their beloved *Blue* members stood waving with family and friends.

The cheers roared, swelling to a crescendo. Not the raucous cheers they heard at their concerts. These were passionate expressions of love and hope. They waved back, Jason patting his hand over his heart to say thank you. JT covered his face with his hands to hide his emotion. Sergio simply stared in disbelief as tears streamed down his face.

Voices young and old drifted up to them.

"We love you!"

"Tell Jackson we love him!"

"God loves you!"

"We're praying for you!"

About that time, blinding lights panned the window as camera crews discovered the impromptu gathering. The special, intimate moment ended. Frank closed the window as the others made their way back to the waiting room.

"That was *awesome*," wowed Micah, Jackson's younger brother. "Wish Jackson could have seen it."

"He knows, Micah," Jason responded with a wink. "Somehow I think he knows."

"Well, it can't hurt to remind him."

They all looked at Gevin with puzzled faces as he headed back down the hallway, pulling Marissa along with him. "C'mon. I think it's time we stopped all this crying. There's something we need to do."

JT, Tracey, Sergio, Alli, Jason and Hannah followed them down the hall. After a few minutes of desperate pleas to the attending doctor, they received reluctant permission to make a group visit into Jackson's room. They filed in silently, reverently aware of Jackson's still form lying so peacefully in that bed. Alli took a seat in the chair beside him again as the others formed a circle around the bed.

It was the first time they had all been together with Jackson like this. Alli looked around from face to face with a renewed hope shining through her glistening eyes.

"Gevin?" Jason looked inquisitively at his cousin.

Gevin took a deep breath, taking a second to look at Marissa beside him.

"Go on, baby," she whispered.

"Okay, Jackson. It's like this," he began, his dark eyes focused on Jackson's face. "We can't stand this anymore, buddy. See, you pretty much scared the hell out of us, but . . . well, we just wanna tell you we love you, man." He swallowed hard and took a moment.

"But you need to know there are *thousands* of people outside pulling for you. They're holding candles and all they want is to hear that you're okay. And that's all *we* want, Jackson. Come on, man. Pull out from under this . . ." He stopped, this time looking at the others, his eyes moist, pleading for someone else to speak.

"Hey, man, it's me, JT," he started, his voice graveled. "Now, you've been lying here on your butt sleeping way too long, man. And we've all decided it's about time you wake up and smell the coffee, know what I mean? Come on, Jax. You can do it. I know you can do it."

"No kiddin', Jackson. Enough already." Jason feigned a tease, his tone not quite convincing. "If you needed a break, all you had to do was ask, man. We'd chill for you—you know we would. But right now—well, right now we need you to wake up." His voice grew quiet. "We all need you, Jackson. We can't make it without you. None of us can. I hope you know that."

Hannah tightened her grip on Jason's hand, urging him to continue. "And the thing is . . . well, we've been praying for you, man. And all those people outside? You should see them. They're praying too. And Jackson, we *know* God's not through with you yet. I think He just reminded us of that when we looked out that window. There's so much more we've gotta do together, Jackson."

Gevin's head suddenly snapped up. He looked Jason straight in the eye. As if a light clicked on, a curious smile crept across his face. "That's right, Jackson." His eyes stayed locked on his cousin's. "Jason is exactly right. We're nowhere *near* through with what we've gotta do together."

Marissa turned to face her fiancé, the confusion written on her face. Hannah watched the exchange of unspoken communication. Gevin nodded, as if answering her question, then hugged her against him.

Marissa's smile broke across her mahogany face until she was beaming. "That's right, Jackson. There's a whole lot of people in here and a lot more out there who are depending on you to get yourself outta this bed."

JT stared at Gevin. "Gev, what—"

"Yeah, Gevin, what are you trying to say?" Sergio interrupted.

"I think this whole thing—all of it . . . well, I think it's just shown me—" he stopped, looking once again at Marissa, "—shown *us* that we still have a job to do. It's pretty clear to me now. Rissa, there's no reason we can't get married and continue with all this, is there?"

"No, there's no reason at all, if it's what you want," she answered. "As long as we're together."

"I mean, things don't just happen without meaning. And somehow I think this whole tragedy . . . it finally opened my eyes." He looked up toward the ceiling of that crowded hospital room, his eyes bright with revelation. When he looked back down at those around him, there was a humbleness in his demeanor.

"I guess I owe you all a big apology. We've all been fighting ever since Rissa and I announced our engagement. This should be the happiest time of my life, but it's been clouded by all these arguments. I *never* wanted that. I guess I just got tired and was looking for the easy way out. I'm really sorry, guys. JT? Sergio? Jason? I hope you'll forgive me. I mean it, guys. I'm really sorry."

They all answered at once. Hannah could feel the collective relief among them, as if a ten-ton boulder had been lifted from their shoulders. They hugged, they laughed. After the heartache they'd suffered, it was a welcomed moment of fresh air.

"I just wish Jackson could hear us," Sergio said softly.

"He does, Sergio. I know it," Jason said. "I don't doubt it for a minute." Their eyes returned to Jackson, his familiar face so peaceful. "And guys, since we're all here like this? Well, if it's okay with you, I think we need to pray over Jackson."

"Hey, JMac—you're not gonna preach to him, are you?" JT teased. "I mean, he's liable to roll over and *never* wake up if he hears one of your sermons."

Their subdued laughter rippled through the room. "Very funny, JT. I just figured we could use all the help we can get. At this point, it seems like God's our only hope. Hands down."

"Go for it, Jason," Tracey chimed in. "Let Jackson hear you praying."

Jason inhaled deeply, reaching a hand out to Hannah and one to JT beside him. The others joined hands around the circle. He lifted his face and closed his eyes. "God, we know that apart from You there *is* no hope. Not just for Jackson here, but for all of us. We screw up so bad sometimes, God. Then we come crawling back to You, asking for forgiveness. But oh God . . . how awesome it is to know You're always there, with open arms, just loving us so much. So we stand here, every one of us, and we ask You to forgive us—for anything that stands in the way of You hearing our prayers. We want You to hear our hearts and forgive us, okay Lord?"

"That's right. Preach it, JMac," JT murmured softly.

Hannah wondered if he was teasing again. She slowly looked up, finding JT's eyes still pressed closed, his expression serious and sincere. Marissa caught her eye, smiled and winked.

Jason continued. "We need You, Lord. We are so hopeless without You. But we know—God, we *know* You can wake up Jackson for us. You can bring him back to us, whole and complete. God, we love him *so much . . .*" His voice cracked. Hannah could feel his body trembling. She pulled her hand free and wrapped her arm snuggly around his waist, nuzzling her head against his shoulder.

Marissa began to hum quietly. It was so like her, knowing it would put Jason at ease. Finally, he took a deep breath and tried again. "But we know that You love him even more than we do. We can't even begin to understand love that deep. So we're asking You, God—no, we're *begging* You—to heal Jackson. Give him back to us, God. Please. *Please.*"

Jason paused only a moment. Then, as he struggled to force the words, he added one more prayer. "But God, we ask . . . for strength. To face *whatever* is Your will for Jackson . . . no matter what that may be."

The words hung in mid-air, the bitter truth of them taking root in each and every one of them. Then, as the whispered prayers of others drifted around the darkened room, Marissa began to sing the words of the familiar hymn she'd been humming. One by one, they joined her, their quiet voices filling the room.

> *When peace, like a river, attendeth my way,*
> *When sorrow like sea billows roll*
> *Whatever my lot, Thou has taught me to say,*
> *It is well, it is well with my soul.*
> *It is well, it is well*
> *It is well, it is well with my soul.*

They paused at the end of the first verse, even as Marissa's voice continued with a soulful climb, as though her heart searched for a secure hiding place. JT's warm, raspy voice joined hers, the blending of their mournful harmony both haunting and utterly beautiful. As Marissa finally broke into the next verse, they joined her again, this time their rich harmonies layering the profound lyrics.

Though Satan should buffet,
though trials should come,
Let this blest assurance control,
That Christ has regarded my helpless estate,
And hast shed His own blood for my soul.

They sang the chorus again, then began the final verse of that old, beloved hymn with such conviction and force, Hannah was sure the entire hospital must be hearing their heartfelt song of prayer.

And Lord, haste the day
when my faith shall be sight,
The clouds be rolled back as a scroll;
The trump shall resound,
and the Lord shall descend,
Even so, it is well with my soul.
It is well, it is well
It is well, it is well with my soul.

When the song ended, their voices echoed off the glass walls of the tiny room. As that last note hung in the air, the tears fell freely. The impact of the words against the convicting melody produced an ongoing rhythm of sniffling noses and quiet sobs. Hannah had never experienced anything so powerful in her entire life. She knew she wasn't the only one.

Alli pressed Jackson's lifeless palm against her cheek. "Please, God . . . please."

CHAPTER 15

Cobwebs everywhere. The more she tried to brush them away, the more entangled they became. They seemed to be growing . . . tying knots in themselves and wrapping around everything in their path—including her. They tickled her face at first, no matter how much she pushed them away. Then, as if someone flipped a switch, the webs morphed into high speed, encircling her face like the tattered rags on a mummy. She fought them, frantically trying to clear them before they strangled her.

"No! No! Get them off me!" she screamed. "Help me! Get them . . . *noooooo!*"

She felt hands gripping her arms. Strong hands shaking her.

"Help me! I can't breathe! I can't—"

"Hannah! Wake up!" Jason gently patted her face. "Wake up! You're just dreaming."

Her eyes flew open. Jason's face was only a couple inches from her own. "But . . . there were cobwebs . . . and they were—"

He wrapped his arms around her and pulled her into his embrace. "Shhhh. There are no cobwebs. Just a bad dream, that's all. I'm here. Everything's okay. I'm right here." He rocked her gently back and forth, until she slowly relaxed against him.

"Jason, it was so *horrible*. I couldn't see anything and these cobwebs were wrapping themselves all around me and—"

"Don't talk about it anymore, okay? Try to get it out of your mind. You're okay, I promise you," he whispered, pulling her face toward him to look at her eye to eye. "I'm right here, Hannah, and I won't leave you, okay? I promise you that."

Still shaking, she stared into his reassuring eyes, wanting to believe him. Embarrassment slowly washed over her. She dropped her head into her hands. "I feel like such an idiot. I'm sorry. I don't know why—"

"Hey, after the last couple of days, it's a wonder we're all not having nightmares." He pulled back, raising his arms over his head with an exaggerated loud yawn.

"No wonder people in hospitals are sick—the beds alone will kill you," he laughed quietly.

During the wee hours of the morning, after leaving the emotional gathering in Jackson's room with all the others, Hannah and Jason had drifted down the hospital wing to one of the rooms set aside for all of them. They sat together, side by side, in one of the narrow hospital beds. With the head of the bed cranked up at almost a ninety-degree angle, they watched television as a diversion. Apparently they had fallen asleep. The television was still on.

Jason dropped his legs off the side of the bed. "Whoa," he moaned, rubbing the small of his back. "My back feels like one huge knot. Ooohhhh . . . that hurts. I'm in serious pain here."

Hannah pulled her hair off her neck. "Jason, I hate to tell you this, but you sound like an old man. You want me to ring the nurse for some oxygen? Maybe some prunes or a laxative or something?"

He looked over his shoulder at her, returning a mischievous smile. "You," he crawled back toward her, "are not nice. After all I've done for you. Easing you out of that nasty nightmare. And this is the thanks I get? Oxygen? Laxatives? Hannah, you know what I do to people who are unkind to me." He grabbed her waist and started tickling.

"No! Jason, stop! You know I hate—ahhhh!" she cried, dissolving into a storm of giggles. She grabbed his neck and pinched it sending him into a pathetic cry of surrender.

"Okay, OKAY! I'll stop! Now let go—let go!"

"What in the world is going on in here?"

They froze, turning their heads toward the door. Laura and Frank stood in the doorway.

"Oh, hey Mom. Dad! Uh, well we were just . . ." he looked at Hannah. A split second later they were laughing again. Jason scrambled to stand up as Hannah fell back against the raised bed. Finally, he let out a long sigh. "Oh never mind. I guess we were just letting off a little steam. Did we wake you guys or what?"

Laura walked over to a blue vinyl chair and sat down. "No, you didn't wake us. In fact we just had breakfast. One of the local radio stations had a hot breakfast buffet delivered for all of us from Cracker Barrel. You all should go eat something."

"Sounds good, but what's the word on Jackson?" Jason asked, finger combing his hair. "I can't believe we fell asleep watching that stupid TV movie. We must have slept all night. Have the doctors said anything?"

Laura looked across the room at her husband who was leaning against the door frame. He dug his hands deep in his pocket and shook his head. "Nothing. There's been no change at all."

Hannah watched Jason take a deep breath. Their momentary relief disappeared, the laughter forgotten.

Frank walked over and tousled Jason's hair. "Why don't the two of you go get a bite to eat. I'm sure we'll hear some news soon."

Jason turned toward Hannah. "You hungry?"

"Yeah, but I think I'd like to take a shower first. Is that okay?"

"No problem. In fact, I could use a shower too. Grab a couple of towels and we can—" He shot a look at his mother just in time to see her jaw drop.

"Jason!" Hannah gasped.

"Jason Thomas McKenzie, I did not raise you to talk to a young lady like that. You apologize to Hannah right this minute."

He held up his hands. "I'm only kidding! I just thought I'd try to get a rise out of you, Mom. Hannah, it's my mission in life to try to shock her socks off." He leaned over her, grabbing his mother in a raucous bear hug.

Hannah felt the heat on her face. "That's okay, Laura. He was just dreaming. *Trust* me on that." Hannah scooted off the edge of the bed. "Jason, I'll go shower in the room across the hall. I won't be long."

She stood up just as Jason's mother pushed her son away and stood up as well. She moved to Hannah's side and enveloped her in a warm, maternal hug. "Good girl. Keep him on his toes, will you?" She laughed, then pulled back and looked into Hannah's face. "Hannah, I'm glad you're here with us. And I know Jason appreciates you're being here with him. He acts tough but underneath all that teasing and carrying on, he's just a big kid. And like it or not, a mother isn't necessarily what he needs at a time like this. You've been wonderful."

"Mom, what kind of fluff are you shoveling her now? Let her go take a shower. I'm starving."

Hannah turned her head toward Jason just as he peeled off his sweatshirt. His lean muscular physique took her breath away.

"Quite a 'hunk,' isn't he?" Laura teased.

Hannah covered her face with her hands. *Tell me I did not just gawk at him right in front of his mother?!* Jason threw himself into a litany of WWF poses again, showing off his build with a straight face. Hannah cleared her voice. "Yes, well, I'm outta here."

"It's about time. Go ahead and get the water heated up. I'll be right there."

Laura rolled her eyes and shook her head.

"Uh, no, Jason." Hannah headed toward the door. "You will shower in here. And I suggest you make it a *cold* shower. Know what I mean?" She threw a towel at him and left the room.

Ten minutes later, Hannah crossed the hall still toweling her hair. She slung the towel around her neck and started brushing out her long, wet curls as she walked into Jason's room. "You done yet?"

"Yeah, just about. Wow. You look great." He smiled, lassoing her neck with his towel. He pulled her into his arms.

She melted into his embrace, her head pressed against his bare chest. The scent of his freshly washed skin sent a warm wave through her body. Jason took a deep breath, his face nuzzled against her wet hair.

"Mmm . . . you smell good." He kissed the tip of her nose and leaned his forehead against hers. "I wish it didn't have to be like this. There are a thousand places

I'd rather be than in this hospital under these circumstances."

"I know," she sighed.

"Hey, I've got an idea. Let's get out of here for a while. What do you say?"

"I don't know, Jason. Do you think we should? I mean, what if Jackson woke up and we weren't here? Or what if something—"

"I have my cell phone. We'll tell Mom and Dad to call us if anything happens. I need some fresh air. We won't go far. Maybe just down the street for some good coffee or something. Oh, I know! Do you like Krispy Kremes? Let's go get some Krispy Kremes. Forget the hot buffet. I'm craving serious carbs. What do you say?"

"I'd love to. If you think it's okay?"

He pulled her along behind him, heading down the hall. "But we'll have to use one of the limos. We'd never get out of here on our own. Do you mind if someone drives us?"

"Whatever." She reached for his hand as they hurried down the hall.

Laura and Frank rounded the corner. When Jason told them their plans, Laura wasn't pleased. "I'm not so sure that's a good idea, honey. I know you're restless, but what if you run into some crowds of well-wishers or—"

"Mom, we'll be fine. I play this game all the time, remember? Besides, we won't be gone that long and we'll be careful. Call us if you need to, okay?"

With that, they picked up their pace and sprinted down the hall to find George, the limo driver. Taking some back hallways, they avoided the crowds and made their way to a secluded section of the parking garage. Hopping into the limousine, they were whisked away from the hospital and down a side road to freedom.

"Any change?" Alli asked as she entered Jackson's room.

"No, sweetheart. No change," Jane Greer answered, giving her a hug.

Bob and Jane stood on opposite sides of their son's bed. Jane reached out, brushing the hair back off his forehead. She traced his strong jaw line with her fingers, smiling wearily.

"I'm still not used to this stubble. It seems like only yesterday his voice had just begun to crack. He couldn't *wait* for some facial hair. So excited when it finally started coming in. Course, it was nothing but the slightest appearance of peach fuzz on that chin. But he was so proud. Now, look at him—he fills this whole bed and he's got a face full of stubble."

"C'mon, honey," Bob said. "We promised to give Alli some time with him before they kick us all out to bathe him." He leaned over and planted a kiss on his son's forehead, pausing to whisper. "Today's the day, Jackson. C'mon, buddy, it's time to wake up. We love you, big guy."

Alli watched Jane place Jackson's arm across his chest again. She leaned over her son, lingering as she kissed his cheek as she had surely done a thousand times in his lifetime. "I love you, sweetheart."

A few moments later, they were gone.

Alone with Jackson for the first time in several hours, Alli fought her despair. She decided to make the best of it, assuming he would hear her every word.

"You know, Jackson, if you'd just snap out of this, you could have hot biscuits and gravy from Cracker Barrel. Does that sound good? There's a ton of food out there. Course, I haven't felt much like eating but I would if you'd just wake up." She looked down at his peaceful face, wishing she could will him to open his eyes.

Instead she blew out a heavy sigh, sitting down beside the bed and taking his hand into hers. She leaned over to kiss his hand, then laid her cheek against his open palm. "Please wake up, Jackson. I'm so lonely without you. Even with all these people around, I feel so empty without you."

She lifted her head, suddenly aware how tired she was. When his eyes remained closed, his expression the same, she slowly laid her head back down and gave in to the fatigue. With her eyes closed, she felt herself drifting off to sleep, the steady beep, beep, beep of Jackson's monitor the only sound she could hear.

She began to stir, thinking she'd surely slept an hour or more. She looked at her watch, surprised it had only been around fifteen minutes. Suddenly, she realized what had awakened her. The beeping had stopped! Still trying to shake off the grogginess, she snapped her head up to look at the monitor. Why was it stuck? Instead of beeping, it shrieked at her.

That's when she noticed the flat line.

"Jackson! JACKSON! NOOOOO!" Her scream bounced off the walls. "SOMEBODY! HELP ME! Oh Jackson—oh God, please don't let him die! Jackson! JACKSON! Nooooooo!"

She stumbled to the door just as it flew open with a team of doctors and nurses racing to Jackson's bedside with a crash cart. They shouted orders and yelled to each other, oblivious to her cries. She tore through them, sobbing and begging them to help him. "PLEASE! You have to save him! You can't let him die!"

"Get her out of here STAT!" one of the doctors yelled.

A nurse grabbed her, quickly propelling her toward the door. "You have to leave right now. You can't help him if you're in the way."

"Noooo! I can't leave him! Oh God, please! Please don't let him die!" She pulled away from the nurse. "Let me go! LEAVE ME ALONE!"

The voices of the doctors and others on the team rose in a feverish pitch. "We're losing him! His blood pressure is plunging . . . Doctor, I can't find a pulse."

The room spun wildly around Alli as she fought against the strong arms of the nurse who kept shoving her out the door. With every ounce of her strength, she screamed—

"JACKSON!"

CHAPTER 16

Across town, the limousine stopped at a deserted city park. Jason and Hannah climbed out of the luxury car, carrying a bag of warm donuts fresh from Krispy Kreme and two large cups of coffee. They had purchased a separate order for George who gladly remained in the warmth of his car. Both wearing sunglasses and ball caps, they looked like a couple of ordinary college kids out for a visit to the park on a winter morning.

They sat on top of a picnic table beside a partially frozen creek. Their breath escaped in puffs of smoke, but they drank in the crisp, fresh air and bright sunshine.

"I'm glad we decided to do this. I don't think I realized how confined I was feeling at the hospital." She looked over the rim of her cup as she sipped the hot brew. He'd become quiet in the last few minutes, his face more serious. She set her cup down. "Are you okay?"

He was looking across the park. She did the same. The swings on a swing-set moved back and forth in the breeze, each one in its own rhythm. The sunlight sparkled off the snow, making both of them glare despite the sunglasses.

He bit into a glazed donut then took a sip of coffee. She wasn't used to seeing him so silent. He had every reason in the world to be that way, but she was surprised how uncomfortable it made her. Attempting to hide her concern, she took a tiny bite of her own donut and looked off another direction. Moments passed. She drained the rest of her coffee only to hear him humming quietly. It was not a melody she recognized.

She took a chance. "Is that a new song?"

He didn't answer right away but kept humming. Finally, "Just something I've been working on for a few days."

"Sing it for me."

He stole a look at her above the rim of his sunglasses and attempted a smile. "I don't think so. Not yet." He turned and looked away again.

Four, maybe five minutes passed. Nothing. Only the pieces of a sad melody drifting through the air between them. She pulled up her legs, hugging her knees, resting her head on them. She closed her eyes.

"Hannah?"

"Yes?" she answered, not looking up.

Silence again. *What was he trying to say?*

She heard him moving but was too afraid to look up. The table shook as he stood up on it. She felt his hands press down on her shoulders as he lowered himself to sit behind her, his legs sliding out on either side of her. Slowly, he wrapped his arms around her waist and laid his head on her shoulder.

Hannah couldn't breathe. She sensed something was wrong, but didn't have a clue why he was acting so strange. Half an hour earlier they'd been laughing, cutting up in the hospital room with his parents. Now he was struggling and she didn't know why. Was it Jackson? Was it all the ups and downs the group had been through this week? What? Jason was never at a loss for words, so why was he so quiet now?

And why is it scaring me?

Despite the thick jackets between them she could feel his heart pounding against her back. That same heart that caused millions of fans around the world to collectively hold their breath when it underwent surgery years ago. What would it have been like to know him then like she knew him now? No, it would have been too frightening to pace the halls of a hospital while the surgeons worked on him for endless hours. She thought of Alli. Could she have handled sitting beside Jason waiting and hoping for him to wake up again as Alli had been doing for Jackson? She shivered at the thought.

She felt Jason's arms tighten around her. "Hannah?"

"Yes?"

"We have to talk."

Her eyes stung. The wave of butterflies rippled through her stomach again. It was the tone of his voice. So different. So, so serious. She swallowed hard. "I'm listening."

He rested his head on her shoulder again. "We have to talk about us."

Oh no. Not now. Please not now. She shook her head. It was the best she could do.

"You know, it's only been ten days since we met." His voice sounded strained. Hushed.

Is he saying good-bye? Here? Now? Please not now. Not yet.

"Can you believe that?" he continued. "It seems like we've been together forever. At least to me it does."

She let out a long breath. "I know," she whispered. "Me too, Jason."

Now it was his turn to take a deep breath and let it out. She shivered at the feel of it against her neck. Out of her periphery she could see the white cloud of his breath.

"Remember that first night we were together at Mom and Dad's? And I told you that on my way home for Christmas I prayed and asked God to make this a really special Christmas?"

"I remember," she smiled, cherishing the memory of that night.

"Well, this last week or so . . . I've thought a lot about that prayer. And I realized something. It was you, Hannah. I have no doubt in my mind. I didn't even know exactly what I was praying for . . . I wasn't even thinking about some*one* coming into my life like this. But there you were—the stray my mom picked up on Christmas Eve."

She poked him gently with her elbow.

"Don't get me wrong. I like strays," he said quietly, the slightest trace of humor in his voice. "But more important, I like *you*. I told you before, Hannah, I love you. I mean that. You probably think you don't know me well enough to trust me, but I promise you, I don't use those words unless I mean it from the bottom of my heart."

She swallowed again. The knot in her stomach squeezed her breath away.

"And the more I've thought about it, the more I've realized . . . it wasn't just a coincidence that God brought you into my life that night. At first I thought, this is great—Hannah's fun, we're having an awesome time together. It's the holidays. Mom and Dad obviously like you a lot. Cool Christmas gift, y'know?

"But then Gevin told us he was quitting the group, and we all started fighting. And then Jackson—" He sighed again. "Jackson got shot and the world stood still."

He lifted his head, taking the ball cap off her head and stroking his fingers through her long hair. "But through every moment of all of that, Hannah, you've been right here with me. I can't even imagine how I would have made it through without you. Mom was right about that. It's like . . . as if God knew I would need you. And He gave you to me right when I needed you most."

She was grateful he was sitting behind her. He couldn't see the tears streaming down her cheeks. When the breeze blew, she thought her tears would freeze before they fell from her face. She pressed her eyes shut.

"And that's why I know there's something very special about us—you and me—together. I know it's only been a few short days and I know you're gonna think I'm crazy, but—"

She turned around to face him, reaching her fingers to press against his lips. Her chin trembled as she looked into his eyes, searching for meaning. "Jason, don't. Please don't."

He took her face in his hands, wiping away her tears with his thumbs. "I have to say this, Hannah. I have to say it now. Today."

She shook her head. "No, Jason. *Please.*" She tore her eyes away from him, looking down instead at the silver cross that hung on a chain against his sweatshirt. She fingered it, her thoughts pricking her mind like so many icicles.

"Hannah, you're making this really difficult for me," he said, a hint of irritation in his tone. "Why won't you let me say what I want to say to you?"

"Because I'm so scared! Don't you see?" She looked into his eyes, needing to make him understand. "Every single moment I've had with you has been a gift to me. I never dreamed—*never dreamed* anything could be so wonderful. And from the moment I realized that *you* were the son of this kind woman who invited me to her home on Christmas Eve, well, I've never known such complete happiness and joy in my entire life." She looked back down at his cross. *God, give me the words. Help me.*

"But over and over and over I've told myself—that's all this is. It's just a dream. A fairy tale come true. And just like Cinderella, there's going to come a time when the clock strikes midnight and I have to wake up from this . . . *amazing* dream."

She laughed, her lips trembling. "And it *has* been an amazing dream for me. You've been incredible. I never imagined I could know you like this—like a regular person. I mean, there are actually times I have to remind myself who you are. Because the one I've fallen in love with isn't a celebrity. He's just Jason. I've never known anything like this. I've never felt so . . ." Her voiced failed her. Only a whisper. "I've never loved anyone the way I—"

"Then why won't you let me finish saying what I have to say? Why won't you hear me out?"

A sob escaped from her throat and she turned her back against him. "Because I know that you're caught up in the emotion of this week and that you're not thinking clearly. I mean, how could you? With what's happened with Jackson and—"

"Shhhh . . . stop, Hannah. You can't tell me what I'm thinking. You don't *know* what I'm thinking. You can't know what I'm feeling right now. This isn't some irrational idea that popped into my head while we drove through the Krispy Kreme! Give me a little credit, okay? I've thought about it a lot."

He turned her around with such force she was afraid she would fall off the table. "Hannah, look at me. This is *real*. It's the real thing. I *know* it is. It's right for me and it's right for you. You know it too, don't you? Tell me because I *know* you do."

She squeezed her eyes, fighting the grip of fear inside her. "I can't, Jason. I can't. It's too soon! This is all too fast for me."

"You know you love me, Hannah. You *know* this is right. I have to hear you say it."

She blinked her eyes, wiping them with her hands. She tried to speak and couldn't. She tried again. "Jason, I—"

"JASON!"

They jumped at the intrusion of George's urgent beckoning. They both looked across the grounds at him standing outside the car, then back at each other. "What is it, George?" Jason shouted.

"Your dad just called. He said to get back to the hospital as fast as you can."

In less than thirty seconds, they slammed the door to the limo as George floored the gas. Gravel spattered against the underside of the long vehicle as it turned a hundred and eighty degree circle and tore out of the city park.

Ten minutes later, as the limousine flew into the hospital complex, they were shocked by the size of the crowds huddled everywhere. "George, what are we gonna do?" Jason asked, their secret entrance blocked by too many people.

"I can try to find another alley but we'll lose time. I think your best shot is to bust through at the main entrance. Looks like plenty of cops—they'll get you through. Your dad said they're expecting you."

"Let's do it," he yelled, throwing open the door as the limo slowed under the porte-cochere at the main entrance. He grabbed her hand and looked her straight in the eye. "Stay right with me, Hannah. No matter what happens, don't leave my side. I won't let go of your hand but the crowds can get pretty rough. Hold on tight, okay? Are you ready?"

The roar of the screaming crowd obliterated her answer as he pulled her swiftly from the car. Hundreds of voices screamed his name until she thought her

171

eardrums would burst. True to his word, his hand gripped hers like a vise. Thankfully, the police formed a barricade that allowed them to slip through the mass without bodily harm. An occasional hand reached for them but the police did their job well.

They ran into the building, an entourage of policemen surrounding them. Still, they were surprised to find themselves blinded by the flashing cameras of the press who had somehow eluded security and snuck into the building.

"Jason! I can't see!"

She heard his voice answer her. "Don't look up! Keep your face down and hold onto my hand!"

As the press yelled one question after another and pressed in closer and closer, the policemen fought back. Hannah wondered how in the world Jason and the other guys survived living with this day in and day out. Finally, they were out of the fray as the elevator doors shut, wiping out the voices and the flashing lights.

"Are you okay?" Jason asked, pulling her against him. She looked up at him, his face wild with fear at what they might be about to discover.

"Yeah, I'm all right."

The doors opened to another pandemonium, this time with more familiar faces. Their agents, their families, their close friends, members of the band—they were all there at once. Laura appeared out of nowhere. The expression on her face frightened both of them.

"Mom! What is it? What's happened?"

She pulled them away from the elevator, hoping for some privacy. Everyone seemed to be talking at once, trying to get close to them. "Mom! Answer me! Is Jackson okay? Is he . . .?"

She drew them into a huddle, shutting out the others surrounding them. "He's okay, Jason. He's okay. He's still in a coma, but he's still alive. But we almost lost him, honey. He stopped breathing—it was horrible. Just horrible," Laura continued, her eyes filling. "Poor Alli was there all alone with him when it happened. The trauma team practically trampled her trying to save him—"

"Is Alli all right?" Hannah interrupted.

"Yes, honey, she's fine. She fainted in the middle of it all. Who wouldn't, for heaven's sake? But she came around and she's resting now. She insisted on seeing for herself that he was all right, then they sedated her a little bit. The poor thing hasn't slept since all this started."

Laura turned abruptly to look Jason straight in the eye. "But son, there's something else. I need to tell you— *both* of you. Hannah, this is going to be a little awkward for you, but—"

"JASON! Oh Jason!"

And just like one of those strange movie scenes, Hannah's world slipped into slow motion. She turned her head toward the urgent voice calling out to Jason. She was tall and blonde and beyond description. The perfect cover girl.

"Jennifer! What are you—"

And then she was there, her arms around his neck, hugging him and crying out his name. Hannah felt Laura's arm on her shoulder. Hannah could see Laura's lips moving, speaking to her, but her voice sounded far away, tunneled somehow.

Hannah looked back toward Jason and Jennifer. Pieces of their conversation drifted in and out of her hearing. "I came as soon as I heard . . . I tried to reach you . . . oh, Jason, I've missed you so much . . ."

Hannah tasted the bile in her throat. This couldn't be happening. Not now. Not after everything else. Not *Jennifer.* Hannah tried to tear her eyes away, to avoid the pain. But she couldn't help it. Jennifer was stunning. Flawless. And far more gorgeous than any of the pictures Hannah had seen in the magazines years ago. As she clung to Jason, they looked so natural, so perfect together.

The cobwebs . . . circling around and around her, obstructing her view. Choking her just like in the horrible nightmare.

Hannah couldn't breathe.

Jennifer's voice drifted toward her again. "I knew I had to come. I had to be with you right now. I couldn't bear watching the reports on television and not being here for you."

People pressed all around them. Everyone knew Jennifer. Of course they would want to speak to her—Gevin, Marissa, JT, Tracey, Sergio. Others wanted to tell Jason what had happened to Jackson. The bodies pressed in on them, separating Hannah from Jason, inadvertently pushing her farther and farther away. Even Laura had been pulled away from her.

She looked up trying to see his face, hoping to find him looking for her. She stood on her toes. She could just make out the back of his head. And then he turned around. He was looking for her!

Jason?" she called out. Her voice was useless. She cried out again. "Jason . . ."

He heard her voice, so frightened. So far from him. He craned his neck looking for her. How had they gotten separated? He couldn't imagine what she must be feeling. Not after the park. Not after the words they'd shared. The words he'd *tried* to share.

And then their eyes met. She looked at him with so much pain and confusion, he couldn't bear it. She mouthed his name and he could almost feel the ache of her heart.

A tall and bulky bodyguard stepped in front of him, breaking their view of each other. Jason looked around him, straining to see her. Suddenly the man moved out of the way.

She was gone.

PART TWO

CHAPTER 17

"That'll be $64.93, ma'am. You can run your card through the slot there when you're ready."

Hannah went through the motions. Customers in. Customers out. She couldn't remember a single face of any of them after working for three straight hours. She finished bagging the groceries and turned off the light over her register, already twenty minutes late for her break.

"Well, look what the cat dragged in!"

Kylie.

"Although I'm too mad to even speak to you, let alone *care* where you've been for the last week."

As Hannah walked into the tiny break room, the sound of her best friend's voice chilled her. She didn't blame her for being mad. Hannah had never returned any of her calls or text messages. It wasn't intentional. It was all just too complicated.

"Kylie, I'm so sorry. I meant to call—"

"Yeah, like I said. Save it for someone who cares." Still, despite the sarcasm, Kylie quirked one of her forgiving smiles and gave her a long, hard hug. She pulled back to look into Hannah's face. "What's going on? Why the mysterious disappearing act, huh?"

Hannah avoided her friend's intense stare. She could never hide anything from Kylie. Ever. But right now, she couldn't bear to talk about the last ten days.

Since slipping out of the hospital after the spectacle with Jennifer's sudden arrival, Hannah had begged George to take her home. She felt like a robot going through the motions, nothing more. She took a long hot shower, letting the scalding water wash over her for almost thirty minutes until it began to run cold. Hoping the water had rinsed away her tears at last, she crawled into bed only to be overwhelmed by a new, fresh wave of emotion.

She cried and cried, then cried some more. She fought every tender feeling she felt for Jason, knowing it was all a terrible mistake. What a fool she had been to let her feelings run away with him, regardless of who he was or what they had experienced.

She tried to sleep, but found herself restless, tossing and turning, and thoroughly frustrated. Finally, around 4:00 in the afternoon, she gave up. She got dressed, deciding work would be the distraction she needed to survive. It was time to step back into reality.

"Hannah, seriously, what's the matter?"

Kylie's words startled Hannah out of her thoughts. She turned away, dialing the combination on her locker.

"Hannah, talk to me! It couldn't have been *that* bad having to work during the holidays. Did something else happen? Is your family okay? Are you sick? Are you—"

Hannah abruptly opened her locker, making it bang loudly. "Kylie—enough! What is this? The third degree? Whatever happened to 'hi-how-are-you-good-to-see-you,

Hannah?' You're wearing me out." She faked a sarcastic laugh and knew it didn't fool either of them.

Kylie plopped down in the orange plastic chair. She ripped open a bag of Nacho Cheese Doritos with an exaggerated flair then popped the lid on her Diet Coke and took a long sip. "Okaaaay . . . So, Hannah, how are you? Good to see you. I'd say you look great, but that would be a bald faced lie." She took a bite of a chip and tried to act nonchalant.

Hannah closed her locker and sat down at the table across from her. The redhead's long wild curls never failed to brighten her spirits. She offered the trace of a smile as she watched the freckles across Kylie's cheeks dance with each deliberate chew.

"I'm fine, Kylie. It's good to see you too. How was your vacation?"

Kylie leveled an impatient glare at her. "I see. So we're going to play a game, are we? Fine. My vacation was fine. Christmas was fine. Jason is fine. The snow is—"

Hannah choked on her orange juice. "What did you say?"

"I said my vacation was fine. Christmas was fine. My brother is fine. The snow—"

"Oh. Yeah, Jason. Your brother." She cleared her throat, forcing her eyes to study her bag of pretzels.

The silence hung between them. "Hannah, I don't know what this is all about but wouldn't it—"

"It's no big deal, Kylie. I just forgot that Jason was going to be home from the Navy for Christmas. That's all. Really."

"Uh huh . . . and of course that explains why your face looks like bruised melons and your eyes look like the Atlanta interstate system. Because of course, we *both* know how much you love Jason."

Hannah froze. She held her drink in mid-air. Her eyes stung then began to fill. *Oh no. Not again.*

"Hannah, what *is* it?"

She quietly closed the bag of pretzels, grabbed her drink and gathered her things. "Look, Kylie. I'm not feeling well. Must be a bug or something. I think I better go home." Her voice cracked. "Just tell . . . tell Jim I'm sorry and that I'll try to be in first thing in the morning."

Kylie stood up, her chair scuffing across the linoleum. "Hannah, why won't you tell me what's wrong?!"

Hannah reopened her locker and grabbed her purse. "Kylie, I just—"

I have to get out of here. Now.

She slammed the locker and ran out the back door.

"Alli, don't you want to go lie down for a while? You're going to make yourself sick if you don't get some rest, and that won't do you or Jackson any good at all. Please?" Tracey pleaded with her friend as they sat beside Jackson's still form.

"No, I can't go. I know that if I leave him for even a second that something terrible will happen again. I can't. As long as the nurses don't chase me out of here, I'm staying."

"I understand." Tracey draped her arm across Alli's shoulders. "I'd do the same thing if it were JT. I don't know how you've done it, Alli. I don't know how you keep your eyes open, much less put a sentence together. But just promise me you'll try to go get some sleep the next time they make you leave. Okay?"

Alli leaned her head on Tracey's shoulder. "I will. I promise. And thanks for looking out for me. Everybody has been so incredible. I felt like such a wimp passing out when Jackson—" She turned to look at him again, then looked into Tracey's face. "Oh Trace, what would I have done if—"

"Don't even think like that, Alli. It doesn't help—" She stopped mid-sentence. "Alli? What is it? What's the matter?"

Alli watched the surprise registering in her friend's eyes. But it was no match for the shock she felt rushing through her.

"Alli, what's wrong?"

Alli slowly lowered her head, looking at Jackson's hand wrapped in her own. "Trace," she whispered. "Look."

"Look at what?"

"Did you see that?"

"See what? What are you talking about?" Tracey's voiced bordered on impatience.

"Look." She motioned with her chin toward her fingers laced through Jackson's.

They both stared at Jackson's hand and then it happened. The tiniest, most imperceptible movement of Jackson's thumb.

Tracey gasped. "Oh my gosh!"

Their eyes were glued to Jackson's hand. Neither of them risked so much as a blink. They watched for any sign of movement. Nothing. Had they imagined it?

"Jackson! Jackson, squeeze my hand. I know you can hear me, baby. Just please . . . *please* squeeze my hand!" Nothing. Alli looked at Tracey for reinforcement, refusing to believe she had imagined what she felt. Tracey nodded her head, signaling she'd seen it too. Alli looked at Jackson's face. He was so still. Not a single sign of life anywhere. Then—

A tear rolled out of his closed eyes and down the side of his face. Alli held her breath. "Jackson?" she whispered. "Jackson, can you hear me?"

Nothing.

The door quietly whooshed open and JT stepped silently behind them. He rested his hands, one on each of their shoulders. "Hey. How's he doin'?"

Neither Tracey nor Alli answered, nor did they look at him.

"Gee, nice to see you too, JT," he mocked, greeting himself.

"Shhh! JT, be quiet!" Tracey still didn't turn to acknowledge his presence.

"Why? What's going on?"

Tracey grabbed JT's hand and pulled him to the other side of Jackson's bed. "Alli felt some movement in Jackson's hand. And then—well, check this out." She took JT's forefinger and moved it gently to the edge of Jackson's eye.

JT took in a sudden breath. He looked at Tracey then straight across the bed to Alli. She felt her entire face light up as the first glimmer of hope filled her soul.

"But if he's crying, that means . . . that means he must be hearing something, or . . . at least trying to pull out of it, right?" JT took hold of Jackson's hand and started patting it. "JAX! Now you listen to me, Jackson Greer—you break through that fog and come back to us, buddy! You can do it, Jackson. I know you can. C'mon, big guy! Please?"

They waited, looking back and forth at each other. Then all of a sudden, Jackson's lifeless hand turned in JT's hand until he gripped it with unbelievable strength.

"Alli! Look at this! He's got me in a vise here!" JT laughed out loud, throwing his head back. "Oh God! Thank You!" He squeezed his eyes shut. "Thank You," he whispered hoarsely.

Alli laughed and cried all at once as she watched her nightmare slowly start to dissipate. She pulled Jackson's hand up to her lips and kissed it. "Oh Jackson, please . . . wake up, baby! I know you can hear me!"

Alli leaned her head over until her forehead was resting on Jackson's. "Please, Jackson?" Her voice husky with emotion, she begged him. "Please? Oh please come back to me, Jax?"

This time it was Alli who felt the strength of Jackson's hand gripping her own. A low guttural sound escaped from somewhere deep inside him, never fully arriving in his throat. His breath sounded strained, as if he was trying so hard . . . Alli pulled her head back, concerned that his breathing had changed. She looked at the monitor. Perfect.

"Jackson?" she whispered once more.

The same guttural sound seemed to push itself until it finally emerged as a bona fide groan. Another tear fell from each eye.

JT cried out with impatient anger. "Come on buddy! Dig out of that hole! DO IT!"

Slowly, Jackson tried to lick his lips. "Where . . . " His eyes fluttered as if glued shut until he finally broke them open. They snapped back shut, his face grimacing.

JT, Tracey, and Alli cheered in unison, beckoning him and begging him to snap out of it once and for all.

"It's too bright in here!" JT yelled, whipping around to close the mini-blinds on the window. The room plunged into a welcomed darkness.

Jackson's eyes opened again, mere slits as he squinted. Alli climbed up on his bed beside him, his face cupped in her hands. "Oh Jackson! You're back! You're finally back," she cried, snuggling into the crook of his neck. He turned his face toward her as she lifted her head back up. Jackson's face contorted with sadness. "Oh Jackson," she wept, resting her forehead against his.

His lips trembled as he attempted to speak. "Alli . . ." he whispered. "Alli."

She buried her face in his chest sobbing and laughing all at the same time. She could hear JT and Tracey doing the same. When she looked back up, she watched Jackson slowly turn his head toward JT as he beheld the tear-stained face of his buddy. The slightest hint of a smile pulled at the corner of his mouth. His head dropped back toward her as she continued crying, the waves of relief washing over her.

"Shhh . . . don't cry," he whispered.

"What do you think you're doing? Young lady, get off that bed!" A nurse they'd never seen before was the first to enter the room, followed by an anxious group of doctors and other nurses.

"Sheila, she's okay," Jackson's primary doctor said, moving to the side of his bed. JT and Tracey made room for him, but JT refused to let go of Jackson's hand. "She's the best medicine he could have right now," the doctor added. "Hello, Jackson. Nice of you to join us. How are you feeling?"

Jackson took a ragged deep breath and nodded. "Kinda strange . . ." he answered softly.

"Did you hear that?" JT shouted. "Did you HEAR that!" JT did the ritual hand gestures with Jackson that he and the guys always gave each other before a performance. "Jax, I've gotta go get the guys! And your mom and dad and—"

"Whoa, whoa—just a minute there, partner," the doctor interrupted. "We need a little time with Jackson here before we invite the troops in. Why don't you all step outside for a minute and give us a chance to check him out first, okay?"

"Oh please don't make me leave, Dr. Williams! Please let me stay?" Alli begged.

Jackson's countenance fell as he shook his head at the doctor. "Please?" he whispered.

"It will only be for a minute. I promise. She hasn't left your side for days, except when we've booted her out to examine you. Alli, I promise this will only take a second and you can come right back in."

Alli turned her face only a couple inches from Jackson's. She smiled, relaxing for the first time since that horrible moment on New Year's Eve. She looked into his eyes and kissed him, oblivious to the roomful of people around them. "I love you, Jackson."

"Always mine?" he mouthed, his smile weary.

She laughed, kissing him again. "Always and forever, Jackson. Always."

"Hannah? Hannah, open this door right this instant. Do you hear me?" Kylie banged on the door of her best friend's apartment. "You either open up or I'll use my key. Did you hear that?"

Exasperated, Kylie dug her keys out of her coat pocket and forced one into the door. She pushed against it, but the door refused to give way. She grumbled, realizing the deadbolt would be in place since Hannah was home. She pulled up another key, shoving it into the deadbolt and pushing her way into the apartment.

"All right, Hannah, all I can say is you better have a darn good reason for all this. Hey! Where are you?" She poked around the small apartment then headed for the bedroom.

She dropped her purse on the floor and put her hands on her hips. "Okay, excuse me, but you're not sick, I'm not stupid, and I'm not leaving here 'til I get some answers. Got it?" She stomped over to the window and yanked on the cord throwing the curtains open. Daylight flooded the room.

The body in the bed moaned. "Kylie! I'm trying to sleep. Do you mind?"

"Yes, I mind!" She yanked back the covers only to have them yanked back.

"Kylie, stop it! I'm freezing—just cut it out!" Hannah rolled over onto her stomach pulling the covers over her head. "Please, just leave me alone and give me some space," she mumbled from deep under the covers.

Kylie picked up the remote control off the bedside table and clicked on the small television resting on the chest of drawers. She plopped onto the end of the bed and pulled her legs up Indian style. "Fine. You go ahead and sleep. I'm gonna watch TV."

She surfed through several channels catching pieces of *Friends* reruns, some old western on AMC, the news on CNN . . . "Oh, look at this. Hannah, did you hear what happened to Jackson Greer of *Out of the Blue* over the holidays?"

No response.

"Well, you *had* to have heard something. It happened right here in Chapel Hill. I mean, I was all the way out in California and I heard about it. Oh wait, look. It's a live report." She pressed the volume control and the voice of a young reporter filled the room. She felt Hannah moving on the bed behind her.

"Word swept across Chapel Hill and certainly all around the world as the good news was announced concerning Jackson Greer."

"Oh my gosh, he's okay?"

Kylie turned to look at Hannah. Best friends since kindergarten, Kylie knew Hannah had once been an avid *Blue* fan, but was surprised at her reaction. "Well, I should have known I could count on *Blue* to still get your attention. Y'know, Hannah, you look awful—"

"Shhh! I want to hear this. Turn it up."

Kylie stared at her, appalled at how bad Hannah looked. Bewildered by her strange behavior, she turned back around to see the reporter extending a microphone to a man in a suit. His name flashed across the screen, identifying him as the hospital spokesperson.

"We are pleased to announce that Jackson Greer regained consciousness a few hours ago. His doctors report that his condition is stable and they are continuing to monitor his progress. His friends and family wish to—"

"I can't believe it. He's really okay."

Kylie cocked her head at an angle, staring at Hannah. "You know, it's been a long, long time since I've heard you even mention the band. I mean, sure— Jackson getting shot is a big deal, but I wouldn't have expected this much of a reaction out of you. Not after all these years. And certainly *not* after the despicable way you've been treating me today."

Hannah looked sideways at her and took a deep breath. "Look, Kylie, I'm sorry about running off from work. And I didn't mean to be rude just now, it's just that . . . you woke me up. That's all." Hannah rubbed her eyes.

The unanswered questions still hung in the air.

"You're not really sick, are you?"

Before Hannah could respond the phone rang. Kylie watched her, realizing she wasn't going to answer it. She peered at Hannah, adding this to the long list of questionable behaviors. While they waited for the recorded message to play out, Kylie looked around the room. She took a double take at the royal blue evening gown sparkling with rhinestones that hung on the doorframe of the closet door.

"And *where* did you get that gorgeous dress? You creep! You had a date for New Year's? Well, c'mon! Out with it. Who was it?"

"Hey, Hannah? Are you there, girl? This is Marissa," the voice on the answering machine asked.

Kylie raised her eyebrows. "Marissa?"

The message continued. "—and we need to talk. You just disappeared and we all got really worried but then George told us he'd taken you home."

Kylie mouthed the name at her. "George?"

"—and the thing is, well, Jackson finally woke up and everybody's goin' nuts over here and—well, Hannah, I know how hard it must have been when—wait, I don't want to leave an epic message here, so here's what I'm going to do. I'm going to have George drive me over there and—"

"Who's Marissa?" Kylie interrupted. "How do I know that name? What a minute . . . wasn't that the name of the tour manager for—"

Hannah snapped up the phone. "Rissa, I'm here. I just . . . yeah, I'm okay. No, really, I'm okay . . . I know, but I just couldn't . . . but I . . . No, no please—you don't need to come over here . . . I know but . . ."

Kylie worked a thousand pieces of the puzzle in her mind. And then, as if reaching for the last piece, it hit her. "Ohmygosh!"

Hannah closed her eyes and lowered her head. "Okay, Rissa. Okay. Yeah, I'll be here. I look like I've been run over by a freight train, but I'll be here . . . Okay, see you in a few minutes." Hannah slowly clicked off the portable phone and tossed it on the covers beside her. She pulled the quilt up to her chin, stole a peek at Kylie's shocked expression, and pulled the quilt over her head.

Kylie exploded. "Oh my GOSH, Hannah! You've been hanging out with—and that's Marissa as in Marissa-the-tour-manager for *Out of the Blue* . . . and you went to some kind of New Year's par—"

It suddenly hit her. It all finally made sense. The air vanished from her lungs so fast, she felt faint. "Hannah! YOU WERE THERE?!" she wheezed. "You were there when Jackson got shot and—but WHY were you there? And who were you there with?" Another gasp. "JASON! It has to be Jason! Because you weren't talking about my *brother* Jason at break—you reacted when I said his name because it was Jason *McKenzie* and—but how did you meet him and—OH MY GOSH, HANNAH!" Kylie finished her rampage with a squeal that echoed all the way back to their groupie days.

Hannah threw back the covers. "Kylie! Stop! You're gonna hyperventilate. Now just calm down, will you?"

Kylie stopped, staring at Hannah as unanswered questions continued to storm her mind. "But—"

"Look, Kylie, I *promise* . . . I'll tell you everything. Everything!" Hannah jumped out of bed. "But I can't right now. You heard her, Rissa is coming over and—"

"Oh, 'Rissa' is it? Well, my, my, my, aren't we all chummy with the celebs? Good grief, I was only gone for two weeks. I left town and you were supposed to be working the entire holiday and I get back and you're all chummy with a bunch of *celebrities*? And for crying out loud, Hannah—you're Jason McKenzie's *girlfriend*?!" Another squeal bounced off the walls of her bedroom.

Hannah stopped in her tracks. Kylie stared at her friend's face, a profound grief covering her countenance. She watched Hannah lean over to pick some clothes off the floor.

Diane Moody

"No, Kylie. No, I am not Jason McKenzie's girlfriend."

Kylie watched a tear roll down her best friend's face. "Hannah?"

Hannah looked up at her. "It seems the clock struck midnight . . . and Cinderella woke up."

CHAPTER 18

"I can't believe this. You are so unbelievable, Hannah. I'm totally freaked out here trying to figure out what in the world has been happening, and look at me! You've got me cleaning your apartment like some maid or something. I feel liked chopped liver."

Hannah stood in the door to her bedroom. "Kylie can you just give it a rest please? I told you we'd talk and we will. Can you just forget about it for now?"

Kylie muttered as she dashed through the room picking up clothes and dirty dishes. Her running commentary only made Hannah more nervous, so she headed back to her bathroom. The ranting from her living room followed her. On any other day, she would have laughed at Kylie's soliloquy.

"So there you are trying to salvage that pitiful crybaby face and here I am cleaning up after you like some hired maid. Don't mind me, missy," Kylie mimicked. "I'll just dust your furniture and mop your floors and scrub your toilet—"

"I heard that," Hannah yelled. She hurried out of the bedroom, pulling her hair up into a ponytail. "How do I look?"

"Like a wet puppy, if you want the truth, but—"

The doorbell rang followed by a series of rapid knocks.

Hannah headed for the door. "Kylie, can you just please try to be nice and stop being so witchy to me?"

"What? I'm not being—"

"Hannah! Oh, girl, how are you?" Marissa immediately rushed into the apartment and engulfed Hannah in a hug. "We've been so worried about you." She pulled back, taking a long look, holding her at arm's length.

"Rissa, the last thing you should be worried about right now is me. I heard about Jackson on the news. I was *so* relieved—is he really okay?"

Hannah was aware of Kylie's presence. It was awkward to talk to Marissa like this, especially since she hadn't had a chance to tell Kylie all that had happened.

"Hannah, why did you just take off like that? You didn't have to run, you know."

"Rissa," Hannah stopped her, stalling for answers as long as she could. "I want you to meet my best friend. Kylie, come over here for a minute."

Kylie twisted the dishtowel in her hands and slowly approached them.

"Kylie, this is Marissa." Hannah smiled, pleased to finally make the introduction. Marissa extended her hand to Kylie who stared at her with the goofiest grin Hannah had ever seen.

"Hey, Kylie, nice to meet you," she said, forcing her hand into Kylie's. She laughed easily at the redhead's reaction.

"Wow, this is such an honor," Kylie responded, shaking hands diplomatically as if meeting the president of the United States.

Marissa looked back at Hannah, her countenance etched with curiosity. "Hannah, she's great. Very . . . *verbose*, isn't she?" They laughed, Kylie joining them at her own expense.

"Okay, Kylie, you can stop shaking her hand now," Hannah teased. "Rissa, come on in and sit down. Can I fix you some tea or something?"

"No, you can't and don't get comfortable because I'm on a mission here."

"What?"

"I came over to see how you were doing, but there's someone who's very anxious to see you right now and—"

"No! No, I can't." Hannah backed away from Rissa, shaking her head.

Marissa looked perplexed then leaned her head back. Her expression changed as she picked up on Hannah's interpretation of her statement. "Oh, Hannah, I'm so sorry. I didn't mean—"

"No, really—it's okay." Hannah sat down on her rocking chair.

"No, you don't understand. I came here to get you because Alli and Jackson want to see you. They've been really worried about you. Everybody has. That's why Gevin suggested I come by and pick you up."

"Oh, wow—*Gevin* . . ." the third voice responded.

Hannah and Marissa turned to look at Kylie. She still had that silly grin on her face. It was a welcome diversion for Hannah who couldn't help smiling despite the anxiety needling her.

"Jackson Greer wants to see you," Kylie muttered. "Jackson Greer wants to see *my* friend, Hannah. Who'da thought . . ."

Hannah turned her attention back to Marissa. "Look, I would love to see Jackson. And I've wanted to talk to Alli, and I'm so thrilled that Jackson's okay and all, but—"

Marissa dug her gloves out of her coat pockets. "Hannah, there's not a lot of time. We're going. Just get your coat." She turned toward the front door.

"But I can't! I won't. I just couldn't bear it if I ran into . . . well, what if—"

Marissa turned around and faced her directly. "Look, I give you my word. You will not run into Jason. Okay?"

"How can you be so sure?"

"Because they . . . I mean, *he* left just before I did. He was going home to get some rest. He said he wouldn't be back for probably five or six hours. So you don't have to worry, okay?"

"But Rissa, this is ridiculous. They don't need *me* there. None of them do. They hardly know me! I told you the other night how out of place I felt. Well, I still do, no matter what you say. Why can't you understand how *I* feel?"

"Because right now, all I care about is how Jackson feels. He asked to see you and I'm gonna make sure he does. Got it?"

The sharp tone of Marissa's voice startled her. She immediately regretted sounding so self-centered. If Jackson had asked to see her, the least she could do was swallow her pride and go see him.

"Rissa, I'm sorry. Of course, I'll go."

"Good. Now grab your coat and let's go. George has to be wondering what's taking me so long." She opened the front door.

"George? Who's George?" Kylie asked, walking toward the door. "Whoa, you're in a limousine. Maybe the *longest* limousine I've ever seen in my entire life."

"Oh, Kylie," Marissa said. "I wouldn't hesitate to invite you, except that—"

"Don't be ridiculous, Rissa—I can call you 'Rissa', right?"

Marissa laughed. "You can call me whatever you want to, girlfriend. And I would really like to get to know you better, only—"

"Only, hey—we can't keep Jackson waiting, can we!" Kylie laughed at herself. "Jackson Greer! I can't believe you're . . . and Hannah . . . and, oh just go!"

Hannah wrapped a wool scarf around her neck then pulled on her long black coat. "Kylie, I'm really sorry. I hope you understand."

"What's not to understand? *Out of the Blue* awaits you! Ha! Can you imagine? They're waiting on *you* . . . I never saw *this* one coming, Hannah. Not in a million years."

"We'll talk later, I promise," Hannah called over her shoulder as she and Marissa hurried out the door.

Hannah and Marissa walked briskly through the back corridors of the hospital. The routes were all too familiar to them after the last few days. Hannah's heart raced as she followed Marissa down the long halls of the hospital basement. She prayed Marissa was true to her word and she would not run into Jason.

They stepped into a service elevator and rode silently up to the seventh floor where Jackson had been moved. When the elevator doors opened, Hannah was relieved to see a familiar hospital security guard. He recognized both Hannah and Marissa and allowed them to pass.

Diane Moody

The closer they got to Jackson's room, the more uncertain Hannah felt. She took a deep breath as Marissa knocked gently on the door.

"Anybody home?"

Gevin appeared at the door, opening it wider for his fiancée to enter. His serious face broke into a wide smile when he saw Hannah behind her. "Ah, mission accomplished. It's about time, Hannah. Come here, girl," he said reaching out for her. He gave her a warm hug. "You okay?"

She had to take another deep breath if she was going to answer. "Yeah, Gevin, I'm good. Your girlfriend here doesn't take no for an answer, but I guess you already know that, huh?"

He draped his arm over Marissa's shoulder. "Yeah, I learned that a long time ago."

"Hey, you guys having a convention out there or what?"

Hannah followed the sound of Jackson's voice and peeked around the corner into the suite. An explosion of color amid hundreds of flowers came into view. Huge bouquets of roses, daisies, sunflowers and every other imaginable flower. Stuffed animals and large fruit baskets dotted the floral scenery. It took a minute before she finally saw him sitting up in the hospital bed, Alli seated on the foot of his bed.

"Oh Jackson . . ." Her tears gave way as she walked to his side, leaning over to hug him. They were silent for a moment. She felt Alli's hand on her back. Finally, she laughed out of pure joy. "I was so happy when I heard the news."

His eyes shone bright and a little moist as well. "Yeah, me too," he quipped. She laughed again then turned to Alli who hugged her hard, laughing through her own tears.

Hannah pulled back, wiping her eyes. "This is just so amazing. I've never seen such a miracle in my entire life. Jackson, how are you feeling? Are you really okay?"

"I'm feeling good. It's like every hour I feel a little stronger," he said, his voice hoarse. "Everybody has been incredible around here. Do you believe all this?" He waved his hand across the massive sea of flowers.

"Hannah, you wouldn't believe it," Alli jumped up. "There are flowers here from all over the world! Look at this gorgeous bouquet. It's from Elton John! There must be three dozen roses in there!" She continued around the room, pointing to various arrangements. "These are from Sting, and this ficus tree is from Will and Jada Smith. Do you believe that? And look—these iris are from Julia Roberts. Aren't they beautiful?

"But this is my favorite—check out this card."

Hannah noticed the royal imprint on the card. She slid the card out and read the enclosed note aloud. "*'Best wishes for a full recovery. Sincerely, William and Kate.'* Are you serious? Wait—did he sign this himself?"

"Yeah, we'll be putting that up on eBay by the end of the day." Jackson smirked.

Alli playfully swatted him. "No we will not! This one goes in our scrapbook, thank you very much. Along with pressed flowers from the arrangement. Imagine, Will and Kate sending flowers? He is *so* fine."

"Excuse me?" Jackson protested.

"Sorry, babe. But he's royalty. What can I say? Oh, and Hannah—look at this poster Jay Leno sent over. It was taken of him and the guys about a year ago when *Blue* played the Tonight Show." Hannah noticed the hand-written message on the lower end of the poster: *Prayers & best wishes, Jay.*

"That is so—"

"Yeah, yeah, but show her *my* favorite," Jackson interrupted.

"Oh yeah." Alli leaned behind the desk and pulled out a large box. Inside was a basketball autographed by Michael Jordan. "Isn't this incredible?"

"You better keep your eye on that one," Gevin warned. "I've already had some interest on it on eBay."

"You touch it and you're history," Jackson teased.

"Well, Jackson, it looks like you made out pretty good, all things considered," Hannah said, taking a seat on the other side of Jackson's bed.

"Not too shabby, I guess. But this is all I really care about, to tell the truth." He reached for Alli's hand. "They told me she never left my side, except maybe when they changed my diapers."

"You weren't wearing diapers. How many times do I have to tell you that?"

He tried to sit up taller, and grimaced at the effort.

"Are you okay?" Hannah asked.

"He's still really tender where the wound is. I keep telling him to take it easy, but that's pretty much a waste of my time."

"Jackson, did you remember what happened that night?" The question slipped out before Hannah realized it. She studied her hands, avoiding his eyes. When she heard no response, she looked up again.

Jackson looked at Alli, giving her a tired smile. "I'm afraid so. Not entirely at first, but it came back to me. I still can't believe it. I was really worried about Sergio, but we had a good talk earlier. It's gonna take some time, but I think he'll be okay. I've slept through all this, but it's still so fresh for him, y'know?"

"We're just glad you're here. That's all that matters," Gevin said.

"What a month this has been, huh?" Marissa added. "I don't know about you guys, but I think we could all use some peace and quiet."

Hannah looked back to find Alli and Jackson watching her. The concern in their eyes touched her deeply. She felt her face warming.

"Hannah, are *you* okay?" Alli asked.

She knew it was useless to attempt to speak and simply looked up at them again, nodding her head slowly.

"It's gotta be so awkward," Jackson said quietly. "It was such a surprise to hear that—"

"No, please. I'd rather not talk about it right now, okay?" Hannah answered with a hoarse whisper.

The silence hung in the air again. Jackson winked at her, expressing more than any words could say. "Just know we're here for you. Nothing has changed that."

"Jackson's right, Hannah," Alli said. "Nothing will *ever* change that. It feels like you've been part of our little family here forever."

Hannah sat up, taking a deep breath, waving her hand through the air. "I know, I really appreciate—"

The door swung open and Hannah's heart stopped. *Oh God, please no.*

"Hey! You guys having a party in here? How come we didn't get an invitation?"

Hannah let out a sigh as Frank McKenzie strolled in behind Laura.

"Hey guys," Jackson welcomed them. "Come on in."

Laura bee-lined for Hannah's side. "Ohhhhh, I was hoping we'd run into you!" She buried her head against Hannah's, embracing her warmly. "Are you okay, sweetheart?"

"Laura, I'm fine. Really. It's so good to see you."

Frank gave her a hug as well. "We've been worried about you."

"We need to talk," Laura whispered maternally.

"I know . . . we will."

Laura smiled with such kindness. Memories of her first night at the McKenzie's came flooding back.

The noise level grew as the conversations multiplied. They laughed mostly, the relief so genuine it covered them like a soft blanket. Hannah absorbed it all, loving these people. When thoughts that she might never be with them like this again began to seep into her mind, she shook them off.

Later, she looked at her watch. She felt the unease creeping back in. Maybe those five or six hours Jason went home to sleep were only two or three? What if he were to show up? She couldn't risk it. She began to say her good-byes. More hugs. More promises to talk.

She gave Jackson one final hug. "I'm so glad I got to see you again," she spoke for his ears only.

He looked at her quizzically. "Come back soon, okay?" He gave her a long kiss on her cheek. She just smiled, not at all sure that would ever be possible again.

As she turned to leave, Gevin followed in step behind her. "Hannah, I'll walk you back to the limo."

She said good-bye to everyone then slipped out the door. Gevin rested his arm over her shoulder as they walked. "You know, Hannah, I really think that—"

"Gevin!"

They stopped in their tracks. At first Hannah wasn't sure who had addressed them. The baseball cap and glasses caught her off guard. Then her heart stopped.

"Uh . . . well, hey Jennifer," Gevin stuttered. Hannah felt his arm tense against her shoulder.

"So how's Jackson? Jason was still asleep so I just called a cab and came back over. He'll probably sleep for a month after all that's—"

"Jackson's doing great," Gevin interrupted. "In fact, I'm sure he'd love to see you. So why don't you—"

"I'm sorry, have we met?" Jennifer asked Hannah as she pulled off her ball cap. Her long blonde hair fell down on her shoulders. She shook her head and it fell perfectly into place. *Of course.*

Hannah took a deep breath, straightening her shoulders.

"Oh, sorry, Jennifer, I apologize," Gevin said. "This is—"

"Hi, Jennifer. My name is Hannah. I'm a friend of . . . Alli's." She held out her hand. "We're friends from way back." *Way back last week.*

There was an uncomfortable pause, then Jennifer's face broke into a dazzling smile. "Oh, don't you just love Alli? She is so down to earth and so *amazing.* I can't imagine what this has been like for her. But how nice of you to be here for her. You all must be very close."

Time simply stopped. Hannah watched this remarkable young woman in front of her. She was warm and friendly, her clear blue eyes conveying a depth of character that surprised Hannah. No wonder Jason had loved her. She remembered Christmas Eve, that first night at Jason's when she'd looked at the gallery of pictures on the McKenzie's game room wall. The one of Jason with Jennifer. *You'd have liked her,* he'd said. *She's terrific . . .*

She snapped back to reality, realizing Gevin and Jennifer were waiting for an answer. Problem was, she couldn't remember the question. "Um, well . . . Jennifer, it was really nice meeting you, but I've got to run."

Gevin came to her rescue. "I'll ride with you downstairs, Hannah. Jennifer, just go ahead up to the room, and I'll see you in a little while, okay?"

"Sure, Gevin. It was really nice to meet you, Hannah. I hope I'll see you again sometime."

Hannah nodded, producing the best smile she could. She and Gevin walked toward the elevator which opened immediately. They stepped in, turning around as the doors began to close. Jennifer waved at them, disappearing around the corner.

If only she had been *obnoxious*. If only she had been some kind of ditzy blonde or arrogant or rude. It would have been so much easier to hate her. To despise her for coming between her and the man Hannah had grown to love. But she was none of those things. In fact, Hannah realized that Jennifer was the kind of person she would be friends with. The thought unsettled her.

And it grieved her more deeply than she ever could have imagined.

CHAPTER 19

"Since we're kind of slow right now, Hannah, go ahead and take your break if you'd like."

"Okay, Jim. I'll finish straightening these shelves then go." The cereal aisle was in shambles when Hannah arrived that morning. Some late night visitors must have ravaged through the selections for their Cocoa Puffs. She only had one small section to go. She reached for a box on the next shelf, but stopped. There on the family-sized box of Wheaties were the smiling faces of JT, Sergio, Jackson, Gevin, and Jason.

She slowly picked up the box. How had she not noticed it before? She gently ran her hand across their faces, the grief surfacing all over again. She sank to the ground, her mind spinning. *Put it back and get back to work. It's just a stupid picture.*

But she couldn't help it. She focused on the details. JT's hair was tinted dark green. Must have been taken long before the holidays. The last time she'd seen him, it was platinum blond and curly on top. Of course with JT, that could all change in a matter of hours. The thought made her smile. What a character he was. Definitely *a bull in a china shop* as Marissa liked to say.

She studied Gevin's picture, wondering what was different. Ah, the goatee. He had a full beard now, closely trimmed. *Nice look, Gevin.* He was smiling, but it was one of his more serious smiles. She remembered the glow on his face when he told them he and Marissa were engaged.

Sergio . . . that incredibly warm smile and those dark bedroom eyes. What a sweetheart. *I wonder how he's doing. With Jackson recovering, has he finally been able to get over the haunting of Liza's attack?*

And Jackson. His boyish grin as precocious as ever. His hair was longer here, the blunt blond locks flowing over his collar. She realized she liked it better the way he wore it now. She thought of Alli and how radiant she looked yesterday at the hospital with Jackson on the road to recovery.

She finally allowed her eyes to track to Jason's beaming face. Why did his smile always look so mischievous? Or maybe she just never noticed it until she got to know him. So full of life. So happy.

Her chest hurt again, the dull ache of her broken heart. She took a deep breath, refusing to allow another invasion of tears. There had been far too many and she was determined never to cry again. Unrealistic perhaps, but the only way she was coping enough to work these days.

She leaned her head back against the shelf and closed her eyes. *Will I ever be able to make it through a single day without this kind of pain? Everywhere I look, I see their faces. On television, on newspapers, on magazine covers . . . on cereal boxes, for crying out loud. Can't I just make it through one hour without these constant reminders?*

"Excuse me, ma'am, do you know where I could find a bag of rancid cranberries?"

Hannah looked up into the smiling eyes of Laura McKenzie. "Laura," she whispered jumping to her feet, hiding the box behind her. She melted in Laura's embrace. "What are you doing here?"

"I haven't been able to get you off my mind for one single minute since I saw you at the hospital yesterday. Are you okay?"

Hannah pushed her hair back behind her ears. "As okay as I'm going to be for a while, I guess." She attempted a smile. She watched Laura's eyes drift to the Wheaties box in her hand. Laura reached for it, a knowing smile spreading across her face.

"Ah, I see you have good taste in cereal. One of my personal favorites, I might add."

"I was just cleaning these shelves and there it was. I hadn't seen it before."

"I must have bought twelve of these boxes. Keeping them sealed, you know. I figured that one of these days my grandkids would want to see their crazy father's picture on a cereal box." She stopped, searching Hannah's face. "Oh Hannah, I'm so sorry. I didn't mean—"

Hannah took Laura's hand. "Laura, you don't have a mean or malicious bone in your body. No need to apologize."

"Still, it was a thoughtless thing to say. Look, do you have a few minutes? I'd really like to talk if we could."

Hannah looked at her watch. "I was just getting ready to take my break, but I'm not sure this is such a good time. I only have a few minutes and—"

"A few minutes will do fine. Besides, there's someone in the car who wants to see you," Laura smiled playfully.

Hannah's eyes grew wide. "Uh . . . I don't think—"

"Well for heaven's sake—there I go again." Laura shook her head. "Why don't I just open wide and put *both* feet in at the same time? Honestly, Hannah. I'm surprised you aren't kicking me out of here. No, no, it isn't—well, just come on." She grabbed Hannah by the hand and started dragging her toward the front of the store. Hannah set the Wheaties box on a shelf as she followed this determined woman.

Kylie shot her a questioning look as they passed the checkout counter. "Hannah? Where are you—"

"I'll be right back. I'm gonna take my break out . . . well, she . . . oh, never mind."

As Laura stepped outside in front of her, Hannah could hear Kylie calling after them. "Who *is* that?"

The brisk January air and bright sunshine made her blink. Laura held her hand firmly, tugging her along against the chilling wind.

She heard the yapping even before she saw the tiny little puppy. "Baby!"

Laura opened the door to her car, careful to make sure Baby wouldn't jump out. She reached for the squirming puppy finally grasping her in her arms. "Look, Baby! Look who's here to see you!"

Hannah reached out, scooping Baby into her arms. After the initial licking and feistiness, the pup settled down, content for Hannah to hold her. Hannah snuggled her close, kissing her miniature head. Baby answered with a quick lick to Hannah's chin. She smiled at the feel of it. "Hey, girl, how are you?" The dog responded with a howl of delight, her chin jutting straight up in the cold morning air. Hannah and Laura laughed at the sight.

"Hannah, come on. Jump in. I'll turn on the heater and we'll be nice and comfortable." Hannah followed the suggestion, welcoming the shelter from the wind.

By the time Baby settled into a cozy nest on Hannah's lap, the car had warmed considerably. They chattered on about the weather, Frank, Jackson . . . until Hannah grew quiet, afraid where the conversation might be going. Finally, Laura broke the silence.

"You know things aren't always as they seem to be."

Hannah gazed across at Jason's mother, curious at the comment.

Laura continued. "Sometimes we look at a situation and notice the obvious and make conclusions based on that alone."

"But—"

"But God has a way of working in ways we can't begin to understand. In fact, that's what He does best. Give him the obvious and—well, somehow I wonder if He isn't maybe a little *bored* with the obvious. Where's the challenge in that? But give Him what seems to be an impossible set of circumstances, then back away and let Him go to work. You never know what will happen."

"Laura, what are you trying to say?"

"Only that it's wrong for you to turn away and throw in the towel."

Hannah shook her head. "You make it sound simple. Like I can just hand all this over to God and everything will work out perfectly."

Laura tilted her head to the side and raised one eyebrow. "I suppose it sounds that way because that's *exactly* what I'm saying."

"But life is more complicated than that, Laura. You and I both know that."

"Of course it is. I don't mean to make it sound like a pie-in-the-sky belief system. But if we truly believe God is who He says He is, then we have to be able to trust Him—not just with the little things in our lives, but the big things as well. The hard things. Just look at what happened with Jackson. Hannah, we almost lost him. Yet I believe with all my heart that God heard our prayers—not just those of us who are close to Jackson but all the thousands of his fans around the world."

Hannah looked down at Baby, scratching her gently behind the ears. "I'm so glad he's okay. I can't imagine what it's been like for Alli. For his family. To come so close to losing him."

"But Alli never gave up, did she? And Jackson's family? They never once lost hope. They believed he would come through it and he did."

"But Laura, that's a whole different situation."

"I know that, Hannah."

"I don't even feel worthy of comparing the two, to be honest."

"I didn't imply that you should."

Hannah looked out the window, watching the wind blow a shopping cart swiftly across the lot. "Laura, this whole crazy thing . . . it happened too fast. It was all just too fast." She paused. "And it ended even faster."

"Nobody said it was over." Laura reached out and placed her hand over Hannah's.

"How can you even suggest that it's not? The minute Jennifer walked into that hospital, everything Jason and I had ended. *Everything*, Laura. In one split second, it ended."

She tried to control the emotion boiling from deep inside, but she couldn't. It was bad enough to be snapping at Jason's mother but to lose control was doubly humiliating. "From the moment you walked into my store that night on Christmas Eve, my whole world changed. Every thought, every dream, every breath I took was forever changed. Falling in love with Jason has been—*was*—the most wonderful thing that ever happened to me. I never—" Her breath caught, the dam broke, and she didn't even care any more. "I never in all of my life could have imagined anything so beautiful and so pure and so—"

"Right?"

"Yes! *So right*. Being with Jason was . . . it felt so perfect. Like it was meant to be. And now it's—" She jerked her head away, holding up her palm toward Laura while fighting her anger.

"It's taken a turn. That's all, Hannah. Not a dead-end. Just a turn. Call it a detour. Jason had no idea Jennifer had broken off her engagement to that attorney in Nashville. He had no clue she'd show up at the hospital like that."

"So she waltzes back in the door and it's like I never existed."

"That's not true."

"Oh sure. And that's why he's been knocking at my door and ringing my cell phone nonstop."

Laura looked away. Hannah's heart ached for the answers she yearned to hear. Instead—silence.

"I can't offer you an explanation. I wish I could." Laura drew a long breath. "Jason's biggest weakness wasn't that hole in his heart, Hannah. It's a heart that's much too tender. Ever since he was a little boy, he never wanted to hurt anyone's feelings or cause anyone pain. When he and Jennifer went their separate ways, he suffered for over a year. Not because he regretted his decision, but because he knew he had hurt her terribly. It wasn't until he heard about her engagement that he finally let himself off the hook about it. I tell you that because I fear he doesn't have the heart to hurt her all over again. She showed up to support him in his hour of need—obviously not knowing *you* were there, giving him all the support he could possibly need. And rather than hurt her all over again—well, I pray he'll be honest with her before he makes a huge mistake."

"I'm afraid your prayer is too late."

"I disagree. I have faith in him. And Hannah, I refuse to stand by and watch you walk away from what you and Jason had together."

"Watch *me* walk away?" Hannah shot back, feeling a fresh wave of anger surge through her veins. "I think you're a little confused, Laura. Jason isn't your little boy anymore. You can't tell him who he can play with and who he can't. He's a grown man. He makes his own decisions. So stop trying to play God and leave us alone."

Laura grew quiet. The silence hung heavily between them. Baby whimpered, looking back and forth between them.

Hannah wiped her face, trying to regain her composure. "I'm sorry. I didn't mean that the way it sounded." She wiped her nose with the hem of her apron. "Look, I know you mean well. I know your heart is in the right place. But I can't handle this right now. You're Jason's mother. And as much as I value our friendship, you will always be Jason's mother. I cannot separate you from him."

"Precisely. Which is exactly why you should listen to me! I know him better than anyone, whether you think so or not. And all I'm trying to tell you is to give it a little time. Give him a chance to—"

"A chance to what? Another chance to break my heart all over again? To parade around with his perfect girlfriend—who I happen to like, by the way. And why wouldn't I? She's perfect. She's gorgeous, she's kind, she's funny . . . she's everything he could possibly want."

Hannah gathered Baby in her arms. She hugged her then handed the tiny pooch to Laura. "I'm sorry. I can't . . . I just can't talk to you anymore. It just hurts too much."

She shoved the door open and jumped out of the car, slamming it behind her. She ran across the parking lot to the store entrance, then hesitated. Remembering her keys were in her pocket, she bolted toward her car. In seconds, she peeled out of the parking lot and headed home.

Laura rubbed away the fog on the window to watch Hannah make her pitiful escape. "Oh Lord, what have I done? I should never have come here." She closed her eyes as she tucked Baby inside her coat, cradling her in its warmth. "Father, please keep Hannah safe. Protect her. She's such a precious child. I don't think for a minute You brought her into our lives as some sort of joke. You're the only one who knows what's going on in all this. Help me know how to pray. For Jason, for Jennifer . . . and for Hannah."

She paused then turned the key and started the car. "And for heaven's sake, help me know when to keep my mouth shut."

"He looks great, doesn't he?" JT asked as they all rummaged through Laura's kitchen for something to eat.

"He does. I can't believe it, but he really does." Gevin handed a plate of cold cuts over to Marissa. "The doctors are even amazed at his progress."

Jason loaded his arms with jars of pickles, mayonnaise, mustard, and a bag of lettuce then kicked the refrigerator door shut.

Sergio pulled out a chair out for Tracey. "Didn't they say they were going to get him up walking in the morning?"

"Yeah, they did," Jennifer answered. "And I have a *great* idea."

Jason watched the familiar spontaneous gestures of his former fiancée. She pushed her sleek blonde hair out of her face, her eyes twinkling with excitement.

"Here's what I'm thinking. Each of us could dress up like different people. Famous people. All there to visit Jackson. Like JT—we could dress you up like Elvis, and—"

"Whoa, whoa, whoa—wait just a minute." JT held up his hands. "You are not gonna put me in sequins and a cape and prance me down that hospital hall. No way." He smirked, looking over the top of his tinted glasses at her.

"Where's your sense of humor, JT? Do this for Jackson if you won't do it for me. C'mon!"

"Jennifer? It ain't gonna happen. Got it?"

"I forgot how stubborn you are," she fussed, shaking her head. "Okay, fine. Be a spoil sport. Just come as you are. That's always a trip anyway. Now Sergio and Gevin. I was thinking we could—"

"Sorry, Jennifer, but I'll pass on this one." Sergio avoided eye contact with her, concentrating on the sandwich he was building.

"Count me out too," Gevin added. "It just doesn't feel right. Not now. Not yet."

"You guys aren't being much help here," Jennifer groaned. "I'm just trying to think of some way to cheer Jackson up. Take his mind off everything. Remember how much he's always loved our pranks? C'mon, you guys."

"I don't know, Jen," Jason said. "I've got to agree with Gevin. It just doesn't feel right. Not now." He caught the disappointment on her face.

"Not now? Jason, why *not* now? Why not let Jackson know how happy we are that he's okay?"

Jason shrugged, slapping a couple pieces of provolone on his sandwich.

Marissa closed the loaf of bread. "I hate to be a party pooper, but I have to agree with the guys. I love a good joke, but I don't know—I guess it feels a little over the top or something. Sorry, Jen."

Jennifer looked around the table. "What's the matter with you all? Where's your spirit of compassion?"

The clatter of knives against plates and jars cluttered the silence.

"Okay, okay. I get the message. So we'll forget the group approach. But surely one of you will help me out here? Jason?"

"Sorry, Jen."

Jason watched her eyes widen with frustration. He knew she meant well and he had to admit he appreciated her intentions. Still.

"JT? C'mon, you'll do this, won't you?"

JT walked over to Jennifer, summoning her into his arms. "Now, now—don't give up on us. We'll come around eventually. It's just been a really rough week. That's all. Cut us some slack here. Okay, babe?"

She rolled her eyes and stepped into his hug with a sigh of defeat.

"You are one crazy woman. I forgot how fun you are to have around. Let me tell you, you're a breath of fresh air after all that's happened. It's good to have you back, Jen."

The awkward silence gnawed at Jason. Jennifer was here because of him. She showed up out of love for him, for Jackson—for all of them. He loved her for that. In spite of everything, he genuinely loved her for that.

So why do I feel so miserable?

He took a deep breath and tried to smile at her as she unwrapped herself from JT's arms and headed his

Diane Moody

way. She tucked herself beneath Jason's arm, wrapping her other arm around his waist.

A palpable strain still permeated the air. Jason didn't miss the uneasy glances from Marissa and Gevin. They all loved Jennifer. She had been part of their "family" for a long, long time. Ordinarily, it would have seemed so natural to have her here again, involved in their lives again.

But it didn't feel natural. At all.

Too much had happened. Too many mixed feelings. Only a few days ago, they had all sat at this same table. Now Jackson was in the hospital, Alli at his side, and Liza was incarcerated.

And Jason's arm was around someone entirely different.

CHAPTER 20

"This is getting a little old, don't you think?"

Hannah sat in her easy chair, a rumpled mess wrapped in her pale pink chenille robe. She watched Kylie survey the damage as she dropped her purse and keys on the table by the front door. She pulled off her coat and tossed it onto the back of the sofa.

"I mean, how long are you going to keep up this ritual of leaving work every time you feel the tears coming on? You planning to hide out here for the rest of your life?" She walked to the kitchen and began picking up the dirty dishes. "And more importantly, am I gonna get paid for being your maid? Geez, Hannah, this place is a pig sty."

Kylie turned on the kitchen faucet then turned to look at her. Hannah stared back at her then looked down at her hands, picking at the chipped nail polish on her thumb.

She heard Kylie blow out an exasperated sigh as she tossed dishes into the sink, attempting to clear off the counter. Finally, the redhead shut off the faucet.

"When was last time you had a hot meal? Huh?" Kylie planted a hand on her hip.

Hannah shrugged.

"Don't give me that. I asked you a question. When was the last time you had a hot meal?"

"Um . . . I don't know. I can't remember."

"Well, you're gonna have one now. I'm gonna make us some spaghetti and you're gonna eat every bite if I have to force-feed you, got it?"

Hannah moved slowly to the counter as Kylie began putting their meal together. In less than twenty minutes, she had prepared two steaming plates of pasta. The loaf of French bread she'd found in the freezer had warmed quickly in the oven, filling the apartment with a delicious aroma.

Hannah's stomach growled. She took a seat at the table. Kylie sat down across from her. Her friend made small talk as they ate, repeating how pleased she was to see Hannah eating a few bites. She tore off a hunk of the crusty bread and put it on Hannah's plate.

"You don't have to be my nursemaid."

"Oh? Funny, it looks to me like *somebody* better take care of you because you're certainly not doing a very good job of it. Go on. Eat. I refuse to let you starve yourself."

They continued in silence. Hannah managed a few more bites of spaghetti then chewed slowly on the bread. Finally, she pushed the plate away. "Thanks, Kylie."

"Don't thank me. In fact, you're the one who's supplying dessert. Come on, let's go sit on the sofa. The coffee's ready. I'll bring it over."

"What dessert?"

They settled into the living area, both nurturing hot mugs of hazelnut coffee.

"You're going to tell me everything. Whether you want to or not. This ridiculous merry-go-round you're on is going to stop for a few minutes, and you're going to tell me every single detail just like you promised. I know it won't be easy. But you owe it to me, and quite frankly, I think it might be good for you."

"I don't see how."

"Because maybe, by just starting at the beginning and running all the way through it, you'll see it more clearly. You'll sort through this heartache you're suffering from and be able to find some way to handle it."

"Kylie, I don't think—"

"I didn't ask you to think. I just want you to talk. Start at the very beginning. If it takes all night, then so be it. Now, tell me. How in the world did you happen to meet Jason McKenzie?"

His name suspended in the air. The ache in her heart gripped her. She traced the rim of the mug with her finger. Finally, she took a deep breath. "It was Laura. Jason's mom. She came into the store right about closing time on Christmas Eve . . ."

And so the story unfolded. They laughed and cried and continued long into the night.

"You were right," Hannah said over a yawn.

"Right about what?" Kylie asked.

"I've told you everything. Every single detail. Talking about it helps. I still feel this sorrow inside me, but somehow, it doesn't hurt quite as much. It was all suffocating me—I couldn't handle it. But now, after telling you everything . . . I don't know, it just helps. A lot." Then she snickered. A little at first, then she laughed out loud.

"What?"

"You. Your forehead is caved like some pitiful arch of empathy or something. It's like you've taken on the pain I've shared, and it's warped your face into this, this—"

"And that's somehow *funny* to you?" Kylie mourned. "I'm distraught from hearing maybe the most depressing story I've ever heard. And you sit there laughing at the expression on my face? Geez, Hannah."

"Oh, c'mon. Let me have a couple moments of laughter." She wiped her eyes. "Because this may all be new to you, but I've been living it for weeks, Kylie. And no offense, but you look like some poor little puppy or—"

"Like Bambi when his mother got shot?"

"What?"

"Well, I kinda *feel* like Bambi must have felt when his mother got shot. Remember? That horrible emptiness you felt when you saw that movie?" Kylie stared at the dust particles floating in the light of the lamp, her mind revisiting the old Disney film scene. "Your story . . . it makes me feel a little like that."

Hannah pulled the quilt over her legs again. "Oh don't be so melodramatic. It's just life. That's all. People fall in and out of love every day. It's no big deal."

Kylie tilted her head, not buying the nonchalant remark. "Well, excuse me, but I don't think so. Not like this. This isn't some college romance or . . . or some silly holiday fling, Hannah."

Hannah yawned and stretched, then snuggled into the sofa. "I know."

"But I'm really sorry. All this time . . . ever since I got back to town and you've been so upset and you wouldn't tell me all this and then I found out about Jason and that you'd been actually *involved* with these people. Well, I was just stunned! I was so shocked that you—and them—and gosh, Hannah—it's *Out of the Blue!*"

"Yeah . . ." Hannah's eyes slowly closed. "Blue . . ."

"But I'm so sorry. I never *dreamed* anything like this had happened. And I feel so awful." Kylie poured out her heart, lamenting her downfall as a friend.

"Awful," Hannah mumbled. "Why do you . . ."

She waited for Hannah to finish her thought. But her own confession couldn't wait. "I feel *awful* because I was so jealous! The minute I put two and two together and realized the one you were so upset about was *Jason McKenzie* and . . . and that you'd been hanging with these people? I was *beyond* jealous. And what kind of friend am I, that I would be jealous when you were so upset? I'm horrible. Just horrible. I'm such a wretched excuse for a friend. How can you ever forgive me? At a time when you were suffering and . . . Hannah?"

A soft snore answered her.

"Hannah?"

The figure buried under the quilt on the sofa turned over and burrowed deeper. "Coffee is on aisle four on your right."

Kylie exhaled. "Oh Hannah, what in the world are you going to do?" She sat there quietly for several more minutes thinking over the strange story she had just absorbed. Finally, her eyes grew weary and she began to drift off to sleep as well. Tonight she would dream of famous people and impossible situations.

"That was an impressive walk you made down that hall, Jax," Sergio said, helping Jackson back into bed. "How're you feeling? Did we wear you out?"

"I'm exhausted. I can't believe a few steps like that can wear me out so much." Alli fluffed the pillows behind him. He grabbed her hand and kissed it.

"Just give it some time," Gevin added. "You'll be outta here in no time."

"You still think you're up to the press conference?" Marissa asked.

"No, probably not," Jackson answered. "But we're going to do it anyway."

"Are you sure, Jax?" JT asked. "We can do it later, man."

"No, I want to. I need to do this. It's like a burden on me. I don't know how else to explain it. It's just something I really need to do."

Marissa tucked the blanket under his legs. "Well, I'm sure it'll relieve all the fans to see that you're okay."

"We'll just make it short and sweet," Jason suggested. "A few words. That's it, okay?"

"No problem. How much time do we have til it starts?"

"About half an hour," Marissa answered. "But hey— the press is on your time schedule, so just take it easy."

"Trust me, they'll wait," JT stated, pulling on his baseball cap. "C'mon, let's give him some time to rest."

They filed out, heading down the hall to a private waiting room. Security remained tight offering them the privacy and protection they still needed.

Forty-five minutes later, they assembled in a hospital conference room on the first floor. A mob of reporters and cameramen lined the opposite wall. A long table set up with microphones banked the front of the room. As he,

JT, Sergio and Gevin filed in, Jason noticed Marissa, Tracey, and Jennifer sitting in chairs against the wall nearest the door. He and the guys made their way behind the table accompanied by the loud staccato frenzy of cameras clicking to capture their every move. Reporters began shouting questions.

A hospital spokesman held up his hands for their silence. "As agreed, the guys will make a few statements. We will not open the floor for questions. Please respect the ground rules or we'll clear the room. Understood?" He looked around as the reporters mumbled a few responses.

After grabbing a seat, Jason took a sip from one of the chilled water bottles on the table. They had done a thousand press conferences, but never had he felt so ill at ease. He looked over at the girls just in time to see Marissa wink at Gevin, mouthing "I love you." He glanced over at Gevin just as his cousin touched his two forefingers to his lips, winking back at his fiancée.

Marissa stood up and moved closer to the door. *Guess I'm not the only one feeling uneasy.* She shifted from one foot to the next and back. Folding her arms across her chest, she looked back at Gevin.

"What's wrong with Rissa?" he whispered to Gevin.

"I wish I knew," Gevin answered under his breath. "You know how she gets a sixth sense about things. Well, we might as well get this over with."

Gevin cleared his voice and pulled the microphone closer to him. "We'd like to thank you all for coming today," he spoke, looking directly into the television camera lens across the room. "There's no way we can begin to describe for you what the last few days have been like for us." They all nodded in agreement. "But we wanted to say a few things, especially to all of our fans out there who have been so incredible . . ." His voice caught. He coughed nervously and reached for his water bottle. Camera lights flashed in milliseconds. Muffled voices rippled through the room.

Jason swallowed hard. *This is not gonna be easy.*

"Ohhhh, my back . . . ooouch." Kylie slowly attempted to sit up.

Hannah stirred, rolling over on the narrow sofa. "What time is it?"

Kylie twisted from one side to the other, moaning. She looked at the digital numbers on the clock. "It's 10:45! Oh no, I'm late for work!" She started scrambling out from under her blanket, then stopped. "Wait—today's Friday. I don't work today. Oh, thank goodness. You're not scheduled either, are you?

Hannah yawned. "No, I don't work again until Monday." She watched as Kylie fell back into the easy chair that had served as her bed for the night. "Why did you sleep in the chair?"

"Same reason you slept on the couch. We fell asleep talking."

Hannah rubbed her eyes. "Oh yeah, I guess we did."

Kylie pulled the cover back up to her chin. "I'm sitting here pouring my heart out to you, begging forgiveness, and all I get back is your snoring."

"What were you apologizing for?"

"For being such a jerk of a friend." She stopped, yawning again. "Oh, skip it. I'm too tired for all that now." She reached for the remote sitting on the table beside her. "I want to see what the weather is supposed to be today. I was hoping to go for a run." She clicked on the television, flying through several cable stations. Suddenly, Gevin Michaels's face filled the screen.

"Wait! Kylie! Stop—" Hannah sat up. "Look!"

Kylie turned up the volume.

Gevin's face was contorted. Suddenly, an arm wrapped around his shoulders. The camera angle widened, showing Jason comforting his cousin.

"Hannah, it's Jason!"

Hannah stopped breathing, watching his every move.

"This has been really hard for us. But I think what Gevin was trying to say, and what we all want to say, is how much we appreciate everything. All the expressions of love that have poured in from literally all over the world."

Jason looked sideways at Sergio and JT, then back at Gevin. "There were times we weren't sure we'd make it another hour. We thought we were losing Jackson." Jason's eyes grew wide, his eyebrows arched up his forehead. He was clearly struggling.

"Oh Jason," Hannah moaned. Her eyes stung.

"And that was just about the time we looked out the window of this hospital and saw this . . . *ocean* of people outside. They were holding candles and signs and—well, it was such an unbelievable outpouring of love. I've never seen anything like it."

"None of us have," Sergio added, his accent sounding thicker than usual. "You think you come to a point in your life where things just can't get any worse." Sergio looked up to the ceiling, blinking back his tears. "Sorry— just give me a minute." He inhaled and blew out his breath rapidly. "I've got something I just really need to say so bear with me." A couple of seconds passed. He pinched the bridge of his nose and looked back at the cameras.

"You all know that the woman who shot Jackson had been involved in a relationship with me . . . And it has been—I can't possibly tell you what that has felt like for me. But it's very important I say this . . . here and right now. Laura and Frank McKenzie helped me understand that this nightmare will live with me the rest of my life if I don't let go of the bitterness I feel in my heart. And the only way—the *only* way—I have survived all this was to come to the point where I could honestly and totally forgive Liza Rochelli. Dios me ayude, yo perdono a Liza Rochelli."

The murmur of voices from the press pool grew louder. More flashes. More incessant clicks.

"Look, I will never forget what happened. But I can honestly say, with the help of God and my friends here, that I have forgiven her. I believe that she should be imprisoned for the rest of her life, granted. But I can no longer harbor the hate I felt toward her for what she did. If I did, I would be no better than her. So—" He sighed loudly. "That's all I have to say."

JT reached over and squeezed his shoulder. "You're a better man than me, Serg," he said quietly. "That took a lot of guts, man. I'm proud of you."

"Well, I know you all didn't come here to see the four of us," Jason said, the camera panning to focus on him. "So—" He looked toward the door, nodding. The camera lens widened to show Alli pushing Jackson's wheelchair into the room.

The live scene became surreal as the room erupted in cheers and applause. The flashing lights created a strobe-like effect. The camera shot back and forth between Jackson and Alli, to the other members of *Blue,* then widened to take in the front half of the room.

When his wheelchair reached the position on the table they had left open for him, Jackson reached out for the table, pulling up to it. He looked up at Alli behind him who immediately buried her face against his shoulder, wrapping her arms around him. He covered his face with his hands, obviously overcome with emotion.

"Oh Jackson . . ." Hannah wept freely. She looked at Kylie who bit the edge of the pillow she held in her arms, tears streaming down her face.

From the television, the cheers and applause continued as the entire Greer family filed in behind Jackson and Alli. They clutched together as one, smiling through their tears.

The ovation continued. When the noise began to diminish, everyone waited to hear what Jackson would have to say. It took him several more minutes to regain his composure. Alli remained steadfast behind him, her hands on his shoulder. He reached up, grasping hold of her hand on his left shoulder.

He attempted to begin and failed. He tried again.

"We love you, man," JT prompted. Jason, Gevin, and Sergio echoed the sentiment.

Finally, he spoke. "You cannot possibly imagine . . . how I feel right now." He looked around the room. "And I'm not even going to attempt to try . . . to express . . . except that I am overwhelmed." His chin trembled.

"When we perform . . . either on stage or wherever, well, we get bombarded." He laughed nervously. "The screaming and the hysteria . . . and after a while, we just get numb to it." He looked at Sergio and JT on one side, Jason and Gevin on the other. They nodded in agreement.

"Maybe we even take it for granted sometimes. That's just part of the whole crazy thing, I guess. But this—" His face slowly began to crumble. "Oh God . . ." He lost his composure, unable to continue. Alli buried her head against his.

Hannah and Kylie both sniffed back tears as they watched the heart-wrenching scene unfold.

A full minute passed before Jackson tried again, taking another deep breath. "I'm sorry. This is so hard. I've just never experienced such *profound . . .* love." He shook his head. "I never knew such an incredible depth of love . . . and I know with all of my heart, I will never be the same. Never."

"None of us will," JT added.

Jackson looked across at him. "And these guys . . ." A smile pulled at one side of his mouth. "Well, these guys are the best. They're a little crazy, but they're the best."

Alli leaned down, whispering something in his ear. He nodded. "There's no way I could possibly thank everyone, but I especially want to thank God for the hospital here—for the doctors and nurses. They've all been awesome." He looked around, acknowledging some of the staff.

"But I also want to thank God for my family," he said, twisting around to find his parents, his brother and sisters. "Mom, Dad, Micah, Ashley, Jaylin, BJ—I love you."

Then his eyes rested on Alli, her face beaming. He turned back at the cameras. "There's just one more thing I have to say. I wouldn't be here except for her." He looked back up at her. "Alli, I love you."

It was as far as he got. He lost it again; this time making no attempt to hide it.

"That's enough," Gevin said, his voice audible over the commotion.

Jason stood, holding his hands up. "Thank you. Thank all of you. That's really all we had to say."

As they quickly wheeled Jackson out of the room, a traffic jam ensued in the doorway. Like piranhas, the press disregarded any promises they'd made.

"Is Jackson going to fully recover?"

"Was there any permanent damage? Will he ever walk again?"

Kylie threw her pillow on the floor. "Those people are horrible! Can't they see what those guys have been through?"

Hannah rubbed her face. "Poor Jackson. That had to be so hard for him. I'm surprised they—"

"When will Jackson be released from the hospital?" On television, the barrage of questions continued.

The hospital spokesman stepped up to the mike again. "That's all. No questions, please."

"Sergio! Have you been to the jail to see Liza?"

He turned his back to the cameras.

"Did you know she has a criminal record for stalking celebrities?"

"Is it true that one of you got engaged over Christmas?" They all stopped, looking at the reporter who blurted the question then back at the camera's lens. The camera pulled back then, focusing toward the side of the room where Marissa, Tracey, and Jennifer remained.

"Oh no," Hannah croaked, taking it all in. "How could—"

"Shhh!"

The camera scanned from one face to the next, first Tracey and Jennifer, then Marissa.

"Is it true that Jennifer Crandle left her fiancé at the altar to reunite with Jason McKenzie?"

The camera focused on Jennifer's face, her own panic apparent. She stood abruptly trying to leave the room, but couldn't make her way through the crowd at the door.

"Where's their security?" Hannah yelled at the television screen. "They should have a path cleared for them!"

Jason, JT, Gevin and Sergio were still cornered behind the table at the front of the room. "No comment. No more questions," Gevin spoke firmly as he tried to make his way closer to Marissa.

"But Jason, who was the woman you were seen entering the hospital with on the night of the shooting?"

Hannah froze. Kylie gasped.

The reporter continued shouting his questions. "You were seen with her entering the hospital after Jackson went into cardiac arrest. If it wasn't Jennifer, then who was it and why were you with her? Are there *two* women in your life at this time?"

Hannah and Kylie watched in disbelief as a split screen divided the screen with the live conference on one side and footage of Hannah and Jason emerging from a limousine on the other. He was leading her, hand in hand, through the barricade. The footage slowed. In slow, jerky motions, the scene played out as Hannah's face was splashed across the screen, then freeze-framed.

"Oh my God!" Kylie cried.

"Who's the mystery woman, Jason?" the reporter insisted, pointing to the television monitor. "Is it true she's a local resident?"

Hannah couldn't breathe. She watched as Jason's eyes tracked to view the television monitor. He did a double-take. Then, as the lens focused closer on his face, he stared straight into it, his face taut with an anger she'd never seen before. *He must feel like a caged animal!*

"Oh Kylie!" Hannah cried, jumping to her feet. "What am I gonna do?"

Jason was still trapped in the clog of people. The temperature in the room felt like a hundred degrees even as the litany of questions continued. The gratitude of Jackson Greer was already forgotten as the questions pelted them over and over, prying into the most private areas of their lives. Normally, they were used to such assaults. They could walk away from it.

But not today. As the verbal attacks continued, Jason felt something ugly inside him begin to boil. In the blink of an eye, he was across the table, grabbing the rude reporter by the throat.

"How dare you! How *dare* you!"

"No! Jason, stop!" JT screamed, scrambling to reach his friend.

The camera jerked around trying to capture the heated exchange on film.

The sweaty reporter backed away, using his microphone as a shield. "What did I—"

"Leave us alone!" Jason shouted, his nose only inches away from the reporter, his hands still clutching the man's shirt. "After all we've been through! Why can't you just LEAVE US ALONE! You're a pig! You're a filthy—"

"I don't have to take that!" the reporter yelled as he shoved Jason back. He quickly turned his face to the camera. "Are you getting this, Joe?" he asked his cameraman.

"Why you—" With every ounce of frustration and pent-up anger, Jason McKenzie coiled back his fist and smashed it into the face of the reporter. The room exploded.

In the bedlam that followed, the camera man lost his balance thrusting the live picture out of control before landing on a still shot of acoustic ceiling tiles.

The voice of the local television reporter updated the unexpected story unfolding from the conference room at the hospital.

"—when *Out of the Blue* singer and Chapel Hill native Jason McKenzie assaulted a local television reporter who had asked repeated questions about his personal life. The mêlée erupted when the reporter questioned McKenzie about this woman, seen here with McKenzie just three days ago entering the hospital. Sources tell us she is Hannah Brooks, a student at the University of North Carolina here in—"

Hannah flew out of the room. Kylie followed her. "Hannah! What are you doing?"

In her bedroom, Hannah threw her luggage on the bed. She yanked open drawers, tossing clothes into the bag.

"What are you doing!?" Kylie yelled.

"I'm leaving. I'm on the next flight out of town, Kylie."

Hannah's tone frightened Kylie. "You can't just—"

"Watch me!"

Kylie grabbed Hannah's arms. "Stop it, Hannah! Just stop it! You can't run away from this! Where could you possibly go?"

Hannah's eyes looked wild. "Don't you get it, Kylie? They know who I am now! They'll be knocking my door down any minute. Didn't you see the way they treated Jason? They're ruthless. They won't stop at anything. I can't . . . I will not play this game for them. I've got to disappear and there's nothing you can say to stop me!" She pulled out of Kylie's grasp.

Kylie jumped on the unmade bed, her heart racing. "Oh, Hannah. I'm so sorry!"

"I don't need your sympathy. I need your help. Get my credit card out of my purse. Call the airlines and book me a flight. I don't care where, just the fastest flight I can get out of here."

Less than twenty minutes later, the front door slammed behind them as they raced to Kylie's car.

"They know my name, Kylie!" Hannah cried in panic as they tossed her bags into the backseat and jumped into the front seat. "They've already found out my name! Hurry! Kylie, hurry!"

Kylie roared the sports car to life, the tires squealing in protest as she floored the gas pedal. Hannah looked back behind them as a News Channel 2 van sped around the corner. "Oh God, please help us! Go! Kylie, GO!"

CHAPTER 21

"I said no."

"I don't care what you said! I'm going and that's final." Kylie pursed her lips.

Hannah popped the kinks out of her neck, closing her eyes behind her sunglasses. "No, Kylie. Stop smothering me." The last thing she wanted to do was cause a scene. "You are *not* going and I'm not going to discuss it further. Got it?"

They moved up in the line as it snaked toward the Delta ticket counter at the Raleigh-Durham International Airport. The twenty minute drive from Chapel Hill had been a blur between their on-going argument and the fear of what they might see in the rearview mirrors. She'd begged Kylie to drop her off at the curb, but the fiery redhead would have no part of it.

Now Kylie's eyes narrowed, her arms folded tight across her chest as she tapped her foot. "You are so . . . so . . . *childish!* You are in no condition to travel anywhere by yourself. So just get a grip, Hannah, and stop playing the brave little soldier off to war. This is ridiculous!"

"Will you leave? Just go home. I don't need this right now, thank you very much," Hannah growled under her breath.

A middle-aged couple in front of them turned around and peered at them over half-glasses perched on their noses. They looked the girls over from head to toe, then looked at each other with raised eyebrows.

Kylie couldn't stand it. "Excuse me, is there a problem?"

They lobbed insulted stares then turned around, moving their luggage closer to them.

"Now look what you've done!" Hannah croaked.

"Oh for heaven's sake, why is it all *my* fault? You're the one who had to go flying out of your apartment like a bat out of hell."

Hannah screwed up her face, standing nose to nose with her best friend. "Well, I guess I had a perfectly good *reason* to fly out of there, if you'll recall. Was there or was there not a news van careening around the corner toward my apartment? Huh? Was there or was there not just the tiniest fraction of a second before we made it off that street? Huh?" She pinched her thumb and forefinger together in Kylie's face. "They were that close, Kylie! They would have eaten me alive and you know it."

She turned her back, folding her arms across her chest. She took a deep breath and blew it out in a huff.

"And exactly *who* was it who drove that successful getaway? Huh? Huh?"

Hannah could feel her friend's breath against the back of her neck, just inches below her broad-rimmed hat that hopefully concealed her identity. She rolled her eyes at the thought of Kylie talking to her back.

"I'll tell you who—it was *me*! You need me and you know it but you're just too STUBBORN to admit it!"

Diane Moody

The couple turned around once again, having completed their business at the counter. "WHAT? What is your problem?" Kylie blasted.

They scurried off, clutching their tickets in hand. Hannah moved up to the counter, Kylie hovering close at her elbow.

The thirty-something man behind the counter, whose astonishing good looks had silenced both of them, already locked eyes with Kylie. "How can I help you today?" he asked with a broad smile.

"We have one reservation for the next flight to Tampa," Kylie instructed, "and we'd like to add an additional ticket on the same flight."

Hannah tipped her head, looking at Kylie over her sunglasses again. She looked back at the ticket agent and tried to maintain her composure. "No, my friend is mistaken. Just one ticket, please."

"Two."

"One."

"Two!"

"ONE!"

"Whoa—hold on there, ladies!" The agent laughed, holding up his hands. "I'm sure we can work this out. Let's all take a calm breath and see what we've got here. Name?"

Hannah edged closer to the counter, giving her name and ID as quietly as she could.

Kylie crowded beside her. "And my name is Kylie Reynolds. Here's my driver's license. I'm sure you won't have any trouble rustling up another ticket, right?"

Hannah felt her pulse rate accelerating. *She's flirting? At a time like this?* She looked up at the agent, noticing his name tag. *Jason.* "Of course. What else would it be?" she muttered to herself. "Why does everyone on the face of this earth have to be named—"

234

"Excuse me?"

"Look . . . *Jason*—."

"Ohmygosh," Kylie gasped.

His brows dipped. "I'm sorry, is there a problem?"

"Your name," Kylie attempted to explain. "It's Jason."

He grinned at her. "Well, actually, I already knew that, but thanks for the reminder."

If he wasn't so handsome, she might have slugged him.

"Never mind." Hannah straightened her back. "What I need right now is my ticket. The one I reserved. I'd appreciate it if you'd process the ticket and let me make my flight in time."

His fingers flew across the keyboard, that same smile spread across his perfect face. Hannah was ticked at his apparent amusement over their squabble. Kylie continued schmoozing, hoping to get her way.

"Well, let's see . . . it looks like we have a solution to your problem here," he offered. "The flight is overbooked. Miss Brooks has a ticket, but there are no more seats available." He looked up at Kylie. "Sorry," he said, obviously meaning it.

"Thank you," Hannah breathed, looking up at the ceiling, her appreciation aimed a lot higher. She closed her eyes, then leveled them at Kylie. Of course Kylie was still staring at *Jason*. The look on her face was all too familiar to Hannah.

"Look, I know there are ways to—"

He cut her off. "Ordinarily, yes—normally there are ways to get you on that plane. But we've already had to ask for volunteers to give up their seats. We've been tweaking this thing for an hour now. I'm afraid there's nothing else we can do." He looked back at Hannah, his fingers continuing to tap the keys. "Miss Brooks, how many bags will you be checking through today?"

"I can't believe this." Kylie turned and stomped her way toward a seating area across from the counter. She plopped down into a seat, crossed one leg over the other and swung it wildly.

"Thank you . . . Jason," Hannah said after she completed her business.

"No problem. Your flight departs in forty-five minutes from Gate 35. Thank you for flying Delta."

She put her billfold back in her purse and walked over to Kylie. "Want to grab some coffee over at that Starbucks before I go through security?" Hannah continued walking, not giving Kylie a chance to stew any longer. Kylie blew out an exasperated sigh and caught up with her.

Hannah pulled her hat down lower over her forehead and avoided looking anyone directly in the eye. She was disappointed to see a long line at the Starbucks counter. *So many people.* She slowed her gait as a knot of fear gripped her stomach again.

"Come on," Kylie said softly, pulling her away from the crowd. She led her to a corner out of the traffic and clusters of travelers.

"You wait here. I'll get us a couple of lattes. Just keep your head down." With that, she blended into the crowd and disappeared.

Hannah lowered herself to the ground, leaning against the wall. She pulled her knees up against her, wrapping her arms around her legs. She closed her eyes, uttering a prayer for calm.

"Anyone here order a vanilla latte?"

She looked up, reaching for the familiar cup with the brown teddy around it. "That was fast. Did you cut in line?"

"As if?" Kylie slid down beside her, careful not to spill her cup as she plopped her backpack between them. "Well, okay, maybe. I saw that hottie from my bio-chem class. Can I help it if he wanted to chat? Next thing I know, I'm ordering and outta there. Works like a charm."

"You're incredible."

"I know. How's your latte?"

Hannah lifted the lid, inhaling the comforting aroma of the espresso blend then took a sip. "It's wonderful. Thanks, Kylie."

"You're welcome. Look, Hannah, I'm really sorry." Kylie spoke quietly, setting the cup on the ground beside her. "With everything else, the last thing you needed was for me to pull a tantrum in the ticket line. Geez. When will I ever learn?"

Hannah looked up, casting a weary smile at her friend. She reached out, squeezing Kylie's shoulder. "Never. None of us ever learn. It's just part of life. But I appreciate what you were trying to do. I know you just want to help. But right now, I need some time alone. I need to think all this through. Sort out my feelings and try to get a grasp on everything. It's been such a circus."

Kylie leaned her head back against the wall. "That's an understatement. Good grief, Hannah. Your life has been like that Montu rollercoaster at Busch Gardens. Don't bother riding it while you're in Tampa. It would seem like a kiddy ride compared to what you've been through lately."

"Kylie, you have to promise me something."

"Oh sure—you won't let me go with you but now you expect me to make a bunch of promises?"

"Stop it. I'm serious."

"I know. I'm sorry. So what's this big promise I've got to make?"

"You've got to swear to me that you won't tell a soul where I am. I mean it. Not anybody. Not Jim or anybody."

"I'll cover for you at work. Don't worry about that."

"Just be really careful not to let it slip, okay? I'm totally serious, Kylie. You saw the press. You know exactly what I'm talking about."

"Okay, okay! I promise! But classes start in a week. This is our last semester. You just make sure you get back in time. Don't blow it when we're so close to graduation."

She set down her cup. "Geez. I forgot all about school." She rubbed her face with her hands, accidentally knocking off her sunglasses. Butterflies drifted through her as she quickly replaced them. With the wall of legs and luggage which had quickly surrounded them, she realized she was still safely out of sight.

"I'll be back in time. I refuse to let all this screw me out of graduation. Fortunately I have a pretty light load this semester."

"You sure you're going to be okay? I'm really worried about you."

"I'll be fine. I'll call you as soon as I get settled into my room."

"Yeah, it's here in my pocket," she said, patting the pocket of her jean jacket. "And don't worry. I won't tell a soul where you are. Where exactly is this place anyway?"

"Belleair Bluffs. It's a tiny little area sandwiched between Clearwater and St. Petersburg. It's a family-owned place right on the beach. We used to go there every summer when we were little. Nothing fancy but quiet and secluded."

"Okay, but now it's my turn to ask for a promise." Kylie pulled her long red curls back into a loose pony tail.

"What kind of promise?"

"You have to promise you'll call me every day. Every single day, Hannah."

"I will."

"And . . . if you have any problems or just need some company, promise you'll let me know. I'll be down there in a heartbeat."

"I promise. You're the best, Kylie."

"Yeah, well if I'm so special then why are you leaving me here? I could use some sunshine about now," she laughed. "Sand between my toes . . . the warm ocean breeze blowing across me as I work on my tan—"

"Ladies and gentleman, Delta Flight 495 with service to Tampa is now boarding at Gate 35."

"That's my flight. I better run."

They stood up simultaneously, Kylie handing Hannah her carry-on bag. "Just take care of yourself, okay?" Kylie hugged her.

"I will. And thanks for understanding." She blinked the pesky tears gathering in her eyes. "I've gotta go. Love you, Kylie."

"Love you too, Hannah. Don't forget to bring me one of those lousy sea shells, okay?"

They hugged again and Hannah dashed for the security gate.

Kylie stood watching her until she passed through the security inspection. Hannah turned to wave a final time then disappeared down the hall. "Well, back you go to your dull and boring life," Kylie mumbled as she turned to leave. "But who knows? Maybe Johnny Depp will be waiting on your doorstep when you get home. Of course, with your luck it'd be someone like Dwight from *The Office*."

Smiling at her joke, she approached the entrance noticing a flock of people rushing through in a near stampede.

"You guys head down that way; Mike—you come with me; Jeff, you and Craig take the other concourse." The guy giving the orders handed them each a paper. As Kylie passed within a couple feet of them, she caught a glimpse of the flyer. There on a wrinkled page was a color eight-by-ten of Hannah Brooks—a still shot from the television freeze-frame that turned Hannah and Kylie's day upside down.

"If you see her, call me on my cell immediately. And whatever you do, do NOT let her get on an airplane!"

"But you don't understand. It's extremely important that I talk to Hannah."

"Yeah, right lady. You and everybody else in this hemisphere."

"That's just it. I'm *not* everybody else!" Laura looked around the store then back at the manager. She'd approached the man behind the service counter hoping to find out if anyone knew where she could find Hannah. "Is there somewhere I could speak to you in private?"

"Look, lady, I don't mean to be rude, but I have a store to run here. So if you have something to say, you'll just have to say it right here." He returned his attention to the schedule in front of him.

Laura sighed in frustration. "Fine. Have it your way." She leaned over the counter, her face only a foot from his. "My name is Laura McKenzie. Does that mean anything to you?"

"Sure it does," he answered, peering over the glasses hanging on his nose. "And I'm Brad Pitt. Nice to meet you."

"Oh for heaven's sake," Laura snapped. She plopped her purse on the counter, pulling out her billfold. She flipped it open to her North Carolina driver's license and shoved it in front of him.

"That's nice, Ms. McKenzie. You're the third Laura McKenzie in here today. Not to mention the two Mrs. Michaels and six Mrs. Greers. You know, I have to be honest with you. If I was a reporter, I think I could come up with something a little more original than trying to pass myself off as Jason McKenzie's *mom*."

She held her tongue, projecting steely eyes at the store manager. She jerked her billfold to the wallet photos, pulled out a picture and held it up to him.

He studied the picture. "This is real nice, lady, but—" He tilted his head closer for a better look through his glasses. His face started to redden and he tried to smile. "Well, now . . . that would sure enough be Jason McKenzie right there with you. Everybody knows Chapel Hill's favorite celebrity . . . and can I assume that's Mr. McKenzie as well?"

Laura plastered a satisfied smile across her face. "Yes, that would be me with my husband and my *son*."

Jim removed his glasses while handing the picture back to her. He pinched the bridge of his nose with his fingers. "I am *so* sorry, Mrs. McKenzie."

"Laura."

He smiled sheepishly. "Laura. I hope you understand my position. Hannah's like one of my own kids. We've been inundated all day with these reporters looking for her, and—well, I was only trying to protect her. I am truly sorry."

Laura slowly put the picture back in her billfold, returning it to her purse. "No problem. In fact, I must apologize too. I'm not usually so pushy. But I'm terribly worried about Hannah and she isn't answering her cell phone. Is she here by any chance?"

Laura was touched by the genuine concern in his eyes. Walking around the counter, he held out his arm, showing her to the break room. As he opened the door for her, a young redhead ran into them—literally.

"Oh Jim, I'm sorry! I didn't—" She stood eyeball to eyeball with Laura. Then, with a sick grin, she bolted without another word.

"Wait a minute!" Laura called out to her. "You're Hannah's friend—I remember you from the other day. Please—I need to talk to you."

"Kylie, come back here," Jim said.

The redhead froze. Slowly, she turned around. "Uh—"

"In the break room. Now."

She offered another peculiar smile then slipped by them back to the break room.

"Mrs. McKenzie here is looking for Hannah, Kylie. Now, you told me she was taking the week off, but you didn't tell me where she was."

They both looked at Kylie, expecting an answer. She scratched the back of her neck, pulling off the blue bandana headband she was wearing. "Well, see the thing is—"

"Kylie, we haven't been introduced, but I take it you know who I am," Laura said, approaching her.

"Oh yeah. I know who you are."

Laura couldn't help smiling at the precocious girl, with her wild curls, bright green eyes, and splash of freckles across her nose. "And I trust Hannah has told you about—"

"Yes."

Laura looked relieved. "Then you know it's very important that I talk to her as soon as possible."

Kylie paced back and forth, twisting the bandana in her hands. "I know . . . I mean, I'm sure that—"

"Where is she, Kylie?" Laura interrupted.

"But you see, I promised."

"Promised what?" Jim asked.

"Not to say anything. She's *so* upset. You have no idea."

Laura's eyes misted. "I've been so worried about her. I haven't known her that long, but Jim—just like you, I've felt like she was one of my own from the first time we met. And then she and Jason—" She looked at Jim, suddenly uncomfortable to be discussing something so personal with Hannah's boss.

"Oh, I'm sorry. How rude of me," Jim apologized. "I'll leave you two alone to talk. But Mrs. McKenzie—please, if there's anything I can do, I hope you won't hesitate to call on me." He thrust his hand toward her. "I never even introduced myself. I'm Jim Carson. Hannah has worked for me since she first came to UNC. Again, I apologize for doubting who you were. It's been a little scary around here today."

"Don't give it another thought. You did exactly what I would have done in your shoes."

As he left, Laura pulled out a chair and took a seat. "Kylie, we have to talk."

Kylie shrugged. She slowly sat down on the other side of the table. "Hannah told me how nice you've been to her. She really thinks the world of you, Mrs. McKenzie."

"Laura. Call me Laura," she insisted. "You and Hannah are close friends, aren't you?"

Kylie drummed her fingers on the table. "Yes, ma'am. We've known each other forever. We've been best friends since we were midgets."

"And she's told you all about—"

"Yes. I was out of town over the holidays. By the time I got back, well, by then Jennifer had come back. See, the thing is, I hadn't even *known* that Hannah was seeing Jason,"

"I know."

Kylie continued. "Mrs. McKen—Laura—she's been really upset about all of this. I've never seen her like this before. She's usually pretty strong, but this has torn her apart." She paused. "And I—" She stopped again, looking Laura in the eye.

"What?" Laura waited. "What is it, Kylie?"

"I don't know. I just suddenly had the feeling I was betraying her by speaking so openly with you. What with you being Jason's mom and all."

Laura reached across the table and patted her hand. "I realize this is awkward for you. You don't even *know* me. But if we're going to help Hannah get through this, then you are going to have to trust me."

Kylie stared at their hands. "I would never do anything to hurt her."

"Nor would I. You have to believe me, Kylie. I only want to help her. If she told you how this whole thing started, then you know why I feel personally responsible for all of it."

Kylie laughed quietly. "Yeah, she told me. You rescued her from a crazy old man on Christmas Eve. Something about cranberries, I think. But she was crazy about you from the start. Both you and your husband. And Jason, of course."

Laura patted her hand again. "Then you must tell me how I can reach her. Is she at your place?"

Kylie's eyes grew wide. "Uh, no. Not exactly . . ."

"Well, I'm sure she's not at her apartment. The press has been disgraceful. I knew she would be smart enough to hide somewhere."

"Uh . . . yeah."

"Where is she, Kylie?"

Kylie looked away. Laura noticed the reddening of her face. "I promised her I wouldn't tell a soul."

"Please. You must tell me. I *have* to talk to her."

"I can't! I promised her. What kind of friend would I be if I broke my promise to the first person who asked?"

"But surely you can see why *I* need to talk to her!"

245

Kylie jumped up, feeling cornered. "I don't want to be rude. You have to believe that. But she's my best friend. And she's really upset . . . and . . . well, to be honest, she'd kill me. I'm pretty sure of it."

Laura laughed. "Somehow I doubt that."

"Have you ever seen Hannah when she's mad?"

Laura leaned head back. "I haven't. But come to think of it, she did tell us about some big football player who—"

"Tommy Joe! Oh, don't you love that story?" Kylie laughed. "You should see him on campus. That big ol' ox is the biggest wimp when he sees Hannah coming anywhere near him. It's too funny!"

Laura laughed along with her. "No, I guess I wouldn't want to see her really angry. But let's be honest—you know she won't be *that* mad. Please. I'm begging you to tell me where I can find her."

Kylie grew quiet, looking at Laura. She closed her eyes and took a deep breath. "I'm sorry. I just can't. I'm really sorry."

Laura lowered her head and closed her eyes. She nodded her head, her lips moving as she uttered the silent prayer.

"Laura, I'm really sorry."

She finished her prayer then looked up at the quizzical face across from her. She smiled and answered. "No, honey, I'm the one who's sorry. I have no business asking you to betray your confidence with Hannah. Trust is something to be taken very seriously, and I admire your loyalty. It's rare these days. But there's a promise I'm going to ask of you as well."

"Geez, all this pressure!" Kylie teased.

"You promise me if she is in trouble or needs help or *anything*, you'll call me." She pulled a pen out of her purse and wrote her cell phone number on a piece of paper. "Obviously this is a private number, so I know you'll keep it to yourself."

"Oh, of course. Here, let me give you my number too. In case you need to get a hold of me. That way you won't have to come by here if you don't have to." She scribbled her number and handed it to Laura.

Laura stood up, heading for the door. "Kylie, call me. Anytime. Please keep in touch with me. And if you talk to Hannah, give her my love, okay? And please ask her to call me. Will you do that for me?"

"Sure. It was nice to meet you, even if it's kind of a strange situation."

Laura smiled over her shoulder. "When we get all this behind us, I want you to come to the house. We'll get acquainted. Deal?"

"Deal."

Laura hurried through the store, tossing a quick wave at Jim as she passed the customer service counter. As she pulled her coat tighter around her, she walked through the automatic doors and out to the parking lot. A mischievous smile curled her lip. "Miss Kylie, you are a faithful friend," she said to herself. "But you are no match for my secret weapon . . ."

CHAPTER 22

"Just the man I was looking for."

Still stomping snow off his boots on the McKenzie's front porch, Sergio Cruz turned at the sound of Laura's voice. "Hi Mrs. M. You were looking for me?"

Her eyes trekked to his luggage on the porch. "Sergio? What are you doing?"

"I'm waiting for George. He's taking me to the airport."

"What? Where are you going?"

"I have some business down in Orlando. And to be honest, I was getting kind of restless so I thought I'd head down there and—"

"Well, you just call George back and tell him you changed your plans. I have a favor to ask."

"But—"

"No 'buts,' Sergio. I need your help."

"But—" He stopped, alarmed at her stern tone. He followed her into the house and into the kitchen.

She took off her coat, tossing it over the back of a chair. "Have a seat. I'll make us some tea."

He wasn't use to this side of Jason's mom. She was ordering him around in a tone bordering on belligerent.

She filled the teapot, then slammed it on the stove's burner. Sergio jumped, then quietly pulled out a chair and took a seat at the kitchen table.

Laura turned around, crossing her arms across her chest. "Here's the deal. I have to find out where Hannah is. Her best friend knows, but she's promised Hannah not to tell a soul. And, of course, I can appreciate that." She spoke in short, clipped sentences. "But I have to talk to her. *We* have to talk to her."

"We?"

"We." She stared him down. "Kylie wouldn't tell me, but she'll tell you."

"Who's Kylie?"

"Hannah's best friend."

Sergio rolled his eyes and avoided hers. "Laura, come on—"

"Sergio?"

He snapped to face her. "Yes, ma'am?"

"You know I wouldn't ask if it wasn't important."

"But—"

"Sergio?"

He let out a groan. "You sound just like my mother."

The teapot squealed and she turned for it. "I'm not surprised. I've had lots of people call me 'Mama Blue' so I'm entitled."

A lopsided grin tugged at the side of his mouth. "'Mama Blue?' Sweet." He laughed until she turned around. She was not smiling.

She poured the hot water over teabags in two large mugs. "I have Kylie's number. I need you to call her. With your charm, she'll spill the beans in no time."

"Now you sound like a *Mafia* Mama. You're quite the versatile little woman today, aren't you?" he teased.

No smile.

"Laura, come on. What am I supposed to say to this girl? 'Hola, this is Sergio. Where's Hannah?'"

"I'd expect a little more charisma, but sure . . . whatever it takes." She took a seat across from him. "I want you to call her, tell her who you are and insist on coming over to see her."

"What?!"

"There's a chance Hannah might be hiding out at her friend's apartment. If she is, she'll talk to you. I'm sure of it."

"Yeah, and chances are if she is, my call will only scare her off somewhere else."

"We'll take our chances."

"We?"

"You."

He nodded his head in resignation, studying her. Laura was like a second mother to him. She'd always been there for all the guys, but after the shooting, he felt a stronger bond to her than he'd ever known. Laura McKenzie was a saint. She and Frank had literally saved his soul last week. And there wasn't anything he wouldn't do for her. He melted at the gentleness hiding in her eyes behind the serious guise. "Jason never told me how stubborn you could be."

"This isn't stubborn. This is determined."

"Where's her number? And what's her name again?"

"Kylie. And she's adorable, Sergio. You'll love her."

Now it was his turn to level a stare at her. "AS IF I'm looking for 'adorable' right now?" He shook his head. "Thanks, but just for the record, I'm giving up women forever. I may become a priest."

Finally Laura laughed. "Oh Sergio, if you become a priest, church membership will skyrocket."

"Kylie, huh? I'll call her but I refuse to be charming."

She slid the piece of paper across the table, her smile lingering. "Don't sell yourself short. One look at that smile of yours and she'll tell us everything we want to know."

"We?" He folded the paper and stood up, stuffing it in his pocket.

She walked around the table then gave him a hug. "Love you, Sergio."

He hugged her back. "You drive a hard bargain, *'Mama Blue.'*"

"Call me after you've talked to Kylie. I'll be waiting."

The sun dropped slowly in the winter sky. Jason parked his Escalade in one of the garages and scuffed his way toward the house. "Anybody home?" he yelled, walking through the back door. No one answered. He assumed they were upstairs or gone. Just as well. He didn't feel like talking to anyone.

He threw his coat on the couch and headed downstairs. As he turned the corner of the staircase, he heard the clink of billiard balls below. *Hannah?* His heart pounded as he descended the stairs two at a time.

"Jennifer."

She looked up at him, a polite smile passing across her face. "Hi." She walked to the other side of the pool table and lined up a shot.

"I looked everywhere for you. I've been all over town, called your cell phone . . . I've been by here twice. Where were you?"

She took her shot, a striped ball in the side pocket. She didn't answer.

"Jennifer?"

"I was around." She continued her game.

He watched her. All afternoon he'd struggled with what to say once he found her. His stomach had been in knots for days. He headed for the bar. "Can I get you something to drink?"

Clink. Four ball in the corner pocket. "Water."

Jason grabbed a bottle for her and one for himself from the small refrigerator. He approached her, handing the chilled bottle to her. She turned slowly, reaching for it but not meeting his eyes. He leaned against the back of the sofa and took a long drink.

Clink. Another ball dropped in the side pocket. She was good. He'd forgotten.

He prayed for wisdom. Draining his bottle, Jason took it to the trash can and headed for the rack of cue sticks. He chalked the tip of one and passed her as she took another shot. She missed.

"Mind if I play?"

No response.

She shot again. Seven ball in the corner pocket. It was her last.

He racked the balls. "You break."

She chalked her stick and aimed at the triangle of shiny balls. *Whack.* Jason winced. The balls flew across the felt-covered table.

He aimed. His cue stick didn't come near the ball. He aimed again. He missed again. He cursed under his breath then immediately prayed a silent plea for forgiveness. She still didn't look at him. He aimed once again.

"There are rules and you're breaking them," she stated just as he made the shot.

It bounced across the table, nowhere close to a pocket. "Excuse me?"

"You're cheating." She moved to the other side of the table lining up her shot.

"Jennifer, what are—"

"You can only take one shot. If you scratch, you lose your turn."

"Oh." He watched her pocket the six ball.

"Sorry, I thought it was just a friendly little game of pool," he answered, attempting humor.

"Even 'friendly little games' should be played fair."

"My mistake. I'm sorry."

"Uh huh." She missed her shot. He noticed she clenched her jaw.

He lined up his shot and missed it. Leaving the stick on the table, he held up his hands. "Your shot."

"You don't have to pout."

"I'm not pouting." He picked up the stick again.

She lobbed the two in the side pocket. "Your shots are lousy. You used to be an excellent pool player."

Her tone was caustic. It grated on his nerves. "So I'm a little tense. It's been a long day."

"Oh? I hadn't noticed."

"Jennifer, stop with the games—no wait. I didn't say that." He hadn't intended to use the lyrics from one of their biggest hits.

"Cute, Jason. Did you want to sing the song or just recite the words?"

"Knock it off, will ya?"

"Or what? Are you going to smack me too? That reporter at the press conference has probably lined up fifteen attorneys by now. I'm surprised you haven't been subpoenaed yet."

He fired his shot, the eight ball slamming into the corner pocket. "Great," he muttered.

"Nice game. Shall we play another?" She stared at him with an expression completely devoid of feeling.

He jammed his stick back into the rack on the wall. The photographs on the wall caught his eye. There he was with Jennifer . . . a picture taken two years ago. He remembered the last time he looked at this picture. Christmas Eve. He was standing right here looking over Hannah's shoulder as she studied it. The fresh lavender fragrance of her hair swept through his memory.

Suddenly, he felt a presence behind him. He snapped out of his daydream.

"That was at the Grammys, wasn't it?" she whispered close behind him.

He turned to face her. There was so much pain in her eyes, those eyes he had loved for so long. Her clear blue eyes seemed to study his face, as though desperate to find . . . what? He reached out to gather her into his arms. She stiffened.

He took a long, hard breath and looked away. When he looked back at her, her face crumbled. A tear broke free, rushing down her flawless cheek.

"Oh Jason . . ."

The coarse whisper broke his heart. His throat tightened as he clutched her in his arms, burying his face in her silky hair. "I know, Jen. I know."

CHAPTER 23

Kylie tossed the empty bag of popcorn on the coffee table. She settled back in her rocking chair, pulling her pajama-covered legs up against her. A chill swept over her. She grabbed the quilt off the sofa and wrapped it around her then rocked, slow at first then faster.

The silent phone on the table beside her drew her attention. She shook her head and rocked faster. She snatched the remote control and surfed for a while. *Tired of sitcoms. Tired of news. Tired of television.* She clicked off the remote and tossed it back on the coffee table.

"Come here, Katy," she beckoned the calico cat rubbing its back against her legs. The Persian pounced into her lap with a loud purr as Kylie rubbed her behind the ears.

She stared at the phone again. *Jason McKenzie's mom. I met Jason McKenzie's mom. I met Laura. She told me to call her 'Laura.' We're on a first-name basis. Laura, Kylie. Kylie, Laura.* She grabbed the piece of paper with Laura's number on it. Not that she needed it. She already knew it by heart now.

"Kylie, when we get all this behind us, I want you to come to the house. We'll get acquainted. Deal?"

She could see it all in her mind . . .

They sat on expensive furniture, sipping tea from exquisite china cups. Delicate pastries rested on hand-painted plates. A butler in full dress tuxedo refilled her teacup. Laura wore a fine linen suit, tailored to fit her perfectly. Kylie was dressed—

She looked down at herself. Her navy plaid pajama bottoms clashed with the oversized orange t-shirt, the one with a big hole near the hem. She patted her wild hair, harnessed into two radical pig-tails and sticking out at crooked angles from her head. She wiped her mouth with the back of her hand, feeling the grease residue from her popcorn dinner.

"Yeah, me and Mrs. McKenzie having our own little tea party . . . riiiiight."

The phone rang, jolting her out of her thoughts. She jumped, Katy's claws digging into her thighs. "AHHH! *Katy!*"

She grabbed the phone and dropped it. "Ouuuuch! Ouch ouch ouch!" Kylie picked up the receiver, grimacing as she answered it. "Hello?"

"Hi, is this Kylie?"

"Yeah, that's me. No! I mean—who wants to know?"

"This is Sergio Cruz. Laura McKenzie gave me your number and—"

Kylie froze. Her mouth fell open.

"Hello?"

She could hear his voice. Hear the accent. *Sergio Cruz's voice. On my phone. Asking for* me*?* Then it hit her. No way. *It has to be the press or someone playing a prank.*

"Oh sure. Sergio Cruz. Right."

"No, really—"

"Uh huh." She rolled her eyes, angry that she'd almost fallen for it.

"This is Sergio. I swear it!"

"Sure it is, sweet cheeks. Then I guess I should tell you right here and now, *Sergi-O*, that I think you're the *hottest* member of *Out of the Blue.*"

I can play this game too, buster.

Laughter drifted through the receiver. "Is that a fact?"

"NO, you pervert! You're not Sergio Cruz. Besides, your lame attempt of an accent sounds ridiculous! So whoever you are, Mr. Paparazzi, just leave me—"

"Laura McKenzie talked to you this afternoon."

The words stopped her cold.

"She wanted to find out where Hannah Brooks is. You refused to tell her. Does any of this sound familiar?

No. No, no, no, it can't be . . . She swallowed hard.

He laughed. It was a great laugh. Even in her horror, she loved the laugh.

"Look, Kylie. I have to talk to you. Would it be okay if I stopped by?"

"No! I mean . . . oh, you can't. I'm not dressed and it's late and—" *I'm saying no to Sergio Cruz?*

"Kylie, I promised Laura I'd talk to you and it won't take but a minute. So if I could just come over—"

"Now?!" Her heart pounded in her chest. Her hand flew to her hair, her face . . .

"Yeah, in fact, I'm in your parking lot as we speak."

"WHAT?!"

"You've got to realize we have a lot of connections. I got your address because I was hoping you'd agree to see me. So what do you say?"

"Now?" Her nervous giggle eclipsed her response before she could stop it. *Just let me die right here, Lord. End the tragedy. Beam me up, God.* "Uh . . . well, uh—"

"Great. I'll be right up."

"NO! I mean, well, can you give me a few minutes?"

"Sure. No problem. Say about five minutes?"

"Make it ten."

"Ten it is. And thanks, Kylie. I really appreciate it. I'm looking forward to meeting you."

Kylie raced through her apartment, peeling off her pajamas, snatching up yesterday's cereal bowl, and the laundry basket of clean underwear waiting to be folded. She threw open three drawers looking for a fresh t-shirt then bolted for the closet to find her jeans.

She narrated her own warped-speed marathon with a running commentary. "Ten-minutes-oh-my-gosh-Sergio-Cruz-is-coming-HERE-right-now-what-does-he-want-what-should-I-say-my-hair-is-a-disaster-glory-these-jeans-are-so-tight-Hannah-how-could-you-do-this-to-me-where's-my-hairbrush-oh-gross-the-litter-box-stinks—"

The doorbell rang.

"Eeeeooooww!"

"Oh Katy! I'm so sorry!" The colorful ball of fur darted under the sofa as Kylie wrestled to zip up her jeans. She lowered her voice, continuing her tirade. "He's-only-a-regular-person-chill-out-Kylie . . . WHAT AM I SAYING?! I'll never pull this off! Never!"

It rang again.

"Okay. I can do this. I can." She charged toward the door. Just before answering, she stopped, yanked the bands off her pigtails then bent over to rake her fingers through her uncontrollable red curls. The blood rushed to her head making her feel even dizzier. She stood back up, hand on the wall to steady herself, then nonchalantly opened the door.

Sergio Cruz pulled off his sunglasses as he looked at her from beneath the curved bill of his baseball cap. His eyes popped.

What? What's he looking at? Kylie patted her hair which seemed to be the focus of his attention, then followed his eyes as they landed on her face. Her hand instinctively went to her cheek. She could feel the heat. *No, please, no. I must be eight shades of purple.*

"Kylie?"

"Uh, hi! Sergio! How-are-you-I'm-Kylie-come-on-in-can-I-get-you-something-to-drink-would-you-like-a-snack-or-maybe—"

"Whoa! Hold up, there. Take a breath, okay?"

"Oh. Sorry! I guess I'm a little nervous here. Sorry. I'll try to calm down. Here, watch—" She blew out a quick breath. "See? Breathing. All better. Now. Please. Come in. Have a seat." She rambled on, turning to point him toward the sofa. As he approached the plaid sofa, they *both* noticed the package of feminine hygiene products sitting there atop an empty Wal-Mart bag.

"Whoa!" she yelped, turning to grab the package behind her back. "Second thought, you can just have a seat over there in that chair. It's comfortable. You'll like it. No problem." She faked a cough.

"Are you always this hyper?" He laughed as she tucked the package under an afghan.

He sat down and pulled off his cap, running his hand through his dark curly hair. The tiny diamond stud on his ear caught her eye. But it was his eyes that grabbed her. She stood there, swimming in those dark brown bedroom eyes . . .

"Aren't you going to sit down?"

She fell back onto the sofa, then tucked her legs beneath her, never losing eye contact with him. She started to say something then stopped. He was smiling at her. *I swear his eyes just twinkled. And look at those perfect white teeth... those dimples... and those eyes... those amazing eyes...* A long sigh escaped but she didn't care. Not one bit. She felt the grin slide across her face.

"Kylie, it's really nice to meet you."

She grinned some more. *I love how he says my name—Kah-lee. With the emphasis on the second syllable. Kah-lee. It just rolls off his tongue with that delicious accent...*

"Laura said you and Hannah are—OUCH! ¿Qué diablos?!"

"Katy! Get down!" Kylie scolded as she sprang toward him. The kitten was climbing up Sergio's leg. She tried to pry the feline loose but Katy scurried around him, tunneling behind Sergio's back. "Uh, well... I don't want to—"

He laughed. "It's okay, don't worry about her. I was just a little shocked, that's all. She's fine. I love cats. As long as she doesn't claw me to death."

"Are you sure? Because I can put her in my bedroom."

"No, she's fine. Really."

Katy proceeded to burrow all over him, finally crawling up on his chest and tucking her head inside his jacket. He laughed at her, stroking her patchwork coat.

Kylie sat back down. "You know, that's really incredible. She doesn't usually like strangers. Normally, she hides until they leave." She smiled at the sight of him with her cat. *Sergio Cruz. Petting my Katy. I wonder where my camera is.*

"Kylie, I apologize for barging in on you at such short notice and all, but Laura begged me to come over and talk with you."

"She's persistent, isn't she? She isn't at all what I expected."

Sergio laughed again. "She's persistent. That she is. I was headed out the door to the airport when she lassoed me into this—" He darted his eyes back to her. "I mean— well, not that she had to—"

"It's okay. I met her. You don't have to explain."

"Sorry."

There's that smile again. "You were leaving town?"

"Yeah, I was making a quick run down to Florida to—"

"Florida?" She blinked her eyes wide. "Why were you going to Flor—" She caught herself, but it was too late. She watched it register on his face. He hadn't missed the slip.

He chuckled. "So Hannah's in Florida, is she?"

His enormous smile melted her like a hair dryer set on high blowing on a bowl of Mint Chocolate Chip. "Hannah? Oh, no, I was asking about you. *You're* going to Florida. Why are you going to Florida? *Where* are you going in Florida? Florida's nice. I love Florida."

"Kylie?"

"Great beaches, great sunshine, great theme parks— what part of Florida did you say you were going to?"

"I didn't say."

"Oh."

Silence. His smile broadened.

She smiled in return then scratched her eyebrow, hoping to avoid his gaze.

"Orlando."

"Orlando! I love Orlando."

"Kylie, where is she?"

"So will you be going to Disney while you're there? Or Universal Studios? Sea World? I hear there's a new—"

"Kylie?"

"Yes?"

"Is Hannah in Orlando?"

"No! No, Hannah is not in Orlando. No."

"But she's in Florida?"

"I didn't say that."

"You didn't have to."

Kylie jumped up. "Sergio, are you sure you don't want something to—"

"Actually I do. But let's go out. Here—" He tossed her the keys. "I can't exactly just walk into a restaurant with all that's happened, but how about we hit the Sonic? You like drive-ins?"

Her face brightened, relieved to have the conversation interrupted. "I love drive-ins! But why do you want *me* to drive?"

"If I drive, the waitress brings out our food, and suddenly the Sonic is crawling with lunáticos. It's been a wild week for us."

Kylie grabbed her coat as they headed for the door. "No problem, I'll drive. You've got insurance, right?"

The cold air sent chills down her back but it felt good to get out of the confinement of her apartment. His questions had cornered her like a caged animal. He led the way to a sleek black convertible coupe.

"Oh my! You're gonna let me drive THIS?"

"Why not? You have a driver's license, don't you?"

"No, it's just a really nice car—a reeeeally nice car."

"It belongs to the McKenzies. I think it's one of Frank's, so you'll have to take it up with him if you wreck it."

Her nervous laughter fell flat as she tried to swallow. "Whatever you say." Kylie climbed into the compact, the soft black leather seats as comfortable as an easy chair. "This is awesome. Oh, I could *so* get used to this. Whoa. My seat is warm. Did you—"

"Heated seats. Just so you know." He nodded as if affirming the fact. Sergio slammed the door on his side, fastening his seat belt as Kylie did hers. "Just take it slow and easy and you'll be fine."

"Look at all these—" A siren wailed as she accidentally hit the panic button on the key.

"THAT WOULD BE THE SECURITY SYSTEM! HERE—" He grabbed the key from her and pressed the button again.

"Sorry. What is all this stuff?"

"All the bells and whistles. I have one of these back home so I'm used to it. But just don't touch anything that—" The wipers began beating a frenzied pattern back and forth with a generous mist of water shooting across the windshield. "Those, of course, are the wipers. Let's hope it doesn't freeze or you won't be able to see." He laughed, shaking his head.

"Okay. Okay, I can do this. Here's the ignition. And here's the four on the floor. Okay, let's go for it."

She eased the car out of the parking space, then shifted to forward and—*SCREEEEEECH!!!*

"¡Tranquila! Slow down! Slow down!"

She jammed her foot on the brakes, jolting them hard against their seat belts. "Sorry."

"Are you sure you know how to drive?"

"Of course! It's just that I'm not used to such a fancy—"

The car peeled out again. Sergio let his head fall back on the headrest, letting out a loud yell. "¡Ayúdame, Jesús!" he shouted, laughing.

"I'm guessing that was a prayer?"

"You could say that." He rattled off another long line of Spanish then laughed again.

They made it to Sonic in one piece and Kylie guided the car into a remote slot at the far end of the drive-in. She put the car in park and turned, giving her passenger a triumphant smile. "See? I did it! We made it safe and—"

"And that would be the top going down."

"Oh no! I'm sorry! Here, let me . . . there! Here it comes back up. No problem." Nervous giggle.

"Kylie, do you live your whole life like this? We've only been together for about—" He looked at his watch. "—twenty minutes now, and frankly, I'm exhausted. And yes, that would be the windshield wipers again. Kylie! Turn it off! I'm getting soaked!"

Finally, the top returned securely in place, the wipers were turned off, and Kylie slumped back in her seat. "I'm *so* embarrassed. I wanted to make such a good impression on you and look at me. I feel like Lucy here." She buried her face in her hands.

"Luuuccccy? You got some 'splainin' to do!" Sergio mimicked.

"Oh, Riiiiiccckkky . . . . waaaaaaah!"

"Now, Luuuccccy, stop that cryin' . . ."

They laughed until they hurt and Kylie wiped tears from her eyes. "I can't believe this! Really. Even for me, this is *most* embarrassing."

Sergio let out a long sigh. "Oh, don't be so hard on yourself. To tell you the truth, it feels great to laugh. I haven't laughed—well, it's been a long time." He winked at her and her heart skipped a beat.

When she and Hannah were younger, they used to swoon at Sergio's signature wink in interviews and music videos. He was a pro at it.

And to think this one was just for me.

They ordered Cokes and a large order of fries to share. When the attendant brought their order, Kylie was pleased to find the right button to roll down the car window. She tossed a smug expression toward Sergio and discovered him huddled against the passenger door, the bill on his cap pulled low.

She handed him his drink. "Here Sergio—uh, KEN! Here, Ken . . . here's your drink, KEN." She shot the attendant a fake smile. "That's Ken. Uh, here . . . keep the change. Thank you. Bye."

"Smooth," he teased. "You're really good at being discreet."

"Hey, it's my first time! You should have seen Hannah when I—" She winced.

"When you what?"

"Nothing."

"Kylie, you can forget the pretense. I know you know where she is. And you and I both know you're going to tell me." He stuffed a couple of French fries in his mouth.

"Oh yeah?"

"Sure. So why don't you just 'splain it all to me, Luuuccccy, and we can get on with it."

Her brow wrinkled quizzically as she took a sip of her Coke. "Get on with what?"

"It was a figure of speech."

"Oh."

"So she's in Florida and you have her number . . . and . . .?"

She bit into a fry.

"And this is where you fill in the rest of the sentence, Kylie."

I love how he says my name. I could listen to that for the rest of my life . . . She snatched another couple of fries.

"You're hogging the fries."

"I'm hungry," she mumbled.

He grabbed the bag away from her. "Nope. No more. Not until you talk."

She wiped her hands on a napkin. "And I thought Laura was stubborn."

"Taught me everything I know." He smiled.

"Sergio, do you really expect me to break my promise and—"

"Yes."

"—tell you where she is—"

"Yes."

"—when she specifically asked me *not* to tell any of you?"

"She told you not to tell *me*?"

"Well, she—"

"She actually said to you, 'Kylie, don't tell Sergio where I am.' She said that to you?"

She took a long sip of Coke until the straw squawked.

"Ah ha! She didn't, did she? So you can tell me. Problem solved."

"Sergio! Stop making this so—"

HONK!

"And that would be the horn you're leaning on, Kylie."

She pulled her elbows back from the steering wheel. "Good grief! This thing is booby-trapped."

"Face it, woman, you are some kind of wicked behind that wheel."

"Oh yeah? I kinda like the sound of that . . . say it again," she flirted.

"Not until you tell me."

She shifted in the seat, careful not to touch anything, tucking her leg beneath her. She tilted her head and studied him. *Why does he have to be so handsome? Why do his teeth have to be so straight? Why are his eyes so sexy . . .*

"Kylie?"

Kah-lee. Kah-lee, Kah-lee, Kah-lee. Who knew I had such a sexy name?

"Hannah. Where. Is. She. We're all worried sick about her. We got really attached to her over the last few weeks. When Jackson got shot and we were all together at the hospital—I mean, she was there for Jason, y'know? She got him through it. But when that press conference exploded and then they plastered her face all over the news—"

"I know all this, Sergio," Kylie interrupted, surprised at the sharp tone of her voice. "I was there. I saw her face on the news. I was there when she watched the news reports with Jason *and Jennifer* all over the screen. I was there when she got so scared she was literally shaking. I was there when the news van came roaring into her parking lot. I was with her through that, Sergio. And I've seen how Jason *broke her heart!* I've had to watch my best friend die inside because of all of you." She stopped, short of breath from the outburst. She looked out her window, not wanting him to see her tears.

"Hey, I'm so sorry, Kylie." He reached out, turning her chin toward him with his finger. "I didn't mean to hurt you."

She closed her eyes, embarrassed to let him see her get so emotional. One minute they were laughing and now huge crocodile tears were spilling down the side of her face. He caught the one nearest him. "I don't know what to say."

"It's just that . . . Sergio, you've got to realize I've known Hannah almost my entire life. She's like a sister to me. And you guys, you all have known her, what—maybe two or three *weeks*? When I left for the holidays, she was bummed about having to work but she was okay. And when I got back she was devastated. I've never seen her like that before.

"So when Laura—and now you—ask me to just forget all that and tell you the one thing she asked me *not* to tell you, well, it's not something I take lightly."

Sergio studied Kylie. Her face was so fair, sprinkled with tiny freckles. He'd never known anyone with that many freckles before. But somehow they were an integral part of who she was. They set her apart, made her special. And they totally matched her personality. What a piece of work she was.

He noticed the laugh lines that crinkled when she smiled. Her shining green eyes. And her hair . . . not even JT ever tried a red that shade! But he had to admit she was cute in her own special way. There was something so unique, so refreshing about her.

Then he remembered that he was no longer interested in women or relationships or getting to know anyone new. He forced himself back to the task.

"First of all, I'm sorry, Kylie. We blew it. What can I say? It was out of line for Laura and me to corner you. Okay?"

She nodded her head without looking at him.

"But you have to believe me when I tell you we are *only* interested in Hannah's well-being. We're concerned about her. We've played the game for years with this kind of notoriety and scandals and the wild chases with the paparazzi. It's not fun and it can be very frightening. Especially to someone who is unfamiliar with all of it.

"But even beyond all that, there's an element of danger. I mean, everyone remembers what happened to Princess Diana. That's the extreme edge where this kind of thing can go. They don't know when to draw the line. They don't know when to stop."

Sergio grew quiet, looking out his window. He traced his finger in the fog that steamed it. "When my kid brother was dying a few years ago, the press was unbelievable. They had no respect for what we were going through. It was horrible. And I've never forgotten it. If it wasn't for what I do, who I am as a 'celebrity,' my family would have been spared a lot of added grief. There's a lot of guilt that goes with that territory."

"That must have been very difficult for you. Especially on top of losing him."

He turned to face her. "Kylie, the deal is, I'm not trying to paint some dark, mystical picture here or be morbid or anything. It's just that we all care about Hannah. And we feel like she's 'out there,' and away from the kind of protection we can give her until this thing blows over."

She leaned her head against the top of the steering wheel. He smiled, grateful no horns or sirens went off. She was struggling. It was obvious.

"So Kylie. Will you tell me? Will you tell us where she is?"

Hannah spread her towel over the lounge chair on the beach. It was the last in a long row that lined the beach in front of the quaint hotel. She took a seat and leaned back, feeling the warm Florida sun against her skin. She reached over for the steaming mug of coffee she had set on the empty chair beside her. It tasted wonderful. *Why do things always taste better outdoors?*

The gentle afternoon surf pounded quietly against the shore in a rhythm that soothed her to the bone. She inhaled deeply, loving the scent of the salt air. The lazy sound of sea gulls in the distance relaxed her. She peeked over her sunglasses just in time to see a line of pelicans gliding in perfect formation overhead.

Oh God, thank you. Thank you for letting me come here.

The flight from North Carolina was the worst she'd ever experienced. The plane was packed and she got stuck in the middle seat between two rather large passengers. Her elbows were smashed against her body as theirs consumed the armrests and then some. She tried to sleep but couldn't get comfortable. The man in the window seat had actually wheezed when he slept.

Finally, she made it to Tampa. She waited in a long queue for her rental car. Fortunately, most of these tourists headed east on Interstate 4 toward Orlando. She broke free of the pack and headed across the Howard Franklin Bridge toward Clearwater then south to her destination. It was late when she arrived at the hotel, but

271

the clerk was accommodating. Her cottage was tucked around a corner, away from the courtyard and pool area, but facing the beach. Perfect.

It was after midnight when she finally crashed. She hadn't awakened until almost noon. She knew she should have called Kylie, but she was desperate to get out on the beach.

As if she just needed to *breathe*.

Now, she welcomed the warm air into her lungs and felt her muscles begin to loosen one by one.

Suddenly, a shadow crossed her face. She opened her eyes, surprised to see a silhouette above her. The sunshine blinded her to anything but the dark outline of a person standing over her. Her heart pounded. She held her hand up to block out the sun, but it didn't help.

"Excuse me, but do you mind?" She hoped the panic in her voice wasn't obvious.

She felt someone touch her hair. A shiver ran down her back as she gasped, yanking her head away from this intruder's touch.

"Well, Hannah, it seems you can run, but you can't hide."

CHAPTER 24

"I can't believe it. I cannot *believe* she would do this to me!"

"I don't see why you're so—"

"Shut up! Just shut up and leave me alone, Sergio!" Hannah yelled, kicking sand at him, as she stomped down the beach.

He looked down at the legs of his jeans and his Nikes, now covered with sand. "Well, gee, Hannah, it's nice to see you too. I come all this way and *this* is the thanks I get?" He looked up and noticed she was already several yards down the beach from him. He brushed off his jeans and rushed after her.

Hannah turned and stopped dead in her tracks to face him, her hands planted on her hips. "What are you doing here anyway? What possible reason could you have to come find me?"

Sergio studied the anger in her eyes. A slow mischievous smile spread across his face. "I was in the neighborhood?"

She snapped her head to one side, still staring him down. "Right. Of course you were. Sergio, be honest with me—do I *look* like a moron? You were 'in the neighborhood'? Like you went out for a stroll in Chapel Hill and just happened to end up here?"

If looks could kill, he'd be a dead man.

"Look, Hannah—" He reached out to touch her shoulder. She jerked out of his reach. He dropped his head and let out a frustrated sigh. "Okay, I know you made Kylie promise not to tell anyone where you were, but—"

"Don't even *mention* her name to me." She turned on her heel and stomped off again.

Sergio shook his head but rushed to catch up with her. "Will you stop this? Will you stop running off like this? I need to talk to you! Can't you just chill for a minute and—"

"I trusted her and she totally betrayed me. I can't believe it! Doesn't *anyone* know how to keep their mouth shut anymore? Is everyone—oh, never mind. What do I care," she mumbled as her strides grew faster.

Sergio grabbed her elbow and spun her around to face him again. "Knock it off, Hannah. Enough of the pity party, okay?"

She stared him down. "How dare you!"

"How dare *me?* Did it ever occur to you that there are a lot of people very concerned about you?"

He released her arm and rubbed his face, then reached back up to knead the muscles in his neck. "Look, Hannah, the only reason I'm here—the *only* reason is because we were so worried about you."

He didn't miss the slow arch of her eyebrows or the misting in her eyes.

"*We?*"

The simple question cut through him, the inference clear. He tore his eyes away to look out across the water. In his periphery, he saw her fold her arms across her chest and walk away again, this time at a much slower pace.

"Hannah, it was Laura who asked me to come find you. Not—well, I'm sorry if I misled you to think . . . I meant . . ."

She continued walking, her face turned away from him.

He fell in step beside her. "But we were all concerned. With all the press pouncing on you, we were afraid you might get—"

"It's okay. You don't have to explain."

"I don't?"

"No."

"So you're not still mad?"

She shot a sideways glance at him. Her eyes smiled even if her mouth didn't.

"And as for Kylie, don't be too hard on her. She didn't have a chance."

"And just what is that supposed to mean?"

"What can I say? I put on the charm. And I twisted her arm. Pretty hard, as a matter of fact."

"So you actually *met* her? Or was this verbal arm-twisting done over the phone?"

He threw his head back laughing. "Oh Hannah, you have to tell me what planet you found her on!"

"Yeah, you met her," she answered knowingly. "Kylie is one of a kind."

"Maybe so, but exactly what 'kind' is that? From the moment she opened her door—I mean, ¡ella es muy loca!"

"¿*Muy loca?*" Hannah teased back. "Crazy? Who, Kylie?"

"You would not believe what that girl did to Frank's car."

He told her the story, describing in great animation his entire encounter with her best friend. The more he got into it, the more she appeared to relax. With each new description of Kylie's eccentric antics, the more easily her laughter spilled. She finally stopped walking, dropping down onto the sand as she continued to query him on his first close encounter with Kylie Reynolds.

He followed Hannah's lead, sitting down beside her. He leaned back, resting on his elbows, still chuckling. When their laughter dissipated, he exhaled, leaning his head back to bask in the warm sunshine. As Hannah slowly regained her composure, she laid back on the sand, folding her arms behind her head and crossing her feet at the ankles.

"Oh, Sergio . . . how did it all get so insane?"

They listened quietly to the lapping of the waves at their feet, enjoying the warm January sun. The silence in their conversation was as soothing as their surroundings. "I don't know, to be honest," he answered sleepily, squinting at her. "One minute, I'm off in Hawaii for the holidays, then my psycho-stalker girlfriend shoots Jackson. In a split second, everything went totally out of control."

"One minute, I'm minding my own business, just doing my job at the store," Hannah added, "then Laura McKenzie comes through my line and everything goes out of control for me too. Suddenly, I find myself in this . . . this fantasy with Jason and you and the rest of the guys. And the next thing I know, I'm sitting on top of a picnic table at a park, eating Krispy Kremes with Jason." She paused, raising her eyes to look up at the deep blue sky above her. "And he's pouring his heart out to me, and . . . I just got so scared."

He turned on his side, facing her. He remained silent, hoping she would continue.

"It all happened too fast. *Way* too fast. And I felt like, if he said one more word that day . . . about us . . . that it would somehow, I don't know . . . like it might *jinx* what we had. I know it sounds silly, but from the first night I met him, I had this constant fear that at any moment, I would close my eyes and open them only to find him gone. The whole incredible experience would just vanish like some cruel, disappearing dream.

"We were sitting there on that picnic table in the park. Jason was . . . I don't know, exactly. Pouring out his heart, as if he might—" She closed her eyes against the sting. "And that's the moment we got the call about Jackson. Sergio, we thought he had died. And then suddenly, we're at the hospital—and there's Jennifer. And my worst fears came true. Jason literally vanished right before my eyes."

Sergio was quiet for several moments before responding. "I've known Jason McKenzie a long time, Hannah. And I can swear to you—he never meant to hurt you. You have to believe that."

"I don't know what to think, Sergio. That's why I had to get away." She sat up, brushing the sand off her arms.

"And you thought running away would somehow help?"

The fire was back in her eyes. "I suppose you think I should have stayed in Chapel Hill with that feeding frenzy by the press? No *thank* you."

"But at least we can give you some protection there. We can hire a security team to keep the press away from you. Coming down here all alone was a big risk."

"It seemed like the thing to do at the time. I'm not a professional at this like you all are."

Sergio sat up, brushing the sand off his clothes. "Well, beyond the hassle with the press, I know you can't run away from your problems. I learned that up close and personal through my nightmare with Liza. More than I ever wanted to learn, believe me. Laura and Frank helped me get through all that. They showed me how important it is to face up to your problems, your disappointments, your anger—whatever—and turn it around for something good."

Hannah folded her arms over her bent knees and rested her head against them. "Laura and Frank are so strong in their faith. It's like some incredible anchor that holds them, y'know? I've never known anyone who lived out their faith like that."

"I know. I wish I had that kind of faith." He stood up, holding his hand out to help her up. They began walking along the water's edge again. "And y'know what?"

"What?"

"You're right about that anchor. I think you ought to let them help you get through this thing just like they helped me."

"I don't know, Sergio. It's different. I was in love with—" She stopped, the words hanging heavy between them. "Jason and I were . . ." She looked out across the water. "It's an entirely different situation."

"But Frank and Laura are your friends now too, Hannah. Just like we all are. This wasn't all some fly by night experience. You're part of us now. When I first met you, it was as if you'd been one of us forever. *Familia.* And I've got to tell you—that's very rare. *Extremely* rare. Normally, we're extraordinarily cautious about 'outsiders' for obvious reasons. But you were totally different. And all I'm trying to say is, we want to help you. I know I do. And Laura does. And I know she can."

She seemed to dismiss his comments. "So Sergio, you said you were in the neighborhood. Was that just a line?"

He laughed easily. "Actually, yes and no. I've got some meetings in Orlando tomorrow. But I would have come even if there were no meetings. Laura can be rather persuasive."

"Well, regardless how you got here, I'm glad you came. I'll admit I was furious when I first saw you here. But it was also nice to see a familiar face." She stopped and turned to face him, taking his hand in hers. "I can't believe you cared enough to go out of your way to find me here."

He squeezed her hand tightly in his. "When are you gonna get it through that stubborn head of yours that we care about you? Huh?" When she returned his smile, he pulled her into a tender hug and felt her relax against him almost immediately.

Sergio pushed a strand of hair out of her eyes and winked at her. "Enough of all this serious stuff. I'm starving. What do you say we find some lunch somewhere?"

They turned around, heading back to the motel. He threw his arm over her shoulder in a brotherly gesture and she laced her arm around his waist. "Sergio?"

"Yeah?"

"Thanks."

He roughed her hair up. "You're welcome, Hannah. De nada."

CHAPTER 25

"Are you ready, Jackson?"

"That's an understatement. I want to go home. To *my* home."

Alli stuffed the last of Jackson's belongings into the duffel bag and heaved it onto the cart supplied by the hospital. "I know, but just be thankful the doctors are letting you go to the McKenzie's for a few days. That's almost like home, right?" She planted a kiss on his forehead.

"I know, I know," he lamented, moving toward the obligatory wheelchair. "Why can't I just walk out of here? I feel like some old geezer in this thing."

"Jackson, enough with the whining." She handed him another bag to hold on his lap. "Are you still sure you want to donate all this stuff?"

They looked around the room, overflowing with flowers, balloons, and stuffed animals. "Yeah, I'm sure. The kids in pediatrics will get a lot more use out of these than I will. Except for MJ's autographed basketball. You packed it, right?"

"Don't worry. I got everything you want to keep. Including the flowers from William and Kate. I'm going to have them pressed. For a keepsake."

"I've gotta watch you like a hawk. I take a bullet and you're flirting with royalty. What's wrong with this picture?" He tossed her a lopsided grin. "And did I mention he's married now? Oh yeah, I believe I did. And boy, is that one *hot* princess."

She planted a fist on her hip. "Jackson."

He grabbed her hands and pressed them to his lips. "I'm just kiddin', babe."

She surveyed him curiously. "Are you okay?"

"I don't know. I feel so *gritchy*. I want to get out of this place. I want to go home. I want to go for a ride in my boat. I want to—"

"—take care of yourself so you don't wind up back in here. All that will come. But your recovery is serious business."

"I know, Alli. We've been all through this already."

"Yeah, at least a hundred times and I still don't think you realize how important it is. You've got to be totally faithful to do all the exercises and take all your medications, and—"

"Excuse me, Nurse Ratched. Can we just go?"

"That's just what I'm talking about! You keep joking about all of this like it's some kind of game. You can't fool around with it, Jax. There's too much at stake. You are so *lucky* to be alive," she whispered.

He took a deep breath. "I don't think luck had anything to do with it."

She attempted a smile, understanding his meaning. "You're absolutely right. And I don't think any of us will ever be the same because of it." She cleared her throat and stood back up. "Okay, let's blow this joint, whad'ya say?"

The endless crowd of well-wishers gathered to see off the celebrity patient. Jackson was gracious to all of them, signing autographs, stopping for others to take photographs of him with nurses, doctors, and other patients, especially those from pediatrics. His parents urged the entourage to keep moving, obviously worried how exhausting this would be for their son.

Finally, loaded in the limousine along with his parents at a back entrance in the parking garage, they headed out for the McKenzie estate. Alli sat beside him, holding his hand in hers. His parents sat on one of the side seats.

"So where's Jason and Sergio?" he asked. Gevin, Marissa, JT, and Tracey had stopped by earlier to visit before they left the hospital.

"Laura said Sergio flew down to Orlando on business," his mother answered. "She said he'd be back in a day or so to see you."

"I'm sure Jason will be at the house," Alli added.

Jackson leaned over to whisper in her ear. "What's going on with him and Jennifer?"

Alli shrugged and looked out the window. "I don't know. He's been really quiet the last couple of times I've talked to him. Very evasive, y'know?"

"He ever mention Hannah?"

"No. Not a word." Even the sound of Hannah's name tugged at her heart. She and Hannah had become good friends in the brief time they'd known each other. Alli missed her. "No one's heard from her either. I can't imagine what she's feeling right now. But then, I have to admit it's been great seeing Jennifer again. I've always liked her. I don't know, Jackson. I have such mixed feelings about everything."

He leaned his head on her shoulder. The conversation died as they drove through the streets of

Chapel Hill. Soon, his steady breathing told her he'd fallen asleep.

Ten minutes later, Bob woke him. "Jackson, wake up. Take a look at this."

"What's going on?" he asked sleepily.

They had just turned the corner onto the McKenzie's street. For as far as they could see, the street was lined with people. Kids, teenagers, adults—all assembled to greet him.

"Unbelievable," he whispered.

"Jackson—look," Alli pointed to a banner held high above the heads of the crowd.

"WE LOVE YOU, JACKSON! WELCOME HOME!"

Colorful balloons danced above the heads of the crowd as they waved and screamed and cheered the passing vehicle. A handful of policemen were on hand to maintain control, but these people were not here to cause trouble. They were here out of love.

After the emotional press conference, Alli thought Jackson had surely cried the last of his tears, but she was wrong. As a single tear trickled down his face, he smiled at the scene surrounding them. Alli laughed through her own tears, hugging him.

Bob handed his wife a handkerchief as she wept openly. "Reminds me of that unforgettable sea of well-wishers that night outside the hospital," he remembered, his voice husky.

But Jackson had missed all that. And while they had described the scene to him over and over, in precise detail, Alli knew it could never have prepared him for seeing this with his own eyes.

Finally, as they neared the gated entrance to the McKenzie's, Jackson regained his voice. Well, almost. "I can't believe it. I had no idea . . ."

Bob Greer smiled. "Well, son, now you do."

"Are you gonna eat that?" Sergio stabbed a fork into Hannah's pie. She'd been toying with it, but hadn't taken a single bite. He sliced a healthy portion and consumed it. "Mmm, this is *delicious*."

She nodded, amused by his antics. In the past few days she had grown accustomed to Sergio Cruz's unpretentious ways. She wasn't the slightest surprised by anything he did. She smiled, sliding the dish across the table to him. "I'm not really hungry, I guess," she teased. "Go ahead, hot shot. Help yourself."

"Really? If you're sure," he asked, already devouring most of the hot pastry. "Thanks, Hannah. But you didn't answer my question."

"What question?"

"About going back with me." He took a sip of coffee between bites, then wiped his mouth with the cloth napkin. Their waiter stopped by, refilling their cups.

"If we keep drinking this coffee, we won't need a plane. We can just *walk* back and probably make it there in a couple hours." She laughed quietly.

"Like I need something else to get me wired," he added, finishing the pie with a flourish. "But we won't have to walk. I told you—I'm flying back in the private jet. I want you to come with me. You'll love it. All the comforts of first class and none of the hassles of flying commercial. Basically, anytime we need to get somewhere, the record company makes it available to us. It's perfect for quick trips like this."

"I don't know, Sergio. I'm not sure I'm ready to go back."

"Look, Hannah—your classes start Monday. You told me yesterday you didn't want to miss any classes. Sounds to me like the perfect excuse to get your life back on track."

She cradled the warm cup in her hands. "You make it sound so easy."

"It's gonna be rough. There's no way around it. But you can handle it. We've had plenty of time to talk through it . . . you've had a chance to relax and bolster your courage a little. It won't be easy, but I know you can do it." His grin was crooked as he smiled across the table at her. "I've seen some pretty serious backbone surfacing the last couple of days. I think you *are* ready."

"Sergio, how can I ever thank you for this?"

"For what? Dinner? No sweat. Besides, I ate your pie."

"You know that's not what I meant. I'm talking about you coming down here like this."

"I told you—I was in the neighborhood."

"Stop it!" She laughed. "I'm trying to be serious here, okay?"

"Okay, okay—I'm sorry. But it wasn't like some major strain to spend time with you, Hannah. I've enjoyed it. I mean that. And besides, I think it's been rather therapeutic."

"How so?"

"Nothing gets you out of yourself like helping someone else with their problems." He shook his head, his dark eyes dancing. "Laura is so devious. She practically roped me into this whole thing—first with Kylie, then with you—but all along I think she knew that *I* needed the help almost as much as you did.

"Think about it. She had to know if I was helping you through all this, I'd be distancing myself from my own pain. And she was absolutely right. Somehow, I think we *both* learned a lot from each other the last couple of days."

He reached across the table, extending his hand toward her. Hannah returned his warm smile, allowing him to take hold of her hand. The gesture seemed to seal the friendship they'd found together.

"So it's settled," Sergio announced, standing to leave. "We'll stop back by the motel and get your things, then we'll fly back to Chapel Hill."

A shiver trickled down Hannah's back as she stood up, taking his hand again. "If you say so. I can't say I'm ready to go home, but I know you're probably right." He led her through the restaurant, threading their way through the tables toward the entrance and carefully avoiding any eye contact on the way out.

Alli smiled at those around her. There was no place she'd rather be at this moment in time.

The McKenzie dining room was expansive but charming. An enormous chandelier with lights turned low reigned over the long linen-covered table, adorned with fine china and elegant crystal. Candles glowed, gently casting a sense of warmth among the guests. Fresh flowers cascaded along the center of the table. Those that lined the table were visibly happy this night as they celebrated Jackson's recovery.

"Laura, you did it again." Jackson patted his stomach. "I'm stuffed and every bite was delicious. It's a good thing we're leaving tomorrow or they'd have to cart me out of here like they did the last time. On a stretcher."

Alli popped him on his arm with her cloth napkin. "Jackson! I can't believe you said that!"

The laughter erupted in agreement. "Keep it up, Jax, and it won't be the food that'll getcha—it'll be Alli," JT teased. "That was a righteous snap, woman!"

Jackson feigned injury to his arm. "Got that right, JT. Do you see how mean she is to me? Hey, Laura, could you use some domestic help? I'll leave her here on maid duty if she doesn't cut me some slack."

Jackson's parents enjoyed the exchange, pleased to see their son's sense of humor back in full gear. "Sorry, Jackson," Bob said, "but Alli's the best thing that ever happened to you. Besides, she keeps you out of *our* hair."

"What hair?" Jackson shot back.

Bob raised his hands in defense then ran a hand over his thinning head of hair. "*This* hair, thank you very much."

Gevin nodded toward Jackson. "I think he's back to his old obnoxious self, don't you, Jason?"

Jason swallowed a bite of his dinner. "I think I liked him better when he was in the coma. Nice and *quiet.*"

"You guys are merciless," Tracey yelled. "Rissa, are you sure you want to marry into this—"

"Oh, she's sure all right," Gevin interrupted before Marissa could open her mouth. "In fact, she is *so* sure—" he paused, grinning from ear to ear as he put his arm over her shoulder, "that she helped me set a date for the wedding."

Congratulations rounded the table as everyone shared in the moment.

"And check this out." Gevin lifted her hand to show the striking diamond marquis solitaire on her left hand.

"Oh Marissa, it's breathtaking!" Laura said, taking a closer look.

Alli jumped up to give her a hug. "Rissa! It's gorgeous! I'm so happy for you!" She looked over at Jackson, warmed by the understanding smile on his face. Their day would come. Things had changed. Maybe she'd have a ring on her finger before long . . .

"Nice rock, Gevin," Jason said. "So when's the big day?"

"Ah, ah, ah," Marissa injected. "Nobody's gonna know but Gevin and me. We're on a 'need-to-know' basis on this thing. It's going to be very small, very private, and *very* secretive. We're not gonna let this wedding turn into another *Blue* spectacle. Until you need to know any more details, that's all you're going to hear from us now. Got it, guys?"

"What?" JT barked. "Well, if that's how you're gonna be, you can forget about asking me to sing at your wedding." He threw his napkin down feigning a fake insult.

"Well, uh, JT, that's not exactly a problem. Stevie Wonder's already agreed to sing at our wedding." Gevin maintained a straight face.

"You asked *Stevie Wonder* to sing at your wedding?" Tracey squealed.

"Tracey?" Jason whispered. "He's kidding."

"Oh. Sure. I knew that," she quipped as her face reddened.

"But why won't you tell us when the wedding is?" JT argued. "You don't think you can trust us? Is that it?"

"AS IF you guys don't leak like a sieve?" Alli laughed, taking her seat again. "Good grief, JT. Give me a break. Just whisper the date to Jackson here and we'd hear it on CNN in half an hour."

Jackson acted shocked. "And just what is *that* supposed to mean?" He looked at his parents. "You see how mean she is to me? You see what I have to put up with? Laura, she's yours. Make her the upstairs maid. Groundskeeper. Whatever. Just take her off my hands."

This time he was prepared when Alli whipped her napkin at him. He grabbed it and wrapped it around her mouth like a gag. "There. Perfect."

Jason leaned back in his chair, his laughter ringing through the room with everyone else's. "Oh, Alli, Alli, what are we gonna do with him?"

"Mmggumm," she mumbled, rolling her eyes then narrowing them on Jackson.

He let the napkin go and kissed her cheek. "Always and forever?"

"Not in this lifetime, bucko."

"Okay, okay, enough," Laura scolded her *sons*. "This is supposed to be a celebration, not a roast."

The chatter slowed as they settled back for coffee and dessert. Finally, setting her cup back down on its saucer, Jane Greer looked at Jason. "Tell me what happened with that ridiculous reporter, Jason. How did you convince him to drop the charges?"

"I wasn't the one who convinced him. Turns out he has a thirteen-year-old daughter who happens to be *Blue* fanatic. Apparently she hammered him when he got home. From what I heard, she threatened to run away from home if he didn't apologize to me and drop the charges."

"That is hilarious!" Jane laughed. "Laura, you must have been so relieved."

Laura poured more coffee for her guests before sitting down again. "That's an understatement. Sweet justice, isn't it? I wish I could hug that little girl's neck."

"Oh, no need for that, Mama Mac," JT added. "Your son personally stopped by her house and delivered her a huge bouquet of red roses along with tons of our merchandise to her—while her dad was at work, I might add. I'd say the case is closed, wouldn't you?"

Jason grinned wide, his eyebrows dancing in mischief. "Hey, we take care of our own. What can I say?"

"So whatever happened to Hannah?" Bob asked. "Wasn't that her name? The one we met at the hospital whose picture got plastered all over the news? Where's she—"

"Dad," Jackson groaned under his breath. When his father looked his way, he shook his head, entreating him to drop the subject.

"I'm sorry, did I—"

"It's okay, Bob," Jason said quietly.

A miserable silence fell over the room. Alli avoided looking at Jason, fixing her eyes on Jackson's dad instead. When he looked her way, she shook her head, willing him to drop the subject. Gevin cleared his voice. Marissa, Tracey, and Alli exchanged nervous looks.

"Oh, Jason," Bob said. "I'm so sorry. I apologize."

Jason held up his hand as he finished taking a drink. "It's okay. Let it go."

Laura took the cue. "Would anyone like more dessert?"

"So . . . when is Sergio due back?" Alli asked, hoping to ease the tension.

"Aunt Laura, didn't you say he was coming back tonight sometime?" Gevin asked.

Jason's mother busied herself attending to her guests. "Did I? I mean, yes. I think so. Yes, tonight." Everyone turned to look at her. She gathered empty plates then stopped, aware of everyone's attention. "I said yes, he should be home tonight." And with that, she popped into the kitchen.

"What was *that* all about?" Tracey asked.

Frank picked up the ball. "Oh, she's just uneasy. What with Jackson leaving and all. She's loved having you all here. Typical mother hen, you know. She likes having all her baby chicks in the house together."

"Don't you be callin' me a 'chick' now, Frank," Jackson teased.

"I don't know, Jackson," JT interrupted. "I love it here. Mama Mac always makes this place feel like our home away from home. Know what I mean? But Tracey and I are heading out tomorrow too, so that's two more little chickies flying the coop."

"Yeah, Rissa and I are going up to New York to tell her family about our engagement," Gevin said. "Then we'll head out to LA and meet up with you all later."

"Well, I propose a toast," Frank announced as he stood up, his glass raised. Everyone followed his lead, raising their glasses.

Laura returned from the kitchen. "What are we toasting, dear?"

"Three things. First, a toast for our guest of honor. Jackson, it's good to have you back, son. We wish you a complete and speedy recovery, and we thank almighty God for sparing your life. To Jackson," he said, raising his glass toward Jackson. Jackson smiled, his eyes glistening as he took a sip.

"Second, we're toasting Gevin and Marissa on their upcoming marriage. May God bless you both as you join your lives together. May He bless you with a strong relationship that sees you through the good times and the tough times, and allows you to grow old together."

"Here, here," they all commended, clinking their glasses together and taking another sip. Gevin leaned over to kiss his beaming fiancée.

"And finally, I want to give a toast to the good Lord for seeing us through a difficult chapter in our lives over these past weeks. I wish Sergio was here with us, but I thank God for helping us stick together through it all. Through the tragedy surrounding Jackson's shooting, to the initial rift at the news of this upcoming marriage, and to all the other heartaches that have been hovering around us."

Alli watched Jason who lowered his gaze. Frank cleared his throat and continued. "It isn't mere chance or luck that has seen us through all this. I think you all know it's much more than that. God has been very gracious to us. His protection has been the only thing that's pulled us through. So I want to offer this toast to Him and to thank Him—for saving Jackson, for uniting Gevin and Marissa, and for keeping our boys together."

"Here, here!"

CHAPTER 26

"So what do you think?" Sergio asked, buckling his seat belt.

Hannah felt like a princess in the middle of a fairy tale. "It's amazing, Sergio. I've never been in a private jet before."

"Would you like something to drink?"

Hannah looked up, shocked to find a flight attendant on the small aircraft, though she was dressed more casually, wearing a pair of tan khaki slacks and a starched white blouse.

Sergio made the introductions. "Hannah, this is Shelby. Shelby, Hannah Brooks."

"Nice to meet you," Shelby said with a genuine smile. "May I bring you a beverage before we take off?"

"Sure. A Pellegrino would be nice if you have it?"

"No problem. Sergio?"

"I'll have the same. Any idea when we're wheels up, Shelby?"

The tall, attractive brunette looked at her watch. "Brad will be right back. We should be in the air in about fifteen minutes. Is that all right?"

"Perfect. I need to make a call before we leave." He pulled out his cell phone.

"Sergio, tell me the truth. Do you *ever* get used to this lifestyle? Is it second-nature to you now?"

He blew out a raspberry, as if astonished she'd think such a thing. "No way," he answered, holding the tiny phone against his ear. "Still gives me goose bumps. See?" He held his arm out to her, laughing. "Laura! It's Sergio," he said, speaking into the phone. "You called?"

Hannah turned her head away, anxious to avoid thoughts of where Laura was and who might be there with her. She swallowed hard. *Oh God. Please give me strength.*

"Yeah, I probably won't get to the house 'til around midnight. Is that a problem?"

Hannah dreaded the hours ahead of her. She searched her heart for courage. She reminded herself of all of Sergio's pep talks over the past three days.

"Yes, I'm going to drop her off at Kylie's. She's expecting her. We thought it would be safer. How's everything there on your end?"

She felt his eyes on her and turned to find she was right. She couldn't read his thoughts or even begin to imagine what Laura might be telling him.

"Okay, Laura. Thanks. See you soon."

Just then, the pilot entered the cabin, greeting them both with a broad smile. Sergio made the introductions. Brad shook her hand then dropped a newspaper on the small table between them. "Thought you might like to read the latest birdcage liner. You two are quite the scandal, I see," he quipped as Sergio grabbed the paper. "But at least they didn't say you were aliens from outer space this time." He turned toward the cockpit. "We'll take off in about five minutes, Sergio."

Hannah looked at Sergio as he unfolded the tabloid. "Oh no," he groaned. "Oh no, no, no . . . what the—"

"What is it? What's wrong?"

He folded the paper and put it in his lap, his face ashen. "I don't think you should see it. It's garbage. Not worth the paper it's printed on."

"Hand me the paper, Sergio."

"No. Trust me on this, Hannah. You don't want to see it. It's just a tabloid. Nobody believes these rags anyway."

"Give me the paper. Now!" Her hand trembled as she extended it toward him.

Reluctantly, he handed the tabloid to her. On the front page in a color spread was a collage of pictures. Hannah was in every one of them. The headline pierced her heart.

Hannah Does the Blue?

Jason Dumps Mystery Girlfriend

into Sergio's Waiting Arms

There she was with Jason at the entrance to the hospital. His arm cradling her to protect her from the throngs of people. Then with Sergio, embracing on the beach . . . lying beside him in the sand . . . holding hands at the restaurant . . . entering a dark motel room together . . .

Her stomach roiled.

She tore through the pages to find the story. Her eyes flew over the copy, a ludicrous tale of a brief and passionate "affair" with Jason McKenzie, home for the holidays, nights filled with raucous sex, all under the roof of his parents' home. The affair supposedly ended once Jason's long lost love showed up at the hospital. Pictures of Jennifer Crandle in all her glory, splashed across the pages along with reports of her broken engagement "so she could rush to Jason's side in his hour of need." More pictures. Jennifer embracing Jason at the hospital. Jennifer kissing Jason, surrounded by family and friends.

The story continued, placing a love-sick Hannah on a beach in Florida. Rescued by fellow *Out of the Blue* member, Sergio Cruz, "recently jilted by his psychotic jailbird girlfriend." More pictures. Sergio and Liza in Hawaii, leis around their necks. Liza, dressed in an orange jumpsuit, hands behind her back in handcuffs, her feet in chains. A forlorn Sergio, standing alone somewhere on a beach. The tale unfolded about "the steamy pairing of two rejected lovers . . . the college coed who won't be satisfied until she has them all . . ."

She wadded the paper into a ball and threw it across the cabin. Shelby entered, barely missing the pitch. Hannah snapped open her seat belt. "Where—"

Shelby pointed to the rear of the cabin, rushing to assist her to the restroom. Hannah made it just in time before throwing up.

Shelby picked up the intercom. "Brad, hold up. Give us a few minutes. We have a sick passenger back here." They could hear the engines' downward whine as the pilot delayed their departure.

Several minutes later, Hannah emerged from the restroom. Shelby handed her a cool wet cloth and helped her back to her seat. She pulled out a couple of the "party bags" in case she should get sick again and set them on the table. "Is there anything I can get for you?"

Hannah nodded her head, closing her eyes. She placed the cool cloth over them.

Shelby fastened the seatbelt for her then addressed Sergio. "Can we take off or do you want to wait?"

"No, get us out of here. Now."

"Leave me alone!"

Kylie felt her kitten's paws clawing at her hair accompanied by a loud symphony of annoyed meows.

"Katy, leave me alone!" she whined, pulling the comforter over her head. Not to be outsmarted, the cat crawled under the covers, cranking up her purring machine as she pressed her paws on Kylie's face.

"What is the matter with you?" she yelled, throwing back the covers. She picked up the cat, not buying the kitten's look of innocence. Then she heard it. The doorbell was ringing. Not one simple ring. Someone was holding the button down causing a non-stop chiming of the bell.

Kylie checked her clock. It was five minutes past midnight. She jumped out of bed and climbed into her robe as she hurried into the living room. She peeked out the peephole and jumped back.

Sergio Cruz!

Her heart raced. She could feel the heat spreading up her neck.

Open the door. She knew she should, but she couldn't. She was too angry.

"Kylie! Open up! It's Sergio." It was an urgent and controlled shout, probably an attempt not to wake her neighbors.

She turned her back against the door and folded her arms across her chest. How could he come here? How could he even *think* of coming here?

The door rattled behind her as he pounded on it. "Kylie! Come on! Open up!"

She threw open the door. It must have caught him by surprise, his hand still fisted to knock again. Behind him stood Hannah.

She looks awful. What a surprise.

Sergio started to walk in. Kylie didn't move.

"What is your problem, Kylie? It's late and we're exhausted and you have no idea what we've—"

"What? A little too much fun in the sun?" Kylie planted her hands on her hips.

He stopped cold, searching her face for an explanation. She hoped her sarcasm covered the anger she felt. But more than that, she prayed he couldn't see the hurt that had riddled her since she picked up the tabloid at the convenience store.

Hannah picked up her bags and moved around Sergio. "Kylie, please—I just want to go to bed. Can we just—"

Kylie didn't budge. "Sorry, Hannah. You know the rule here. No overnight male guests."

Hannah looked as if Kylie had slapped her. Then her face crumbled. She pushed Kylie out of the way and ran into the apartment. Sergio followed, grabbing Kylie by the elbow and kicking the door shut behind him.

"What is the *matter* with you?! That was out of line, Kylie. *Way* out of line."

He dragged her to the sofa and gently pushed her onto it. He sat on the coffee table directly in front of her, knee to knee. They looked up simultaneously as Hannah slammed the bedroom door.

"Kylie. Listen to me. If you have one shred of loyalty in your heart—"

"*Loyalty?* That's pretty ironic coming from—"

He put his hand over her mouth. "Will you *please* just shut up and listen to me?"

She glared at him with the meanest eyes she could muster. Then she relented, slowly nodding her head. He lowered his hand.

"If you care anything at all about your friend in there—the one I believe you once told me was *like a sister* to you—then I suggest you hear me out. That tabloid is trash. It was all contrived . . . twisted. *Nothing* happened between Hannah and me. I can't believe I'm even having to defend myself—or her—because there was—is— nothing between us."

Kylie folded her arms again. "How do you explain those pictures?"

The exasperation on his face startled her. "I told you before I left. I had business in Orlando," he continued, his tone impatient. "I stopped by to check in on Hannah, talk to her, just like I told you I was going to do. We spent time together between my meetings. We walked on the beach. We talked. Mostly about what she's been through with Jason. We ate a couple meals together. Kylie, I went as a friend and I've come back as a friend. Nothing more. You have to believe that."

Kylie rolled her neck, her eyes locked on his face. Seeing that tabloid at the convenience store had thrust her heart into a meat grinder. She didn't want to believe it but the pictures were too convincing. She thought she knew Hannah better than that. But then she'd remembered—hadn't she also been charmed by Sergio Cruz herself? So charmed that she betrayed her best friend's secret whereabouts?

Hannah had left town so upset, so devastated by what the press had done to her. She was still grieving over the sudden loss of Jason. Of *course* she would be vulnerable, wouldn't she? The thoughts, the pictures, the story that accompanied them. And while Kylie knew it probably wasn't as "steamy" as the paper espoused, she allowed herself to believe that Hannah and Sergio had found comfort in each other's arms. It actually made sense, considering what Sergio had just been through as well.

Now she wasn't so sure.

"But you were embracing each other! I saw the picture, Sergio. That was hardly a friendly hug."

He gripped her pajama-covered knees with both hands. It hurt. "But don't you get it, Kylie? That's how these rags work! They take a picture, most of them photoshopped, and put a caption below it to say whatever they want. You *know* that! Think about it. They could take a picture of the president standing beside some child star, put some bogus caption under it, and the whole world thinks there's some kind of kinky relationship going on there. They don't bother with truth because they peddle lies. It's been done thousands of times to thousands of people.

"I'm telling you, Kylie, it's a farce. And instead of being angry at your best friend, you might think about giving her a little credit. She took this really hard. She's been throwing up all the way home."

"She has?" Kylie felt her countenance melt instantly. "But Hannah *never* throws up. She must be—oh, Sergio, I'm so sorry!" She jumped up, starting toward her bedroom. "I can't believe I let myself be taken in by all that stuff."

He dropped his head back, raising his hands in triumphant resignation. "Finally! Thank God, we've got *that* settled. Why don't you go see how she's doing? I think she could really use a friend right now. Besides, I'm starving. You got anything to eat?" He jumped up, ambling into her kitchen.

"How can you even think of eating at a time like this?"

He opened the cabinets, the refrigerator, then the freezer compartment. "Ah. Cookies & Cream. Want some?"

"No, but by all means, help yourself."

Still, she dreaded facing Hannah after her heartless accusations. *Some friend I am! I can't face her. Not yet.* She stalled the apology by turning back toward the kitchen and sitting down at the small kitchen table. She watched as Sergio tried a couple of drawers before he found the utensils, fishing out a large wooden spoon. He didn't bother finding a bowl.

"Uh—" Kylie started, watching him dig right into the carton. He looked up at her. She pasted a smile on her face and said nothing. He winked. *Oh no. Not that wink again.* She felt the blush and prayed it wasn't splotchy.

"So what can I do to help her?" she asked. "She's been through so much. How can I—"

The bedroom door flew open. Hannah stood in the doorway. Fresh from a shower, she'd changed into plaid PJ bottoms and a thermal shirt, her wet hair wrapped in a towel. "Sergio. You're still here. Good. I have something I need to say to both of you."

She joined them in the kitchen, grabbing a spoon out of the open drawer. She snatched the carton out of Sergio's hands and scooped a big spoonful before handing it back to him. She pulled out a bar stool and sat down.

"Kylie, I don't know what you're thinking or what—"

"It's okay, Hannah," Kylie interrupted, jumping up to give her a hug. "Sergio explained everything. I'm *so sorry* I doubted you."

"Good. Then I won't bother with that speech. I've made a decision."

They both looked at her expectantly. Her tone was unusually assertive. Sergio set the carton of ice cream on the table.

"I took a long, hard look at myself in the mirror just now. And I didn't like what a saw at all. I saw a shriveled up, coward of a woman who's let one too many people stomp all over her. I've let them tear me to shreds, reducing me to this . . . this little *wuss* of a person who just threw her guts up all the way from Florida to North Carolina.

"And I decided I'm not going to live like this anymore. I'm not gonna take it anymore. Not the press, not the lies, not the harassment . . . and no offense, Sergio, but not even *Out of the Blue*."

He leaned back in his chair.

"My life has been a total wreck since that night Laura came into my store. I know it was all unintentional. Nobody meant for *any* of this to happen, but that's beside the point. I'm sick and tired of being a victim to all of it, and I'm not going to stand for it anymore. I'm done. With *all* of it."

"Well, Hannah, that's great but—"

"No, Sergio. Let me finish. Day after tomorrow, I'm going to grab my backpack, go to class, and finish my senior year. If I get hassled every step of the way, then so be it. If the press is camping at my doorstep, let them. If they call me a slut or a tramp or a nymphomaniac, let them. Because *I* know the truth. I know who Hannah Brooks is, and she's none of those things. Their words can't hurt me anymore because I refuse to *let* them hurt me."

"You go girl!" Kylie shouted, shoving her fist into the air. "I am *so proud* of you! Preach it, sister!"

"I'm not kidding, Kylie. I'm totally serious." Hannah's face mirrored her words. "I will not run and I will not hide. Those days are *over*. I'm going to get my degree, then I'm going to show the world what *real* journalism is. Somebody has to make these people accountable for their lies and for the way they flippantly attempt to destroy the lives of others. And I think I'm just the person to do it."

"All this from looking in the mirror just now?" Kylie asked, smiling.

Hannah pulled the towel from her hair and tossed it toward the bedroom door. She shook her head then finger-combed her wet curls and blew out a long, slow breath. "Not entirely. I had a lot of time to think in Florida." Her angst gave way to a sense of relief. She paused, looking down at her hands. "And, to be honest, I prayed a lot too. More than I ever have."

She looked up at Sergio. "It's really kind of ironic, if you stop and think about it. I've learned more about prayer from hanging out with a bunch of rock stars than I ever learned at Sunday school." She tried to smile, but it just wasn't there. "I watched what can happen when people pray. I mean, c'mon—Jackson's miracle didn't just 'happen,' did it? I believe with all my heart God saved him because of the thousands of prayers that went up for him. And I figured, well, maybe God would help me too if I'd ask Him."

Hannah stood up and walked to the faucet where she rinsed the spoon and placed it in the sink. "And in spite of everything that went down the last few hours, I refuse to be distracted from what I've learned. I feel like this change of heart is a result of those prayers I prayed in Florida. No, I take that back—I don't just *feel* it, I *know* it. Because God showed me I can either roll over and die, or stand up and face the challenge . . . change the direction I'm headed and get on with my life."

She turned to face Sergio, her intense exterior completely softened now. "And I don't think for a minute your trip to Florida was a coincidence. I think God sent me an angel in my time of need. I really do. Thanks for being there for me, Sergio."

He stood up, pulling her into a bear hug. "I am so proud of you, Hannah. I knew you had it in you."

Kylie piled into the hug. "He's right, Hannah. Maybe the reason you had to go through all this was to find out who you really are. Find out just what you're made of. I don't know much about the prayer stuff, but if that's what it took, then all I can say is . . . amen, girlfriend!"

CHAPTER 27

"Well, that was . . . *different,*" Hannah muttered as she slid into her seat beside Kylie in the large auditorium. Well over a hundred UNC students filed into the old lecture hall, climbing row after row up the creaking wooden steps. Far below, in the "pit" on the first level, the professor thumbed through his briefcase retrieving a stack of papers.

Seated only three rows from the top of the auditorium, Kylie handed Hannah a cup of Starbucks. "But you did it, Hannah. You did it!" she whispered, excitement threading her words. "From the minute you left the apartment, you were cool as a cucumber."

"Yeah, yeah. No big deal," Hannah shrugged, popping open the lid on her vanilla latte.

"No big deal? Are you kidding me? You rocked, girlfriend! They pelted you with questions. You ignored them," she continued, doing her best animated sportscaster impression. "They hurled assaults like missiles. You ignored them. They scrambled after you in their mysterious black sedans, tailing you every step of the way to campus. And like the champ, heading into the ring to face your opponent, you—"

"Okay, okay! I get the picture!" Hannah laughed, crossing her legs.

"You were *amazing,*" Kylie whispered loudly.

Hannah smiled mischievously and blew on her latte before taking a sip. "I *was* good, wasn't I, Kylie? Who knew I had it in me?"

"You were better than good. You were *killer* good."

Hannah slid down into her seat, settling in for the class. "Thank goodness the campus security refused to let them follow us any further. You have no idea how scared I was! I was terrified to open my door this morning!"

"I know you were but you did it. You *did* it, Hannah. And now it won't be so hard the next time. Or the time after that. Until they finally get the message that they can't offend you any more. I'm telling you, you knocked 'em dead. You were *incredible.* I am so more proud of you!"

"Ladies and gentlemen, welcome to Advanced Literary Communications. My name is Dr. Stafford and I'll be guiding you through these next few weeks of journalistic excellence—"

"Just think, Kylie," Hannah whispered out the side of her mouth, her eyes never leaving the professor. "This is our last semester. The last time we ever have to put up with any more of these dumb welcome speeches. The last time we have to load up on textbooks and homework and all-night cramming for impossible exams . . ."

"I know, but it kind of makes me sad in a way," Kylie answered discreetly, opening her new spiral notebook to the first page.

Hannah turned to face her. "Are you crazy?"

"Not at all. Come on, admit it. You'll miss this campus. The sun coming up as you go to those early labs. The cute frat boys—they may be snobs but they're still hot. The smell of freshly mown grass on the commons . . . or leaves burning in the fall . . . homecoming . . . the band playing the fight song at football games . . . the student center—"

"The sticky buns at The Bakery."

"The pizza at Vitto's."

"As my assistant hands out your syllabus for the course work, I'll ask you to open it to page three where we'll go over the objectives for our time together these next few months."

After the overview, the professor began his lecture, lulling most of the class to a drowsy early morning nap.

Hannah tried to keep her mind on the lecture, but found herself doodling in the margins of her paper. She propped her elbow on the corner of the desk, resting her chin in her hand. She hoped the professor would assume she was taking copious notes. Not that he would care. This was, after all, college.

Sometime later, a strange sound roused her from her artwork. She stole a glance at Kylie whose jaw dropped, almost disappearing into her blue turtleneck. Slowly she turned to face Hannah. Her lips moved. She was trying to say something.

Hannah's brows knitted the question. *What?*

Kylie motioned her head toward the front of the room. There was panic in her eyes. Hannah was afraid to look. *More reporters? More cameras?*

Without moving her head, she let her eyes crawl toward the main level. Two campus security guards stood at the door as if on patrol, their hands folded behind their backs. At the podium stood another, his back to the class as he talked privately with the professor. And beside him—

It can't be . . .

Hannah froze. Kylie groaned next to her, trying unsuccessfully to verbalize something. Hannah groaned in return. Somehow, they understood each other.

The fourth man shook hands with the professor. They chatted out of earshot. It was obvious they'd met before. Then, the men in the pit of the auditorium turned around as the professor moved to speak to his assistant. Hannah slid down in her seat, trying to hide her face under her hand. She peeked through a slit between her fingers, watching the scene unfold below. The assistant looked through the papers on her desk. She pulled one from the pile and handed it to him. He ran his finger down the sheet of paper then returned to the guard and the man standing next to him. They conferred. Then they all looked up.

"Is Miss Brooks present today? Hannah Brooks?"

Whispers swept through the room. Hannah felt her face glowing. Her pulse pounded in her head. She started to perspire.

"Hannah Brooks?"

"Hannah, do something!" Kylie hissed.

That was all it took. The students turned en masse to look at them, along with the men down front. Hannah watched Kylie's face wilt with guilt; the realization of what she'd done washing over her.

Great. Why don't you just turn a spotlight on me, Kylie?

Kylie offered a weak smile and mouthed, "Sorry?"

Hannah looked back down to the front of the room. The professor nodded agreeably to the guy in the ball cap, and sat down on the stool beside his podium. Dr. Stafford boasted a conspiratorial smile. He was enjoying this.

The guard stood aside. The fourth man took off his ball cap and his sunglasses. A collective gasp arose from the room. The whispers grew louder.

"Hannah?" he called up to her. "Dr. Stafford—who happens to be a friend of the family, by the way—has allowed me a few moments of his time—*your* time," he corrected, waving his hand across the room, "to do something I should have done a long time ago."

She couldn't bear to look up. Kylie's elbow struck her in the ribs. She groaned but kept her face hidden behind her hand.

This isn't happening.

It's just a dream.

It's just another one of my stupid dreams.

Hannah could hear his footsteps creaking as he began slowly climbing the steps, one after another. "And I know this isn't the normal way to handle this sort of thing, but then—well, nothing has ever been normal between us, has it?"

A few catcalls pierced the air. Others shouted to quiet their class members.

She couldn't stand it. She had to look. She lifted her head only enough to see over her fingers.

And there he was. Jason McKenzie, his hat in his hands, his forehead scrunched up like a little kid begging to be heard. When their eyes met, the crease in his brow deepened, but a hint of a smile touched his lips.

"See, I owe you a huge apology, and it just can't wait another minute. And I need all these witnesses here to hear what I have to say so they can vouch for me in case you don't understand me."

He continued slowly climbing the steps, his familiar smile breaking through the walls of her heart.

"Now, I've allowed the, uh . . . *circumstances* to disorient me the past few days. I got confused about things. About the past . . . and some of the people in my past. I think you know what I'm talking about. I was distracted. Like I took my eyes off what was important and lost my way."

Hannah bit the side of her lip. She hoped it would stop the trembling. Her eyes burned. She could hardly see now. Kylie's sniffles only made it worse.

More steps. More creaking.

"And then, it suddenly dawned on me." He was only three steps below her now. "Like somebody took the blinders off my eyes. And I knew exactly what I wanted."

Two steps away.

"*Who* I wanted."

"Ahhhh," the class sighed in sympathetic unison, laughter crackling across the room.

"Isn't that sweet?" someone sneered on the far side of the room.

Jason didn't even blink.

"Who does this guy think he is?"

"You dufus!" A girl shot back from five rows down. "It's Jason McKenzie!" She turned back around, her face bright with anticipation.

"What's he got that I don't have?" It was the football player just across the aisle from her.

Kylie let out a huff. "A limo, a couple of mansions, and millions of fans. Okay? So shut up!" She looked back to Jason and plastered a smile on her face. "Go ahead."

Jason smirked at Kylie. The dimples beside his mouth seemed to pull his smile even wider. He nodded his head in gratitude toward her.

She nodded back. "You're welcome."

The class laughed then slowly hushed.

He took the final step, standing directly beside her on the aisle. "The thing is, Hannah," he began, slowly dropping to one knee. He reached for her hand, covering it with both of his. Hannah cried silently, her shoulders shaking. She blinked, feeling the tears run down her face.

Jason smiled at her, but this time it was a serious smile. Hannah noticed the slight tremble of his chin, a glistening in his eyes. He cleared his throat, never taking his eyes off her.

"Hannah, I won't even begin to make a lot of promises to you. You know what my life is like. Don't you?"

She nodded, a knowing smile trying to form.

He continued. "But I know—*I know* that I can't even think about another day if you aren't a part of it."

Another "ahhhh" echoed across the room.

"So what I'm saying to you, what I'm asking you in front of all these people here with God as my witness is this."

He stopped.

She waited.

"I want my Christmas present back."

The question pushed her brows upward.

"What?" a voice shot from behind her. "What kind of stupid line is that?"

"Smooth. Really smooth, Blue man," the football player mimicked.

"Shut up!" shouted a chorus of female voices.

Jason nodded, tuning them out. "You know what I'm talking about, don't you, Hannah. You remember, don't you?"

Her head tilted as she searched for his meaning. She had no idea.

Then it came to her. She nodded, a laugh and a tiny sob escaping at the same time. "Yes, Jason," she whispered. "I remember."

"*You* were my Christmas gift. And now I want you back, Hannah. I don't know what tomorrow will bring, or the day after that. But I know that I want you there, with me, all the way." His face melted into a huge smile. "I love you, Hannah Brooks."

"Oh, please tell me he's *not* gonna sing to her."

"*I will never ever hurt you,*" a falsetto male voice sang, teasing them.

The women shouted again. "SHUT UP!"

More voices joined in. "*I will never make you cry . . .*"

The room swelled in chorus as the class teased them with a miserable rendition of the *Blue* hit song.

I will never leave you all alone,
Just take my hand,
Baby, understand,
I want nothing more,
Than to love you
Forever.

Jason looked around at the impromptu choir surrounding them, then back at Hannah. He laughed as hard as Hannah had ever seen him laugh. When he looked back at her, he shrugged, holding up his hands. "Couldn't have said it better myself!" he shouted over the singing.

Hannah shook her head, surrendering to the surreal scene absorbing them. She looked at Kylie for support and found her singing along as they continued to repeat the chorus. She looked down at her professor who seemed to be enjoying a good laugh along with the three security guards. Hannah joined the laughter, blown away by the circus around her. It felt like she'd been transported into a melodramatic scene in some ridiculous cheesy movie.

Then, scrambling to her feet, she fell into Jason's arms, laughing and crying all at the same time. "I love you, Jason McKenzie, I love you!" He drew her into his embrace, kissing her passionately to the roaring approval of her classmates. Their cheers rivaled that of any Tar Heel touchdown, except this touchdown had its own theme song.

I will never ever hurt you,
I will never make you cry . . .

EPILOGUE

I will never ever hurt you,
I will never make you cry,
I will never leave you all alone,
Just take my hand,
Baby, understand,
I want nothing more,
Than to love you
Forever.

The arena reverberated as thousands of fans screamed in adoration. Hannah's earplugs were of little help. *Out of the Blue* continued singing on stage above her. It was her favorite song. Small wonder.

She knew Jason would make his way to her side of the stage. Yep. Here he came. He was sweating. They all were by this time in the show. He walked dangerously close to the edge of the platform, singing with every ounce of his heart.

He looked down at her, seated in the hidden pit that buffeted the stage. He placed his hand over his heart, his fingers mimicking a beating heart, pounding against his shirt. He sang to her alone. It was their secret signal.

"I love you," she mouthed.

He winked at her and moved away, joining Gevin, Jackson, JT and Sergio for the finale of the song. Above, just behind her on the front row, a young teenage girl screamed to her friend. "Oh my gosh! Did you see that? Jason winked at me! Jason McKenzie knows I'm alive!"

Hannah dissolved in laughter. *What goes around comes around.* She remembered saying those very words not so many years ago. *Who would ever have thought . . .*

The months had flown by following that unforgettable day in her Advanced Literary Communications class. Hannah graduated with honors in May, her famous boyfriend there with Laura and Frank along with her own family to celebrate the occasion. With persistent effort enabled by her new-found grit and determination, she landed a dream assignment for the *Chapel Hill Herald* chronicling life on the road with *Out of the Blue.*

The endless opportunities for stories flavored by an insider's touch kept her busy. Behind-the-scenes mishaps. Life on a luxury bus. Encounters with celebrities they met up with along the way. Heartwarming stories from fans across the country. Compassionate stops at pediatric wards and children's homes. Then always, the inner dynamics between five gifted and talented (and stubborn and opinionated) musicians who made their living in the unique and often surreal world of entertainment. When her column was picked up by *Rolling Stone* magazine, Hannah could hardly believe it. Her newly acquired agent assured her of a future that was bright and promising. She'd never been happier in her entire life.

Alli and Marissa made this leg of the tour, keeping Hannah company when the guys were busy.

As did another friend who'd made the trip.

"Hannah! Let's go see the guys between sets. C'mon." Kylie yelled, grabbing her hand.

By the time the tour had resumed after graduation, Sergio and Kylie were inseparable. They provided the rest of the entourage with endless laughter. While Kylie may have been dangerous behind the wheel of an expensive sports car, she was surprisingly talented behind the set, keeping the guys on schedule, assisting the staff with wardrobe, make-up, and hairstyling.

"Ser-gi-o!"

Bare to the waist in the middle of a clothing change, he held his arms out to her. "Kylie, ¡mi amor! ¡Bésame! ¡Bésame!" he shouted, all smiles, pleading for a kiss. He shuffled quickly over to her while buttoning his shirt.

"I'll beseme you all night long, my sweet Spaniard!" Kylie wrapped her arms around his neck and smacked a wet one right on his lips.

Hannah laughed at their exchange. Kylie's crash course in Spanish seemed to be paying off.

"I sang to you," Jason shouted into Hannah's ear, sneaking up from behind her. He kissed her cheek then turned his back to her. "Here, help me put this back on." She strapped the power pack onto his belt, snapping it in place as he finished buttoning his shirt. "Thanks, babe." He kissed her again then tweaked her nose. "I'm outta here." And off he flew with the others as the music pounded above them.

And so it went. Night after night. City after city.

And despite the enormous pressures of the lifestyle they led, Hannah and Jason's love grew deeper with each passing day. It wasn't easy. It never would be.

But that was okay. As long as they were together, they would survive.

Hannah made her way back to her seat, Kylie following close behind. She sipped from her bottle of water and relaxed into her seat. She absently fingered the heart made of diamonds that hung from a slender chain around her neck. Her graduation gift from Jason.

In reality, it was a belated Christmas gift—the one he'd promised her from that first week they were together. Graduation, Christmas. It didn't matter to her. It was her most prized possession.

After all, he'd given her his heart.

ThE End

ABOUT THE AUTHOR

Born in Texas and raised in Oklahoma, Diane Moody writes both fiction and non-fiction. Her first book, *Confessions of a Prayer Slacker,* released in 2010 followed by *Don't Ever Look Down: Surviving Cancer Together,* co-authored with Dick and Debbie Church. *The Runaway Pastor's Wife,* her first novel, debuted in 2011 followed by *Tea with Emma,* Book One in *The Teacup Novellas* series, published by OBT Bookz.

A graduate of Oklahoma State University and a former pastor's wife, Diane and husband Ken live in the rolling hills just outside of Nashville, Tennessee. Celebrating over thirty years together, they are the proud parents of two grown and extraordinary children, Hannah and Ben. When she's not reading or writing, Diane enjoys an eclectic taste in music, movies, great coffee, the company of good friends, and the adoration of a peculiar little puppy named Darby.

Visit Diane's webpage at www.dianemoody.net

ACKNOWLEDGMENTS

A tremendous thanks to my friends and family for their support and encouragement along the way for this story with its unique history—especially to Sally Wilson and Joy DeKok. Couldn't have done it without you!

A special thanks to ol' Eagle Eyes himself—Glenn Hale. Beyond your gifted editing expertise, thank you for *liking* my story so much. Who knew a World War II vet would enjoy a love story about a girl and her teen heartthrob? Love you, Dad.

To Dana Myers—best friend from high school, former college roommate, and my all-time favorite Spanish linguist. Thanks also to your Spanish colleague, Maria Waldrup. Dana, you haven't met Sergio yet, but he appreciates you correcting the words I put in his mouth. Or, as he would say, "¡Muchas gracias!"

To my amazing friend and former co-worker Denise Wells who was there at the start and made the writing of this story so much more fun. Thanks for reading my story as I wrote it, chapter by chapter, and giving me such great feedback and encouragement. Thanks also for not mocking this middle-age mom for listening to her daughter's "boys in the band" while she worked in the cubby across the room from you. And don't worry, I won't tell a soul about that concert we went to that summer night. The one at LP Field with all those teenage girls screaming about those cute boys up on stage. Your secret is safe with me, Dee.

To Allison Greer, Jenny Burke and the rest of my daughter's best friends from Harpeth High School in Kingston Springs, Tennessee, who read each and every installment of our story and kept asking for more. You inspired me to keep writing, and I'll forever thank you for that. Thanks for the memories!

To my best friend and the love of my life—my husband Ken who has made this whole publishing adventure such a great ride. Thanks for your eternal optimism, your continued belief in me as an author, and for all your help in designing a book cover to do justice to this story. (Rumor has it, the cover really pops!) Maybe this one will get us to that beach in Hawaii!

And last but not least, to my daughter Hannah. I will never forget this incredible larger-than-life journey we shared, sweetheart. Thanks for inspiring me to write this story, for all those brainstorming sessions dreaming up plot twists and turns, and for those unforgettable front row seats in the up close and personal shadows of your boys in the band. Didn't we make the best memories? I am so, so proud of the woman you've become. Love you, Nanner.

Other Books by Diane Moody

<u>The War Trilogy</u>
Of Windmills and War
Beyond the Shadow of War
From the Ashes of War

<u>The Teacup Novellas</u>
Tea with Emma
Strike the Match
Home to Walnut Ridge
At Legend's End
A Christmas Peril

The Collection
(All five Teacup Novellas in one book)

<u>The Braxton Mysteries</u>
The Demise
The Legacy
The Sibling

Memphis & Me

Confessions of a Prayer Slacker

The Runaway Pastor's Wife

Hale Hale the Gang's All Here
(Family Cookbook)

Printed in the USA
CPSIA information can be obtained
at www.ICGtesting.com
LVHW091555161023
761244LV00007B/40